THE LOST SOULS

A DCI ROHAN ROY CRIME THRILLER

BOOK 4

M.L. ROSE

CHAPTER 1

Jayden Budden ran for his life. He didn't know where he was going, but fear drove him forward, a blind, angst-ridden urge to get as far from home as possible. He ran out of the alley and skidded to a stop.

It was still daylight, and there were people on the street. He pulled down the peak of his baseball cap, and forced himself to slow down. He was close to Burngreaves, and the main drag was crowded. He could lose himself here, and wait for a bus. He had put enough distance between himself and the flat.

Approaching DCI Rohan Roy's daughter, Anna, to warn her about Lydia was a mistake. He'd made himself do it, but it left a peculiar feeling inside him, like a gravestone had slid aside and the demons of his miserable childhood were let loose. They were tormenting him now, banging against his skull, laughing in his ears.

Once he saw Anna and Lydia together, he had to warn her though. Lydia's dangerous presence apart, Anna seemed surprisingly familiar to him. He didn't know why, but he had the same feeling when he had first looked at Inspector Rohan Roy. He had the vague impression he had seen Roy somewhere before. He had looked the man up on the internet, but there wasn't much. He saw an old BBC news article about how Roy had once caught the leader of a paedophile gang, a man called Charles Mason.

A couple of men brushed past Jayden, and he stiffened. His panicked eyes roved around, expecting to see a uniformed copper, or maybe a plainclothes one. What was he thinking, talking to Anna about Jerry and Lydia, when she was the daughter of a detective? He had to, but it had also landed him in trouble now. He knew the police would be at his flat, searching and asking questions.

Jayden was parched, and he saw a newsagent on the left. He pulled his cap down lower, as he knew the shop would have CCTV. He had stolen enough stuff from these places to know that. Luckily, he'd never been caught. He got a bottle of water, put some cash on the till, and waited impatiently while the shop keeper counted the change.

Outside, he walked to join the bus queue. He kept watching for the police. Then his worst fears were confirmed. A blue and red police car with the South Yorkshire Police logo went by slowly. The three cops in the car were clearly scanning the streets, looking for someone. Jayden shrank behind a street sign next to the bus stop. He didn't move, as movement attracted more attention.

His heart rate kicked up a notch when the police car stopped. He kept his head down, pretending to look at his phone. He could tell the cops were looking out the window. An age seemed to pass, but in reality it was a few seconds. The traffic groaned, and engines whirred, the police car inched forward.

Jayden glanced furtively to make sure the car had gone past him. Then he breathed a sigh of relief. He'd had brushes with the police in the past, but nothing serious. He had received a couple of cautions, which didn't stay in the records for more than ten years, and he had never been convicted of any crime. It was mostly buying and selling cannabis, and once he got in a fight outside a pub. In those crazy, sad days when he was homeless, he had broken into a couple of homes as well, but he was never caught. He stopped that soon, an inner voice telling him it was wrong. He might have nothing, but that didn't mean he could steal what others had worked hard to earn.

In those days, Jayden went from hostel to YMCA, living in council flats, smoking weed, and messing around. It was a miracle he never got arrested, despite his skirmishes with the cops. But he was never a serious criminal. He was always released with a slap on the wrist, and he didn't have a police record. Eventually, Jayden learnt how to become a car mechanic, and that became his job. Looking back, he now knew that had saved his life. If he hadn't learnt a trade, he would've ended up hooked on serious drugs, or dead.

The bus arrived, and he got on. The bus would go all the way to Sculthorpe, a village outside Meadowhall, a bumble fuck place in the middle of nowhere. Just what he needed. He got a window seat, and sank down, exhausted. His forehead rested against the cold pane of the window.

3

Talking to Anna about Jerry had let the cat out of the bag. He wondered if Jerry had a police record. Did he? Well, if he did, then why was he never caught? When he thought about the horrible man who had been his stepfather, the chainsaw split his body and soul apart. He could feel the burn of metal and he cringed as if in pain, his face twisted. He gasped and his eyes opened. The bus was wheezing through traffic. The streets outside were thronged with people of every colour and ethnicity. That meant they were still in Sheffield.

Jayden tried to distract himself, but the pain remained. Jerry – that man had destroyed his life, but according to Jerry, also saved Jayden from ruin. Jayden had no one, that much he knew. And now, he had also lost his flat. He couldn't go back there, just to get arrested for talking about Jerry. He had tried telling the police about Jerry in the past. He remembered speaking to a stern-faced detective in Leeds.

'There's no one called Jerry Budden who ever lived here,' the detective told him. His face said he didn't believe a word of what Jayden was saying.

Jayden had tried it once again, but he soon realised there was no point. It was hard to talk about his shame. He braved it once, twice, and then carried it around like an invisible cloak.

He couldn't open up to Anna. Still, there was something about that girl that told him she might understand more than any policeman ever had. But she could also get him arrested, especially as her father was a detective. He couldn't cope with that right now.

Neither could he think. His head hurt like mad. He closed his eyes but terrible visions from his childhood filled his mind. He gasped again, and forced himself to look outside the window. The city was slipping past. Soon, they were on the road that took them past Meadowhall, and into the outskirts of Sheffield.

CHAPTER 2

Ahmedabad, India

Layla Patil watched the glass and metal multiplexes and shopping malls shining in the torrid sun as her bus crossed the four-lane Nehru Bridge. The bridge lay over the wide Sabarmati River, which divided Ahmedabad, Gujrat's biggest city, into eastern and western parts.

The bus was packed. The seats were all taken, and people stood closer than matchsticks in a box. Some also hung out of the doors, holding on to the window grills, their feet gaining a marginal toehold on the steps. The sight reminded Layla of a bunch of bananas hanging from the banana trees in her father's village.

Breeze from the wide angle of the massive river filtered in through the spaces between the packed human bodies, offering some relief from the sweltering heat. Layla wanted the journey to be over as soon as possible, but she knew traffic would be heavy on the other side of the bridge.

Eventually, she got to her destination. Her office was in one of the shiny new multiplexes visible across the river. Layla worked as a secretary for an IT company. She was eighteen, and her education was basic. Her job was a dead-end one, with no prospect of improvement. Her office was huge, filled with men and women sitting in rows in front of computer terminals. She sat down at her desk, and logged in. In her inbox she saw the number of cold calls she had to make, and her heart sank.

Layla was like millions of other Indian girls from the slums in the big Indian cities. They couldn't afford an education, and neither did they have any connections to the new, booming business world of modern India. Layla smiled to herself. Maybe, just maybe, all that was about to change.

Layla lived in a shanty hut with eight other family members, and she was the breadwinner. Her dad had had a stroke and was paralysed. Her mother looked after the home, and cleaned houses to earn a meagre living, but she was getting old. She had four siblings, and her disabled aunt from the village had also joined them after the recent floods swept away her home.

Layla knew she had to leave this hopeless job, and find a new one. But she needed more training in IT. Ideally, a degree would help. Her phone pinged, and she snatched at it. It was from Paresh Mallya, the man she'd met at the employment office. Paresh did well for himself. He lived in a nice flat facing the river, in the affluent, western side of Ahmedabad, not far from this office.

She answered when he called. 'Hi. I'm at work. Can't talk.' She looked around the room. Everyone seemed to be minding their own business. Her supervisor was hovering around, leaning over the desk of an employee and his screen.

'We need to meet today. I heard back from Don Valley College in Sheffield, UK. They like your application. You're just the kind of student they're looking for.' Paresh sounded excited, and Layla's heart thrummed loudly in response.

'Really?'

'Yes. I spoke to the bank for a loan to cover your tuition fees. You can work in the evenings on the college campus to pay the loan off. Once your degree is completed, you can easily find work anywhere in UK.'

From the corner of her eye, Layla saw her supervisor approaching her desk with a frown on his face.

'I've got to go.'

'Meet me outside at lunchtime.'

Layla hung up as the supervisor, Mr Mathur, approached. He had scrawny arms, a thin face marked with old small pox scars, and a pot belly.

'Why aren't you making your calls?'

'I am.' Layla reached for the headphone on her desk, and snapped them on.

'Hurry up, and stop chatting to your boyfriend,' Mr Mathur grumbled, and slouched off.

The hours couldn't pass any quicker. In between calls

where customers shouted at her, or just hung up, she found time to look up the Don Valley College online, which was close to Sheffield University. The College offered short one to two-year courses in a variety of disciplines; IT and Accountancy being two of them. Layla couldn't help grinning as she read the prospectus. If this actually happened, her life would change. She could come back to Ahmedabad, and get a managerial job. She would be Mr Mathur's boss, and save up enough to buy her family a large apartment on Ahmedabad's coveted western bank.

At lunchtime, she logged out, and checked her phone. Paresh was already downstairs, on his scooter. She ran down the five flights of stairs as the lifts were crowded, and slow. Paresh was waiting in one of the side alleys. She got on the back seat and he drove off.

They went to the Sabarmati River, where new promenades were built, replacing the mud huts of the fishing villages. New restaurants and cafes were springing up everywhere, vying for space with American food chain outlets. India was changing, but the lot of women like Layla it seemed, would never change.

Paresh bought ice creams from a Baskin Robbins shop, and gave one to Layla. They sat down on one of the benches. Paresh had come back from UK a week ago, and he showed her the photos on his phone.

'This man is the admission tutor of the college,' Paresh said, pointing to a photo of him shaking hands with an older white man in a suit.

'What's his name?'

Paresh didn't miss a beat. 'Mr Ludlow. He's been there

for more than ten years. He liked your application.'

Layla wasn't a fool. She had checked up on the promises Paresh had made. He was an education broker, the men who arranged for talented Indians to get scholarships to study abroad. In a country of 1.4 billion, there were millions of clever Indian youths who never got to the university of their choice. Many of them got scholarships to a college in the West.

Layla had checked Paresh's background, and that of Don Valley College. Mr Ludlow, the website said, was certainly the admissions tutor.

'That's great,' she enthused. Paresh smiled, and leant over to kiss her. Layla grew self-conscious immediately, but eventually kissed him quickly. Society was changing. Twenty years ago, a couple kissing in broad daylight was considered shameful. Now, it was commonplace. But Layla was still from the poor slums, she wasn't part of the educated middle class like Paresh was. She'd taken her time to trust him. At first, she didn't understand what a man like him saw in her. He was rich, successful, although she'd never seen his office. She had been to his flat, and stayed during the day. She couldn't stay overnight, her family would be too worried.

'It's time I met your parents,' Paresh said, becoming serious. Layla stopped eating her ice cream.

'We need money for your visa, and you need to sign the loan documents. I can arrange all of it, but your parents will feel better if I spoke to them. Don't worry.' He smiled at her look of discomfort. 'I won't tell them what we get up to.'

Warmth crept up Layla's neck, fanning her cheeks. She lowered her head. Paresh touched her chin gently and lifted her face.

'I love you. Remember that. I know you can do this.'

Right then, despite her embarrassment, she wanted to hug him. Paresh had believed in her from the day they met. He had swept her off her feet, and aroused her body, mind and soul. She would do anything for him.

'When do I leave for UK?' She asked, breathless.

'As soon as the visa's done, we can go. I'll come with you, as I have business with the other colleges in Sheffield. Visa are usually issued within four weeks of applying. Your application should be approved next week. Then we can apply.'

'So next month…

Paresh grinned, showing his perfect white teeth. 'You and I will be on a flight to England. Yes, that's right.'

Layla stared at him, her mouth open, heart dancing faster. Then she nodded. 'Yes. It's time you met my parents.'

CHAPTER 3

Sheffield, England

Layla had been in England for a week, and she wasn't quite seeing what she'd expected from the shiny prospectus photos. It was cold and wet, and she felt homesick. Her mum, Karuna, had hugged her and cried when she left home, saying she might never see Layla again. But Karuna had never left Gujrat, never mind taking a flight abroad. Now, Layla desperately wished she could hug Karuna once again.

She was living in a dreary council flat in the aptly named Grimesthorpe. There was damp in the walls, and mould growing in the bathroom. She was sharing the single bedroom with Paresh, but he was hardly around. He left early in the morning, and last night, he didn't come home, or reply to her messages.

Layla didn't know much about England, but she knew

she wasn't in college accommodation. From her window, she could see the kids playing in the communal garden, and the mothers standing around, smoking. Burkha-clad Muslim women walked down the side. Groups of unemployed youth hung around the corner shop just outside the estate. All around her, like needles on a hedgehog's back, stood tall concrete flat blocks. The estate was large, and far below, she could see the twinkling lights of Sheffield.

How did she end up here?

The door opened, and she went to it. Paresh staggered in, his tie absent, shirt sticking out of the trousers. His eyes were red, and he hiccupped.

'How long are we staying here for?' Layla demanded. 'When do I start college? That's not here, is it?'

Paresh barked out a laugh as he headed into the bathroom. She waited until he came out. He brushed past her, eyes hooded, and went into the bedroom. He started taking his clothes off.

'I don't like it here anymore. When do I start college?' She got closer, and touched his forearm. He lashed out suddenly, the backhanded slap catching her unawares. It stung her cheeks, and she fell against the cupboard. Paresh advanced on her, his teeth bared.

'College?' He swore at her in Hindi. 'With the few pounds you paid, you're lucky you're not out on the streets, you stupid bitch.'

Layla felt her heart sink like a stone. 'What do you mean?' A cold fear was numbing her soul. Paresh swore at her again, and went out, but she grabbed him. He flung her hand off, then slapped her again, grabbing her hair. He didn't stop this time, but kept beating her till she was on the bed, then jumped on her and sat on her chest. He squeezed her throat till she couldn't breathe.

He let go of her neck, and she gasped, sucking air in. Paresh leant in, his face only inches from hers.

'You'll do as I say, or I'll kill you.' She stared at him in shock and disbelief, and he slapped her once again.

'Do you understand?'

She nodded in dumb fear, her entire body frozen. Paresh patted her down, and took the five pounds of change she had in her pockets. She didn't have a phone, her Indian mobile didn't work here. Paresh leered at her, then started taking her clothes off. She wept and tried to resist, but he hit her again till she succumbed.

When he was done, he left her on the bed, and went outside. Layla dried her eyes, but the tears kept flowing. She covered herself in the bedsheet, trying to hide her shame. She could hear Paresh's muffled voice outside, speaking on the phone.

She searched the bedside table drawers for her phone, but Paresh must've taken it. In any case, she couldn't call anyone on it. A thought struck her, and she checked under the bed. Her suitcase was still there. She pulled it out, and looked inside for her passport. Her heart chilled when she couldn't find it. Tears rolled down her cheeks. She searched the room, but couldn't find it. She had nothing now, she couldn't even go out and make a phone call. She crawled back in the bed and wept.

After a while, she heard the front door open. Voices

drifted through the wall, and footsteps stopped outside the bedroom. Layla clutched the pillow, her heart thumping. The door opened, and two big men walked in. They were both Asian, either Indian or Pakistani. Layla screamed in fear. One of the men dragged her out of the bed, and she resisted. They beat her till she thought she was going to pass out. Then both men took turns forcing themselves onto her. Layla bore the ordeal in silence, her whole body numb and frozen. She lay there like a lifeless doll when they got off her. In a gruff voice one man told her to get dressed. When she didn't obey, he slapped her till she did.

Then the men took her into the living room, where Paresh was sitting, watching TV.

'Take her to the *randi khana*,' Paresh said. The last two words meant brothel in Hindi. Layla bent over, and vomited on the floor.

'Clean it up, you dumb bitch,' Paresh roared. He stood up and kicked her in the ribs. Layla curled herself into a tight ball as he kicked her again. Then she picked herself up, and went into the kitchen. She now knew the price of not listening. Despite the nausea churning in her guts, she forced herself to swallow back the vomit. She cleaned up the mess. One of the men had stuffed her clothes into a bag. The other pushed her towards the door.

Layla took one last look back at the man she once loved, and who had promised to change her life. Paresh had his back to them, watching the TV. He didn't move as the door shut behind Layla.

CHAPTER 4

'You get in first,' John Garnett said to Sarah, and indicated the back seat of the car. He held Matt, Sarah's son, close to his body. The knife was in his pocket. They were standing outside Sarah's house, and to any passerby, John and Matt looked like father and son, standing close. Sarah looked on helplessly.

'Wait,' John said. 'Where's your phone?'

Sarah patted her pockets as John watched her like a hawk. 'In the house,' she said.

He narrowed his eyes. 'You better not be lying.' He pulled Matt closer to himself.

Sarah turned out the pockets on her jeans. She had some cash, and nothing else. Her purse was also on the kitchen counter. 'See?'

John seemed satisfied. 'In the backseat,' he whispered,

his lips tight. 'What the hell are you waiting for?' He reached for his pocket, and Sarah's lips trembled.

'He's your son, John,' she said. 'How can you do this?'

'Get in the car now, or you know what happens.'

Sarah didn't have a choice. She got in the car and strapped herself in. John put Matt in the front passenger seat, then jumped in the driver's seat. The car zoomed ahead as John floored the accelerator. Matt was flung forward, restrained by his seat belt. Sarah held his shoulder from behind and pleaded to John. She had to think. She needed to buy time. Her radio was at the nick, and she didn't have her phone.

'There's still time to stop. Think about what you're doing, John. You're going to be in worse trouble than before.'

His short laugh chilled her to the bone. 'I've got what I wanted. Surely you can see that.'

Outside the window, the streets were a blur. John knew his way around. He was taking the back roads, avoiding the traffic. He came up to the junction of the A57 and stopped at the traffic lights. Sarah tried the handle.

'It's locked,' John said, his eyes on the rear-view mirror. He put one hand inside his coat pocket, while the other held the steering. Sarah knew he had the knife in his pocket. The lights changed, and the car moved ahead. The A57 was a busy dual carriageway, and the car had to pick up speed.

John put both hands on the steering wheel. Sarah thought about her options quickly. It seemed John was headed for the motorway. She could fight him, but an accident on the motorway could be lethal for all of them, particularly Matt. Sarah had one advantage. Her hands and legs were free, and she had a hair pin at the back of her scalp to hold her hair tin place. It was a large pin. She smoothed down her hair and, in a quick motion, pulled the pin into her left hand. She held it down, away from John's eyes in the rear-view mirror.

Ahead, she saw the sign for the M62 motorway. She had to do something now. A roundabout was approaching, and the car slowed. On the right, it was the thick steel rods of the lane dividers, capable of stopping a car at speed. To her left, a line of traffic. If John lost control, he would veer to the right. Matt, on the left, would be safer.

Sarah didn't have her seat belt on. She seized her moment.

She moved the hair pin into her right hand. Holding it like a weapon, she launched herself at John. She aimed for his eye with her right hand, while the left went for the gear box. She grunted as the pin hit the side of his left eye, and she shoved it in as hard as she could. John screamed in pain, and his hand came off the steering wheel. Sarah kept up the momentum, shoving herself into the driver's seat, pushing John to the side.

John groped in his pocket for the knife, but Sarah had wedged him against herself and the door, and her hand was clamped on his. John fought to free himself, and he was stronger. He was twisting, turning in the seat, pushing Sarah back. But the pin was still stuck to the side of his eye, and Sarah slammed the flat of her hand on it and John howled in anguish, his head falling back. Blood spurted from his eye, a warm red flow on Sarah's hand.

The car's front bumper smashed against the car in front, and Sarah fell forward, her head hitting the dashboard. The car's rear swung out, and it slid to the left, hitting the lane dividers. The impact crunched the driver's door, smashing the window and raining shards of glass on John and Sarah.

John was a ghoulish sight – blood dripping down the left eye, face burning, twisting with hate. He screamed once, and his left hand rose, holding the knife. Sarah tried to move away, and she stopped for the blur of movement on her right. It was Matt. He grabbed John's knife hand with both of his. But Matt wasn't strong enough to stop him. It did buy Sarah the few precious seconds she needed. She lifted herself against the dashboard, and pushed Matt away, holding John's knife arm. His macabre face was close to hers, and she headbutted him as hard as she could, hearing the satisfying crunch of his nose bone fracturing.

John screamed again, and Sarah didn't stop. She headbutted him twice more, her forehead becoming a mass of blood and scratches. They were both dazed, and Sarah's eyes began to swim. She had hit the back of her head hard against the dash, and the pain was getting worse.

John had slumped to the left, but he was stirring. His left hand had now lost the knife, but it closed around Sarah's throat. His fingers were strong, and they squeezed. Sarah didn't have the strength to resist. Matt flung himself at John, hitting and scratching his face. John brushed him off, but Matt came back. Sarah tried to raise herself, but her head was still swimming, eyes blurred. John snarled, and fought with her.

Dimly, Sarah became aware of people around the car. They tried to open the doors, but they were locked. An object smashed through the rear window. Voices were heard, shouting. The passenger side door opened, and Matt was pulled out. The driver's door was wedged on the lane divider. A man entered the front, and another from the rear. They held John back, and helped Sarah get out of the car. She stumbled on the road, but arms held her up.

'Matt!' she cried out, and saw her son come running from the side. She gripped him hard, and almost collapsed on the tarmac.

CHAPTER 5

Detective Chief Inspector Rohan Roy was pacing the garden of his house in Dore village. He had tried Sarah's phone once again, feeling more than a touch guilty as she was on her day off. She didn't answer, and he didn't bother to leave a message. She deserved a day off. But it didn't lessen his worries.

He looked up at the window of Anna's room, which faced the garden, and was open now. He rang Sergeant David Bloomsdale of the traffic department. David had provided him with the live link to track Lydia Moran's car. Lydia had befriended Anna, and she also turned out to be the partner of the notorious child-killer, Stephen Burns.

And Roy had every reason to now believe the man Jayden Budden, who came to warn Anna about Lydia, might well be his estranged brother, Robin.

'DCI Roy,' he said, when David answered. 'Any

movement from the car?' Roy had tracked the car to an isolated spot in the Peak District, but Lydia had vanished from her car. She had to be close by, which was frustrating. How could she disappear from the middle of acres of farmland? Roy was forced to come back, because at the back of his mind was the gnawing worry that Lydia had some friends who might still try to do something to Anna.

Bloomsdale said, 'Nothing, guv. It's still there.'

There was obviously no CCTV in the Dales, one thing that would really have helped in this situation. Roy tried to put himself in Lydia's mind. She had planned this. She was meeting someone in that remote spot, right after she met Stephen Burns. Did she even meet him? She left Manchester HMP, formerly called Strangeways Prison, rather swiftly. Perhaps Dr Parsons alerting the prison security of what Lydia was up to had helped.

'Keep an eye on it, David. Thank you.'

Roy hung up, and called Dr Parsons. The psychiatrist listened to him, then spoke rapidly. 'I believe Lydia did see Steven Burns. I informed the prison governor, but by the time the security guards got to her, she was already in the meeting room, talking to him.'

'Did they ask her to leave immediately?'

'Yes. They didn't follow her, as they're not authorised to do so. She left promptly.'

Roy swore under his breath. 'Harold, I need to speak to Burns now. You know this is important.'

The psychiatrist was silent for a few seconds. 'Alright then,' he said quietly. 'Remember the rules, Rohan.'

'See you soon.'

Roy hung up, and went inside. Anna was still upstairs. He knew better than to call for her, as she was probably submerged in a group chat with her friends, or checking out the latest on TikTok. He made himself a cup of tea, sat down, and pulled out his old, dog-eared leather notebook. His hand gripped the pen, and the white page shimmered in his eyes. He couldn't jot down a word.

What if it was true? What if Jayden Budden really was Robin? It stood to reason. He had told Anna to stay away from Lydia and her partner – his stepfather. The man's name was Jerry Budden, but that was clearly a fake name. Nothing had turned up on Home Office records, council tax, electoral rolls, HMRC, and HOLMES (Home Office Large Major Enquiry System). The police database was similarly matchless.

Jerry Budden was a fake name that Steven Burns had adopted, to fool Jayden. Why? Steven perhaps knew that sooner or later he might escape from his clutches. Unless he was dead before that. And if he escaped… Burns didn't want him to go the police with his real name.

The evil bastard was clever, Roy had to give him that. Cruel, but clever. Perhaps the worse combination imaginable.

He put the pen down, closed the notebook, and hung his head. Where was Jayden now? Why did he run away? The questions tormented him. It was possible that Jayden was guilty of something. He was clearly afraid of the police. Roy knew he had to find him, and fast, before he got too far away. If Jayden was indeed Robin, he couldn't afford to lose him for the second time in his life.

His elbows rested on the table, and his head lowered into his hands. He could feel his brain pulsating. That sharp-toothed, shark-faced frustration was nibbling away inside, cutting away his sense of peace. He left these demons in the dungeon, where he didn't have to face them. They were emerging now, their thin, long, bloody fingers raking into his head.

He closed his eyes, gritted his teeth. Get a grip, he told himself. He needed to—

'Dad?'

He lowered his hands slowly, and turned to face Anna. His frozen lips tried to twitch a smile, but failed. Anna came closer, and put a hand on his shoulder. For a young person, she was surprisingly perceptive.

'Are you okay?'

'Yes, fine. All good.' He took a long sip of the tea. 'How're you?'

'What's happened?' Her large, beautiful black eyes probed his soul. He trembled, then looked away. He couldn't face the question, not now.

'Nothing, darling.' He took the cup into the kitchen, and her gaze followed him. Anna heard it before he did.

'Your phone's ringing,' she called out. Roy dashed back from the kitchen.

'DCI Roy.'

'Guv, you won't believe this,' Detective Constable Oliver Walmsley's breathless voice came over the line.

'Sarah and Matt were abducted by John Garnett, Matt's father. She overpowered him, but the car crashed at the first M62 roundabout. Low-speed RTA, thankfully. They're all alive, just so you know.'

'What?' Roy couldn't believe what he was hearing.

'They've taken her and Matt to the Northern General. I'm going there now.'

'See you there.'

CHAPTER 6

Layla leant over the table in the restaurant, picking up the plates. It was an Indian restaurant in the Hillsborough area of Sheffield called Mumtaz, one that did brisk trade, especially on a Friday evening. She could feel the eyes of the four men on the table linger on her. They had been drinking, and were in good spirits.

'Now then,' one of the men leered at her, then hiccupped. 'What's a nice girl like you doin' clearing tables, like?'

His friends tittered. 'She's too good for you, mate.'

'Jimbo, you're full of shit. When was your last shag, eh?'

Layla ignored all of them, and walked away with the plates. It wasn't the first time her pretty looks had drawn a comment from a drunk customer, and it wouldn't be the last.

She didn't care. She was living in virtual slavery. She had no right to be in the UK as her so-called student visa had expired, if it even existed in the first place. She didn't have a passport, and the only money she got from being a waitress was spent on food and clothes.

Her friend, Noor, was working along with several others, in the kitchen. The head chef was a rotund, thick-armed man who sweated profusely, and swore just as badly. His name was Mansour, and he was directing the work of three sous chefs. All the staff in the kitchen came from villages in Pakistan, in the southern region of Punjab.

Noor, who was washing the big pans, cast an eye towards Layla as she stacked up the plates on the counter next to her. The kitchen was steaming hot, and the girls were sweating buckets. Layla wiped the tendrils of black hair sticking to her forehead. Both girls knew better than to speak to one another while Mansour was around. He kept an evil eye on all of them. Fat Mans, as they called him, was a disgusting character. He had forced himself on Layla once, and she had borne the terrible ordeal in silence. She knew what happened if she complained.

Noor had suffered a similar fate. If not Mansour, there was always someone else. Now, she knew from the blank, desolate look on Noor's face that something bad had happened. Layla nudged her friend once with her elbow. Noor shook her head, and carried on scrubbing. Both girls wore full-sleeved black shirts and trousers. It was stifling to work in their uniforms, but they had no choice.

Layla scraped the plates into the bin, then put them in

the dishwasher. Her only comfort was that it was close to half eleven, when the restaurant shut down.

'Hurry up, you stupid slag,' Mansour shouted from across the kitchen. Layla turned, the voice too close for comfort. Mansour had both hands on the counter that separated them, sweat pouring down his corpulent cheeks, and the bulbous neck that sagged with gravity. He was a disgusting, vile man, and Layla hated the sight of him.

'Take these out to table seven and twenty.' He pointed to three dishes with food on them, laid out on the outgoing tray. Layla nodded in silence and hurried to do his bidding. She had to get close to him to reach for the trays, and her body tensed as she felt him move towards her. She was too quick for him though, picking up the trays deftly and making for the revolving doors.

The only saving grace for the Mumtaz restaurant was its busy atmosphere. Time passed quickly.

Once the last punter had left, Layla and Akbar, one of the other waiters, shut the door and sighed in relief. Akbar had been here four years, and he was in a similar situation. He came here on a student visa, and now his traffickers had taken his passport off him and his visa had expired. He had no right to remain in the country.

Layla joined Akbar outside the kitchen for a cigarette.

'Going home?' he asked, taking a deep drag.

'Yes. I'm exhausted.' She glanced at her cheap Timex watch. It was almost one in the morning. Fat Mansour had gone home, thank god. The back door opened and Noor came out. She shivered in the cold.

'I've called a cab,' Noor said, and Layla nodded. Noor slid closer to Akbar, and they went off to have a chat. Layla knew they were seeing each other, and she was glad. After the trauma that Noor had suffered, she deserved a little kindness. Noor and Akbar's story was pitifully similar to hers

Akbar and Noor came from Fatehpur, a remote village in outskirts of northern Punjab. They worked in the fields, helping their parents eke out a meagre living from the land.

One day, a woman who was a distant relative of their mother came to see them. She wore a salwar kameez, the traditional dress for women, and covered her head with a scarf, but she spoke English very well. Her name was Aliyah, and she explained to Noor's parents that colleges in England wanted overseas students. Once they graduated, they got jobs that earned them twenty times what they would do in a big city like Karachi or Lahore.

Once Noor arrived in England, she realised there was no college. The admission documents were excellent forgeries, and the promise of education was nothing but a lie. A man called Afzal met her at Manchester Airport and drove her to Sheffield. She was put in a two-bed flat with six other girls.

The girls were raped repeatedly by Afzal and his men, and they were videotaped. The videos would be sent back to their families, the girls were told, and also be circulated on social media. If they went to the police, their parents would be killed back home. If the girls went to the police in England, they would be killed and their bodies dismembered and thrown in the sea. No one would ever find them, and the police wouldn't believe them in any case.

Layla and Noor had met in one of the so-called brothels, which were flats across Sheffield. They discovered that Paresh, who had kidnapped Layla, and Afzal, were friends. They were probably part of the same gang that trafficked young Asian girls into England and Europe.

A car came through the back entrance. Layla stiffened. It was the black BMW that Paresh drove. The car looked menacing with its tinted window, and headlights glowing like the eyes of a beast. The car stopped, and the tinted window descended. A bearded man sat in the passenger seat. Layla had seen him before. His name was Sunil, or Sunny in short, and he was one of Paresh's men.

'Where's Noor?' Sunny asked in a gruff voice.

'I don't know,' Layla lied. Her heart beat faster. If Sunny was asking, it could only mean one thing. The car's engine died down. Sunny stared at her and Layla looked away. They were distracted by the sounds of footsteps approaching. Noor and Akbar came around the corner of the building, holding hands. They stopped, and Noor turned, but Akbar stopped her. Then he dragged her towards the car, while Noor resisted. Layla couldn't believe her eyes.

Sunny got out of the car, and so did Paresh, from the driver's seat. He held the rear door open while Akbar and Bilal forced Noor into the back seat, then Paresh slammed the door shut. From inside, Layla could hear Noor's pitiful cries. Layla's heart was breaking.

Sunny got back in the passenger side. 'Keep your mouth shut if you know what's good for you,' he snarled at

Layla. Then the car reversed, and drove away.

CHAPTER 7

Detective Inspector Sarah Botham was propped up on pillows, her eyes closed. She didn't stir as Roy gently closed the door behind him. He had already spoken to Oliver and Rizwan, the two DCs who were outside, along with a uniformed constable.

The room was silent, even the beeping of the monitor above Sarah's head was on quiet. Roy didn't understand the red and blue squiggly lines on it, but Sarah was breathing and she was reclining, not lying flat. There was no bandage on her head. She had an intravenous line going into the back of her left hand, and the saline drip was almost finished. Just fluids, nothing else. She didn't have an oxygen mask on, which meant her lungs were working alright. So far, so good.

He tiptoed into the room, lifted a chair, then placed it slowly by the bed.

'Your shoes are bigger than your mouth, guv,' Sarah said, her eyes still shut. 'They creak all the time.'

'That's a relief.' Roy smiled. 'I thought my joints would be creaking.' He became serious as he looked at her pale, tired face. 'I'm sorry.'

Sarah shook her head, and then winced in pain. 'Not your fault.'

'I can't help feeling it is,' he said. In a way, it was. He had caught the wrong man, although he had his doubts. Damien Russell, while a career criminal, had not been the murderer they were hunting for. Now they knew for sure who it was. The reality, as always, defied expectation. Time and again in his career, Roy had realised that truth could be stranger than fiction – because everyone expected their lives to be normal and sensible, but the reality was always warped and weird.

'How are you?' he asked. 'Matt's alright, by the way. I've just seen him in the paediatric ward. Melanie's upstairs with him, and so is your mother.' Sergeant Melanie Sparkes was a member of their team.

Sarah's eyelids flickered open. He knew then she had been awake the whole time. Sarah was a tough cookie. It would take more than a madman with a knife to cower her.

'Thanks,' she whispered.

'I hear you're pretty handy with a hair pin. If I ever kidnap you, I'll make sure your hair's either loose or in a ponytail.'

Sarah laughed, and immediately her face creased in pain. Her eyes screwed shut.

'Sorry,' Roy said. He covered her hand with his, then withdrew it, suddenly self-conscious. Sarah seemed to stiffen as well, and he cursed himself.

'Just don't move,' he said. He gave her the glass of water by the bedside table, and she took a sip, then sank down on the pillows. Her eyes focused on him, and they were clear.

'No one could've known about John. I'm glad he was never a part of Matt's life. We got him in the end, and that's what matters.'

Roy thought of what Sarah and Matt had been through, and his heart withered in pain. Right or wrong, he blamed himself. He'd had his doubts about John, and he kept them quiet. But Sarah was right. No one could've foreseen that John had killed all those women. It was shocking, but true.

Sarah seemed to sense his mood. 'It's alright, Rohan,' she whispered.

He nodded without speaking. The guilt would stay with him, but at least John would now be behind bars, and no further harm was done.

'What's going on your end?' Sarah asked. He told her and as she listened with her eyes closed, he saw her neck muscles tighten, and her body go rigid. She sat up in bed, frowning. He couldn't stop her.

'Are you sure about this? Jayden could really be your missing brother?'

'I think so,' he said, hoping desperately he was correct. 'How else would he know who Lydia was? And why does Lydia keep going to see Burns?'

'You still don't know what Lydia's relationship to Burns is,' Sarah said. 'But she's vanished, right? You need to get hold of her.'

'We're looking. We also need to find Jayden, which is more important. I'm going to see Burns now.' His jaws relaxed. 'You rest here. Get better.'

'I'm fine. I was just dazed from the bump, that's all.'

'No.' Roy shook his head. 'No way you're getting out of here till the doctors say so. You need to look after Matt as well.' He rose. 'I'll let you know how it goes.'

***

An hour later, Roy stood in front of the grey steel door that led to the small living quarters of England's most notorious child killer. Steven Burns. Evil incarnate. Lawrence, the prison security guard, who was as wide as the door, and as tall as Roy, glanced at him. The man looked like he could stop a truck in his tracks. A strange discomfort glimmered in his eyes. He knew what Roy was here for. He had seen Roy before, and each time, they went through the same routine.

'Ready?' Lawrence asked. Roy steeled himself, and nodded. Lawrence pressed his ID badge against the digital pad on the side, and the door clicked open. He pressed the handle down, and the heavy door had to be pushed, even by Lawrence. Then he stood to one side, and Roy stepped across, and inside.

CHAPTER 8

Roy heard the sound of strenuous breathing, and stopped dead in his tracks. He was in the small landing that was boxed in, and through the open door he could see the window of Burns room, and the table and chair in front. Books were stacked to one side, and papers arranged neatly opposite. Roy went in further, his fists clenched.

Then he saw Burns. He was on the floor, doing push-ups. He was in his late fifties, and in incredible physical shape. Prison life, if anything, had made Burns stronger, it seemed. Rivulets of sweat course down his head and back as he continued doing his push-ups, oblivious to Roy's presence behind him.

Roy walked inside, and sat down on the chair. Burns stopped, then sat with his back to the bed. His chest was heaving, and his face crimson.

'Inspector Roy. To what do I owe this pleasure?' Burns

had a face like a kind school teacher. His blue eyes had a twinkle, and when he smiled, his cheeks had dimples. It made Roy want to vomit. It was hard to restrain himself. If only he could reach forward and grab that miserable neck… He blinked, snapping himself out of it.

He got straight to the point. 'How are you, Jerry?'

The smile evaporated from Burns face, which was pleasing to see. A shift occurred, and Burns' jaws tightened, then his lips spread thin.

'Jerry Budden. A nice name, I must say. Did you have to think long for that?'

Burns got to his feet and reached for a towel. Roy got a whiff of his sweaty body, and he crinkled his nose in disgust. But he didn't move, forcing Burns to sit down on the bed.

Burns avoided his gaze, and remained silent, and Roy knew he had touched a nerve.

'Tell us about Jayden Budden,' Roy said, sitting back, acting casual. He had to be careful. He knew Burns was now aware of what was at stake. He didn't want to give the bastard the satisfaction of telling him he didn't know what happened to Robin – yet again.

'Is there a point to these questions?' Burns sighed. 'You come in here talking rubbish, as usual.'

Roy knew Burns had been told of his visit, Dr Parsons would've seen to that. They had to do things officially. He didn't know if Lydia had been approached by Jayden. If she had, she would've told Burns this morning. And if Jayden didn't contact Lydia, she would still have given Burns a progress report of whatever plan they were hatching for Anna. The mere thought of it made rage surge through him. He bit down on his back teeth, fire in his eyes.

If Burns noticed it, he treated it with the same indifference a duck might have for water running down its back. He stood, his shoulder and chest muscles rippling. For a man in his late fifties, it seemed he was in the shape of his life. Far more ripped than he had been a few months ago, when Roy met him for the first time. Ignoring Roy, Burns went into the bathroom. He returned presently, wearing a t-shirt and a pair of jeans. He feigned surprise when he saw Roy.

'Is there anything else, Inspector? I'm sure you have better things to do than sit here.'

'Jerry Budden,' Roy repeated. Burns stiffened slightly, but this time his response was more measured, as if he was expecting it. Roy suspected Jayden hadn't approached Lydia as yet. If he had, Burns would be more prepared.

'Funny how you stayed under the radar all these years,' Roy said, stretching out his feet, and crossing his ankles. 'Now I know. Did you get a fake ID as well, to go with that name? Your pal Keith Burgess was into his photography, he probably made you a driving licence with Jerry's name.'

Burns shrugged, but Roy could see the tightness in his posture. He wasn't relaxed, far from it. He was as uneasy as a circus lion with the trainer in his cage.

'But at work you were Steven Burns, the forensic psychologist. Your victims, even when they came to age, never knew your real identity. Clever, I have to admit. Tell me, Jerry, I mean Steven, how many boys did you abduct?'

Burns sat down on the bed, and leant against the back wall. He blew out his cheeks. 'I'm going to complain about this, Inspector. You really must leave now. This is harassment.'

Roy smiled. Burns' lips tightened, and he averted his face. This was good, Roy thought. For once, he was getting under Burns' skin.

'Jayden's out and about, Steven. He's making contact with us. He knows about Lydia. You won't be seeing her again, by the way. We know all about your little plans.'

Burns ignored him, but his eyes glimmered with a sudden light, and his breathing increased.

'That's right, Jerry. I mean, Steven. Jayden's talking about you. His very dangerous stepfather. We know what you did to Jayden.' The last sentence wasn't true, but it wasn't a lie, either. Jayden had told Anna to stay away for a reason.

'But Jayden's not his real name, is it?' Roy whispered. 'Of all the boys you abducted, there was one you kept alive. Robin Roy. That's Jayden.' Roy leant back in his chair, acting as casual as he was strolling in the park. He didn't want to ask Burns. He knew what answer he'd get. A denial, as the countless times before.

Burns slanted his eyes towards him. 'You think you know so much, don't you? Well, I'm afraid to disappoint you. I don't know what you're talking about.'

'No? Lydia Moran is your ex-partner, isn't she? You can't deny the fact that you see her every week. We've got it on camera. You two are so close. Almost touching each other when you talk. So much emotion on your face.

Amazing.'

Roy smiled, and Burns returned it. His blue eyes were cold and mirthless.

'She's gone now, Steven. You'll never see her again. Who's next in your messed-up world out there? Running out of options now, aren't you?' Roy shook his head in mock sympathy. Burns ignored him.

'And Jayden was raised as your stepson. He hates your guts, and he's spilled the beans. You abused him as long as you could, but he escaped in the end.' A veil dropped over Roy's mind, blackening it with rust and regret. Black, like a moonless, starless night sky. Dark, like the pain twisting inside.

Burns shook his head in a gesture of supreme boredom. But his hands moved like his feet. He was restless, muscles taut with tension. His indifference was an act.

'And he's Robin Roy, the only boy you didn't kill. And no, he didn't turn out like you. He's alright, just a normal bloke. Not fucked-up like you. Maybe that's why he had to escape.' Roy smiled, and this time his pleasure was genuine. He noted the rigid expression on Burns face now, a clash of anger firming up his jaw.

Roy stood. His work here was done. He had the answer he wanted. Burns would never admit to it, but his silence spoke more volumes than the man realised. Guilt had a way of seeping out like blood from a wound.

He went to the door, and pressed on the buzzer to be let out. Before he did, he cast one last look back at Burns. He was looking down, his chest heaving, nose flaring. He clasped and unclasped his hands.

The lock clicked open, and Roy turned the handle. His head rested against the cold steel of the door.

'I hope you suffer,' Roy whispered. 'Suffer the torment you unleashed on all of us.'

He walked out, but Burns' words halted him in his tracks. 'I never suffered. I enjoyed life, and that's the difference.'

Like a bullet train smashing into a sheet of glass, Roy lost his mental balance. His hand gripped the door handle, till his knuckles turned bone-white. He shook, controlling every fibre of his being from grabbing the bastard and knocking his teeth out. He exhaled, then shut the door behind him.

CHAPTER 9

Dr Parsons called out as Roy walked down the corridor of Manchester prison. 'Rohan.'

He halted in his tracks, but didn't turn round. Dr Parsons caught up with him. The psychiatrist had his hands folded behind his back and a mild question in his inquisitive face as his eyes rested on Roy's.

'Would you like to come into my office?'

'Not particularly. I've got two missing people I need to find. One of them just might be my brother.'

'That's big news,' Dr Parsons said softly. 'Very big indeed. Come on,' he indicated a door to the left. It was his office. Dr Parson said, 'I won't take up much of your time. I just need to know what happened.'

Roy sighed, wishing he could get away. But Dr Parsons had done him a favour by alerting the prison governor about Lydia. He walked in after the psychiatrist, who shut the door after he entered.

The room smelt of old journals and paper. The bookshelves were stacked with tomes of medical textbooks, the walls covered in framed certificates. Dr Parsons sat down in his chair, his expression thoughtful.

'Did Burns confess? About your brother, I mean.'

Ray shook his head. 'By now, you should know what he's like. But, I've got enough from him. He's worried. He didn't expect me to know about his fake identity, or about Lydia. There's only one logical conclusion. Either Jayden is my brother, or another boy that he abducted, and kept till the boy was older.'

Roy spread his hands. 'I doubt another boy was abducted, but his parents, or the authorities didn't report it. Burns definitely didn't have any children of his own. Hence…' His words died out.

The psychiatrist nodded slowly, and passed a hand down his mane of white hair.

'Jayden has to be your missing brother. Robin. I know you hate being asked how you feel. But are you ready for this?'

Roy clenched his jaw, and looked down at his feet. A storm of emotions was battling for release in his soul. He just wanted to get along with the job, and see what came his way. That's how he had lived his life, and today wouldn't be any different.

'I've waited twenty-seven years for this,' he said quietly. 'I'll be glad when it's put to rest.'

Dr Parsons stared at him for a while. 'I know there're tests you can do to confirm family linkage. I suspect Jayden either knows what happened to him, or he's got some type of retrograde amnesia. Which means he suffered so much trauma he's forgotten about his childhood. That's the only way he could deal with it, and stay alive. Does he have a police record?'

'No. That doesn't mean he didn't get into trouble, it's just that he didn't get convicted. Once I find him, I'll know more.'

'When you do, go easy on him,' Dr Parson said. 'And on yourself.'

The two men stared at each other for a while, and Roy was the first to look away. Dr Parsons asked, 'Did Burns say anything else?'

'As usual, he barely spoke, and denied everything. But at the end the bastard did say he had enjoyed his life. He didn't suffer like his victims.' Roy grimaced.

'He said that to provoke you.'

Roy sighed. 'Yes, I know.' He grabbed the chair arms. 'I should get going.'

Dr Parsons stood with him and extended his hand. Roy shook it. 'I hope this is the end of a long road. Good luck with it. Let me know what happens.'

'Thanks, Doc, I will.'

'And remember, in the unlikely event of Jayden not being your brother… His words trailed off.

Roy shrugged. His voice was now a whisper. 'Yes, I

know.' He turned and left, closing the door softly.

***

Roy walked into the nick to find Detective Constables Rizwan and Oliver busy at work. Oliver looked up as he walked in. He was facing the corridor of the open-plan office. Rizwan turned in his seat to see what was distracting Oliver, then he waved at Roy.

''ey up, guv. David Bloomsdale from Traffic was trying to get in touch with you. He couldn't get through.'

'I was at HMP Manchester, reception there is not great.' Roy took out his phone and checked. He had a couple of missed calls.

Rizwan said, 'Nothing to report about Lydia's car. Do you want to bring it back to base and let Scene of Crime go over it?'

'That's a good idea. I think Lydia's abandoned the car, anyway.'

At the corner of his mind, a worry surfaced. Was Lydia still alive? It was unusual for her to ditch the car in a deserted sport and do a runner. Either someone picked up, or she was in grave danger.

Drones had been activated over the farmlands where Lydia was last seen. He asked the two DCs, and they both shook their heads.

Oliver said, 'Patrol cars have gone around the farms. There's only so far they can go on the roads before the fields begin. Drone footage shows a few pedestrians, some cars, but no sign of Lydia, nor anyone matching her description.'

'Phone signal?'

Rizwan said, 'Her phone's not been used recently. We're triangulating the signal, but the last location is the city centre, yesterday evening.'

'I guess we keep looking,' Roy said. Melanie Sparks, the detective sergeant, appeared. She had a cup of tea in her hand. 'Would you like one?' She indicated the cup of tea, and Roy nodded, but then waved for her to sit down first.

Melanie had gone round to Lydia Moran's house in Totnes, and Roy asked her about it.

Melanie shrugged. 'She lives in a two-bed flat in a purpose-built block. Nicely decorated, just average, really. I took a sample of her underwear and toothbrush for DNA. Also confiscated the laptop. That's with Cyber-crime now. If it shows anything, I'll let you know.'

'One strange thing, I must say.' Melanie tapped her chin. 'There weren't any photos. Normally, people have some photos of the family, however distant, and friends. Lydia had none.'

'Maybe she's trying to hide her past. We know that she was in a relationship with Stephen Burns.'

'She didn't have any old albums,' Lydia said. No phone either, she must have that on her. Let's see what the laptop shows. We spoke to her neighbours, by the way. They describe her as a normal, nice person. They knew she was a History teacher at Totnes high school. They never had any trouble with her. No one came into her flat late at night, or made noise. They were happy to have her there.'

'Any sightings of Lydia with little boys and girls?' Roy

asked. Even as he thought of the implications, a shudder of nausea shook him.

'I didn't ask the neighbours about that specifically. But there weren't any photos of children, or any toys in the flat. She seems like a loner, to be honest.'

Melanie sipped her tea. She asked Roy, 'You went to her school, anything from there?'

'I spoke to the principal, who was as shocked as I was to learn she is the former partner of Stephen Burns. She's got a clean sheet at school obviously, her CRB checks, going back ten years, are all clean. Without a DBS check she couldn't be a teacher.'

Rizwan said, 'But no checks would mention her former partner. And Jayden seem to think Lydia was dangerous. That's reason enough to arrest her, if you ask me.'

Melanie agreed. 'Now that she's approached Anna there is all the more reason.' She glanced meaningfully at Roy.

Roy couldn't help but worry. With Lydia still out there, Anna wasn't safe. He wondered if Jayden knew where Lydia was. Was Jayden following Lydia around? Perhaps that's how he found her with Anna in the first place.

He turned to the DCs. 'Ollie, you stay here and help Mel lead the search for Lydia. I want to go back and check Jayden Budden's flat. Riz, will you come with me?

'Of course, guv,' said the young DC.

Melanie got Roy's attention before they left. 'I've put out all points bulletins for Lydia and Jayden. No sign of them as yet.'

Roy thanked her, and left with Rizwan. They took Rizwan's car because, frankly, it was far more dependable. Roy glanced morosely at his VW rust bucket, languishing in the light drizzle that had started.

'I really need to get a new car,' he said to no one in particular.

'To be honest, guv, I don't know how you drive that thing. It's too small for you, for starters. And it belongs in a museum, if you don't mind me saying.'

'I don't,' Roy said as they got into Rizwan's Peugeot 405. 'That car's earned its stripes, going up and down the country. It's even done a couple of chases, believe it or not. But it's time for me to say goodbye. I kind of find it hard, though. I know it's rubbish, but I'm used to it.'

'Aye, I get that,' Rizwan said. 'But it's going to stop working one day when you need it the most. Best not to wait that long.'

'I've been dreading that for the last year. Not happened as yet. Which means it probably will happen soon.'

'That makes sense,' Rizwan said. They drove along, talking about how strange it was that John Garnett turned out to be the killer. Both of them were glad that Sarah and Matt were okay.

'You met him, didn't you?' Rizwan asked. 'What did you think?'

'I had my doubts, I'll be honest. Didn't like the guy, but what can I do? I only saw him once. Something about him though. I didn't say anything because it was important for Matt.'

'Yes.' Riz shook his head sadly. 'That poor lad must be in pieces. But still, he's better off without a dad like that.'

'True,' Roy agreed. 'It's just a shame the way he had to find out.'

The weather was rapidly turning as gloomy as their moods. Steel-grey clouds deepened to black on the horizon, and the wind picked up a notch. All of a sudden, thunder flashed overhead, then the first big drops splattered on the windscreen.

To his left, Roy could see the ring of hills on the Peak District. The rainclouds had crossed the valleys, and still had enough moisture left to soak the city.

With the traffic, it took them almost half an hour to get to the area north of Vernon Greaves, where Jayden lived. Rizwan parked the car in front of the tall, shabby terraced building. Roy didn't have keys, so they had to press on the buzzer and wait. No one came down, but someone picked up the call from a flat upstairs. Roy introduced themselves, and they were buzzed in.

The door to Jayden's room was as broken as Roy had left it. The blue-and-white crime scene tape that Roy had stretched across the door frame was untouched.

Rizwan was the first one in, and he stopped suddenly. Roy almost bumped into him.

'Bloody hell, Rizwan said. 'Was it like this when you came in?'

'No,' Roy said, frowning. The place was a mess. The shelves had been emptied of books and photographs. The

TV lay on the floor, shards of glass around it. The carpet had been lifted up in the corners. Someone had even stabbed a knife into the upholstery of the sofa to check if there was anything hidden within.

The bedroom had been a mess when Roy had seen it, but now it looked like a tornado had ripped through it. All the clothes were on the floor, and the cupboards were empty. The drawers had been open, and the bed had been turned upside down.

Roy whistled. 'Good job I took the laptop when I did.'

'I'll ask next door, and on the floor above,' Riz said.

'I'll do the floor below,' Roy said. 'But whoever did this was looking for Jayden, or something that he has. I wonder why.'

CHAPTER 10

Thornseat Lodge is a derelict country house in the Peak District, perched above a hill with magnificent views of the surrounding countryside. It's close to the ancient village of Low Bradfield, and surrounded by acres of woodlands and rolling hills. It was once a hunting lodge, built for a wealthy steel industrialist, and it went the way of Sheffield's once world-famous steel industry – irreversible decline. Today, the huge hunting lodge stands like a giant skull on a hilltop, the empty windows like the black gaps of missing teeth.

The car's headlights picked out the eerie structure, the light beams reflecting from the few shards of glass that remained on the upper-floor windows.

'You sure this is the right spot?' Derby asked, looking around apprehensively.

'That's what the geezer said.' His friend Marcus pulled

on the joint between his lips. Marcus was driving. He was acting nonchalant, but Derby could tell it was an act. Marcus pulled the car into the grass verge on the road and turned the lights off. They were plunged into sudden darkness. It took a while for their eyes to get used to the inky-blackness of the night.

Derby could make out the shapes of the hills that rose all around them. They had come off Mortimer Road, the main route that snaked into through the valleys in this region of the Peak District. At this time of the night, there was no traffic.

Marcus handed Derby the joint. They rolled their windows down. The only sound they could hear was the wind rushing, moving through the trees. The smell of sage, heather and bracken floated in the breeze. Both boys looked at the rear-view mirrors when they saw the light behind them. Another car, coming slowly up the hill.

'Shit, that's him,' Derby said, a little breathless.

'He should cut his headlights. That's weird,' Marcus frowned. He was the taller of the two, and the natural leader. Both boys were in the first year of their A levels. They liked smoking cannabis, and Marcus had found a dealer who could sell them two nine bars – slang for nine ounces of cannabis resin. It was a large amount of cannabis, and the boys could sell some to their friends as well to make some profit. They sold small amounts already, but this deal would make them a big fish in the admittedly tiny pond of their school. They were known as the bad boys of Ashford High School for a reason. It was a reputation both boys were proud to have, and some girls liked it too.

The car appeared to speed up once they were spotted. It parked right behind, blinding them both. Derby was looking less sure of himself by the minute.

'This guy is weird, Marc.' He put his hand on the door handle. 'What if he does something to us? I'm getting out.'

Marcus grabbed his friend's hand before he could move. 'Don't be stupid. These guys are serious. Don't make a bad move.'

'I'm only going to be standing outside,' Derby protested.

'You look shifty. Like you might run away. Not a good look.'

The car behind turned its headlights off. The door opened and a figure stepped out. Derby took one last pull on the joint and then dropped it. Normally he was relaxed with a chilled buzz when he was stoned, but tonight was the opposite. He felt shaky and on edge.

'Relax,' Marcus warned. 'What's the matter with you?'

Derby could feel his heart pounding. He opened his mouth to exhale. 'Why do they want to meet inside that creepy place? What if they kill us?'

'They won't,' Marcus sounded reassuring. 'If they do, then they don't get their money.'

'Yeah? If they kill us then they take our money and keep their drugs. Have you thought about that?'

'Yes, you idiot. We've got our phones, right? We can make a 999 call. I'll tell them others know we're here.

Besides, these are Darren's mates, okay? They won't do that shit, don't worry.'

Derby wished he shared Marcus's confidence. He watched, heart in his mouth, as the figure got closer to the car. He strained his eyes, but couldn't tell if the person was alone. The car was too far back.

As the figure got closer, both boys frowned. It was a slim, smallish person, with long hair. They could tell it was a girl by the time the rap came on Marcus's window. He wound it down slowly.

'Hello? Who's that with you?' A female voice said.

'Lucy?' Marcus was incredulous. 'What the hell are you doing here?'

'Me?' Lucy sounded indignant. 'Why don't you answer your calls? You didn't tell me you were coming here.'

Marcus got out of the car. Lucy was his girlfriend, and she was also an A level student in the lower sixth, a year below him.

Marcus faced his girlfriend, bending forward to speak in hushed tones. 'I told you I was going to be busy.'

'Doing what?' Lucy spread her arms. 'Meeting your other girl over here?' Her voice trembled. 'Tell her to come out of the car.' Lucy took a step back and looked at the windscreen. 'Come out here, you bitch!' She moved towards the car and Marcus grabbed her arm, pulling her back.

'Whoa, whoa, what's wrong with you?'

Lucy struggled to get free, and Marcus let her go. 'Who's with you?' Her words wobbled, and she seemed on the verge of tears.

'Oh god,' Marcus looked towards the heavens and shook his head. 'Derby. Come on out.'

The passenger side door opened and Derby stepped out. He came closer to them. He was shorted than Marcus, who towered above both of them.

'Lucy? What're you doing here?' Derby asked.

Lucy stood very still, and suddenly very ashamed. Her awkwardness radiated from her in waves.

'Would you like to check the boot?' Marcus said. 'Someone might be hiding there.'

'Fuck you, Marc. You flirt with girls right in my face. Then you say not to bother you tonight. What the hell was I supposed to think?'

'What girls? What're you talking about?'

'You shared a spliff with Donna outside school and walked home with her. You walked right past me, you dickhead.'

'Donna's your friend! And I thought you'd already gone, I didn't even see you.'

Lucy folded her arms across her chest. 'Obviously engrossed in her.'

'Look, I don't have time for this. You need to get out of here now.'

For the first time, and from the warning note in

Marcus's voice, Lucy seemed to realise something was going on. Something other than an illicit romantic liaison.

'What're you up to?' She looked around the darkness, and shivered.

'Just go home. Now.' Marcus turned away and spoke to Derby. 'We need to get moving.'

'You've been smoking,' Lucy said. 'Weird place to come for a smoke. Why not Kinder Hill?'

Kinder Hill was the highest point in the Peak District. It's car park was also a favourite spot for teenagers to hang out and get stoned.

'Lucy, do yourself a favour,' Marcus said. 'Go home now.'

Derby was squinting at Lucy's car. 'Is that your mum's new car?' His eyes widened as he strolled over to the new BMW. 'Cool. Is it nice to drive?'

'Derby, get back here. Lucy, I won't ask you again. Go home.'

Lucy shook her head. 'First tell me what you're doing here. You told Derby to get moving. Move where?' She glanced around and her eyes fell on the massive derelict house a few yards away.

'Are you going in there?'

Marcus didn't answer. He shook his head in frustration, and locked up his car. With Derby, he started towards the stone wall that acted as the fence for Thornseat Lodge. The wall was waist high, and leant so far to the left it was practically leaning on the dense shrubbery that had grown wild in the massive front lawn of the property. The boys walked through the gate, their steps audible in the silence. Marcus stopped, and turned. Lucy was walking behind them.

'What the fuck are you doing?' he growled.

'I'm coming with you.'

'Like hell you are.' Marcus walked back to Lucy, and pointed a finger at her chest. 'Go. Back. Now.'

'What will you do if I don't?'

Marcus stared at her for a while. There was hardly any light now, and he could make out only the dim outline of her face. Marcus was only seventeen, and this was his first lesson in realising a stubborn woman is far harder to persuade than a similar-minded man.

'You're unbelievable,' he said through clenched teeth.

He saw Lucy raise her eyebrows. 'If you told me the truth I would've stayed at home. Is this some kind of a drug deal? Are you selling or buying?'

Lucy was rather partial to getting stoned herself. Not as frequently as the boys, but she had her moments.

Derby said, 'It's a good deal. We're getting—'

'Shut up, you idiot,' Marcus hissed. 'You know what? Do what you want. I haven't got time for this.' He turned on his heels and walked up the path to the derelict house.

CHAPTER 11

The huge double doors of the once imperial Thornseat Lodge yawned in front of them like the black mouth of a cave. Wind and rain had laid waste to the heavy wooden doors. The stench of rotting wood, and something more pungent, acrid, hit them like a wave.

Lucy stopped and covered her mouth with the sleeve of her jumper. 'Eeew.'

Marcus put his hand on the door and pushed. The creak was loud enough to make them jump. Marcus was scared, but he tried not to show it. He kept pushing, despite the loud grating that was now like the sound of an animal being tortured.

'God, that sound is awful,' Lucy said, covering her ears.

Marcus stopped. 'Will you stop moaning? It's bad

enough that you're here, do you have to talk as well?'

Lucy put her hands on her hips and pointed at the door. 'That's pretty rich, given that you're making enough sound to raise the dead.'

Darby said, 'I'm not sure if this is a good idea. Do we have to go in? Why can't they just meet us outside?'

'In case some passer-by spots us. You never know. It's not worth the risk.'

'Yes,' Lucy said, 'because the aliens landing in the field over there might report us to another galaxy.'

'We can't escape once we are in there,' Darby pointed out.

'That's why we are not going too far inside. I've told them that.' Marcus took out his torchlight and flush it around. The walls had caved in, and the rubble of plasterboard filled the floor. The ceiling joints were exposed, long wooden beams with termites crawling on them.

The awful smell was stronger now, like a mist that was enveloping them. Darby held his nose. 'Has something died in here? That smells horrible.'

Marcus said nothing. He went inside, his trainers brushing against dust and the rubble that had accumulated over the years. After a small entrance lobby, the reception area opened out into a large hall. Damp had seeped in, and the elements had wasted the structure. The ceilings were high, but only the wooden joists remained. The rubbish on the floor was so thick, they couldn't wade through it.

'This way,' Lucy said, skirting around the edge.

Marcus and Derby tried to walk through the middle, then gave up and followed her example. Lucy was using the light of her phone, and she suddenly stopped dead in her tracks. Something skittered away through the rubbish on the floor.

Lucy whirled round, her eyes wide with fear. 'Was that a mouse?'

'Probably a big rat,' Marcus said, with evident satisfaction. 'There are giant rats around here, with teeth this big.' He held up two fingers three inches apart. Lucy smacked him on the arm, and turned away.

'There's still time for you to go back. Just do it,' Marcus said.

'I'm the leader now,' Lucy said, speaking over her shoulder. 'Just follow me.'

'Yeah, but you're scared of mice,' Darby said, and the boys laughed lightly. The place was deathly quiet, and the sound of their voices echoed against the walls.

They moved on, and another opening, which had once been guarded with doors, led into a large hallway. To the left, a series of doors opened up, and on the right lay huge windows that had now caved in. Glass lay shattered on the floor, mixed with the general rubble. A breeze filtered in, and the moonless night sky was like a heavy weight, pressing in through the broken windows. They could see the outline of the hills and trees. An owl hooted somewhere, a long, mournful sound.

The three teenagers stood huddled together. 'I don't think we should go any further,' Darby said. Marcus had turned his flashlight off, but now he switched it on, cupping his hand over the beam. He turned the beam to his feet, and looked around.

'This way,' he whispered. They saw a staircase going down into a basement. 'He told me to go downstairs. Come on, don't worry. And if you are, just go and wait for me outside.'

'I'm not going down there,' Darby whispered. 'There's no way out.'

'I agree,' Lucy said.

'Fine.' 'See you pussies later.' He went to move past them, but Lucy caught his arm. She put a finger over her mouth.

'Shh, Listen.'

All of them went quiet. They had to strain their ears, but then they heard the sound. Two voices, speaking softly. It sounded like they were having an argument. Lucy went past the basement, and through an opening that led to a set of stairs going up. The boys followed her. The sound of the voices was stronger now, and it clearly came from the floor above. Marcus went past Lucy, and up the staircase. He could now hear the conversation.

A woman's voice said, 'You said you could help us. We can work for you, that's not a problem.'

A man's voice said something in a language that Marcus didn't understand. The woman spoke back in the same language, and again, the argument got heated. The woman raised her voice, and there was a sound of a scuffle. It was followed by the third of what sounded like bodies dropping to the floor. Then came grunting and heaving. Lucy grabbed Marcus's hand. Her whisper was urgent.

'What's going on?'

They heard that had again, something hitting the floor. The grunting was louder now, as were the sounds of a struggle.

Lucy said, 'We need to stop them. I think someone's getting hurt.

Darby whispered, 'I knew this was a bad idea. We need to get out of here now.'

Marcus thought for a while, then made his mind up. He knew the woman was being attacked, and the sounds of her struggle were fading. She was losing strength. It sounded like she was being strangled from the choked cries he could hear.

He flashed his torchlight up the stairs, and went up quickly. 'What's going on here?'

The torch beam illuminated the back of a man. He was sitting astride another figure on the floor. The man didn't look back. He got up swiftly, and ran for one of the windows. Before Marcus could do anything, the figure had jumped through the open space of the glassless window, and crashed into a tree that leant its branches close. He scrambled down the tree, and disappeared. Lucy and Derby stood next to Marcus, rooted to the spot with fear.

The beam from Marcus's torchlight showed a woman's body on the floor. She wasn't moving. There was a dark gash in her abdomen, and blood was pouring out, soaking the wood beneath. Lucy screamed, and covered her face in Marcus's chest.

Darby was panting, his eyes bulging. He tried to speak,

and he stammered. 'I... I... Think she's dead.'

Marcus gave Lucy the torch. Then he knelt, and felt for a pulse at the neck. Ugly bruises had appeared on the woman's cheek and neck. He felt for a pulse. It was very faint, and fast. He fished out his phone. He called 999, and for an ambulance.

CHAPTER 12

Roy was cradling a glass of red wine, his head slowly succumbing to the stupor of a post-prandial haze. Anna had made a pasta sauce of chorizo and tomatoes, and it had been delicious. He knew he would miss her terribly when she went home. He glanced at her. Anna was watching a nature show on TV.

'What time is your train tomorrow?' Roy asked.

'Half twelve. Will you drop me off?'

'Yes. If the car starts, that is.'

'Not this again. It's quite hilly around here. You really need to get a new car.'

'I was having this conversation with Rizwan today. Part me of thinks I've grown so used to the car I can't let go.'

Anna rolled her eyes. 'The car might let you go, Dad.

When you're going up a hill one day.'

'Yes,' Roy drained the dregs of wine from his glass and smacked his lips in appreciation. That had been a lovely red from the Napa Valley. He burped, and Anna frowned in disgust.

'Sorry.' Roy covered his mouth. He was used to doing it when he lived alone. 'Life can be an uphill battle sometimes.'

He wondered how much he should tell Anna about Jayden. Anna had met him, obviously, when he warned her to stay away from Lydia. Should he let Anna know that Jayden might well be her long-lost uncle?

Anna knew about the scar from his past, and how much it affected him. As she'd grown older he was able to talk to her more, which was heart-warming. But he still kept the normal parent–child boundaries.

It was maddeningly frustrating now, that Jayden was still on the run. Without having a proper conversation with him, and then the genetic tests, it was unwise to tell Anna. But he knew that she wondered who Jayden was, and it pained Roy not to be able to reveal the potential news.

And yet…just on the off chance he was wrong about Jayden being Robin, it was best if he waited. Damned if he did, and damned if he didn't. Life remained an uphill battle.

Roy was on a train, but he didn't know the destination. He called his mother and, surprisingly, Maya picked up, despite it being the dead of night. The train hurtled through the darkness, and went over a bridge at full speed, the carriages rattling. Roy asked his mother where the train was headed, but she wouldn't answer. She kept asking the same question repeatedly.

'Where's Robin? I know you found him. If you don't tell me where he is, I won't tell you where the train's headed.'

Roy tried to reason with her, but Maya could be stubborn when she wanted to be.

'If you don't tell me, you'll be on this train for the rest of your life!' She started to scream, her face turning red and furious. Her hair was white and straggly, and she pointed a long, crooked nail at him.

'It's all your fault,' she screeched. 'You were with him that day he was stolen. You could have stopped it, and you did nothing. You let that monster take my son!'

'No!' Roy howled. 'Stop the train, I want to get off.'

His mother refused, and the questions remain the same. Roy had no answer. He hung up, and called his father. The phone kept ringing. The ringing got louder, and that's when he woke up with a start.

The work phone was buzzing on the bedside table. It was pitch-black, and he blinked a few times. He groped for the phone, and finally managed to press the green button. He was duty senior investigating officer for the week.

'DCI Roy.'

'Hello, guv. Inspector Adams reporting. We've found an IC4 female, deceased. We're in Thornseat Lodge, by Burbank village in the Peak District.'

Roy slipped his legs out of the bed, and rubbed his eyes, stifling a yawn. 'Who alerted you?'

'999 call from a teenager. Three of them came up here, to have a party of some sort, I think. They found the dead body. The teenagers are okay. They're giving statements.'

'Send me the location please.'

'See you soon, guv.'

Roy got up, and went to the loo. He splashed water on his face, forcing himself to wake up. His mind was still on that horrible dream. It was a recurrent one, and it stayed with him during his waking hours.

He got dressed, then wrote a note for Anna. It was four in the morning. He checked all the doors and windows, ensuring they were shut. CCTV was on in every room, and also outside, including motion sensor flashlights. He checked the app on his phone, for the CCTV live view. Satisfied, he went out the door and got into his car. The headlights sliced through the darkness of a chilly morning. The rains had mercifully stayed away, but as summer was drawing to an end, a shroud of cold was descending on the hills.

Roy followed the directions on his satnav. The wonders of satellite communications meant even the remote areas of the Peak District were well served by road directions. Phone communication was a different matter, and radio signals often got lost out here. The police used satellite phones when phone communication suffered.

From the A57, Roy took a right onto Mortimer Road, which snaked into the heart of a deep valley, where the rolling land undulated into invisible hills that rose like juggernauts, blotting out the night sky. His headlight beams did the best they could, but darkness eventually swallowed them up, limiting his vision. As expected, he didn't pass a single car in the opposite direction. He eventually saw the flashing blue lights in the black breast of the hills, like a lonely spaceship sending out a distress signal.

The road became a wide dirt track and he slowed down, avoiding a couple of potholes that his headlights mercifully picked up. The road sloped gently upwards. The car bounced and shuddered its way up to the two vans and police cars, and an ambulance parked next to a gigantic, derelict house.

Uniforms had set up a perimeter with tape. Roy got out of his car and walked to the uniformed officers, one of whom he recognised. Halogen lights had been set up on tripods inside the derelict house, visible in the upstairs windows. It gave the building an eerie quality, as if lights had appeared in its empty eye sockets.

'Hello, guv,' Inspector Jonty Adams, in his peaked cap and high visibility top, nodded as Roy approached.

A stiff wind blew across the road, skittering dirt and pebbles on the road. Roy shook hands with Jonty, who gave him a situation report.

'The teenagers arrived here at midnight, according to them. They came to meet some friends for a rave party that never happened. I'm not sure how true that is, given the absence of electricity generators and sound systems. However, they went inside, and found a man attacking a woman upstairs. The woman was already on the floor and wounded. The man ran off. However, her injuries were fatal. She died before the ambulance could arrive.'

'Where are the teenagers?' Roy asked.

Jonty led Roy to the ambulance. Two paramedics were standing outside, and one of them opened the door. Two boys and a girl were sitting inside. They looked no more than sixteen or seventeen years old. One of the boys was taller, bigger, with longer hair. He was whispering something in the girl's ear, but straightened as the door opened fully. Roy clambered into the ambulance, shutting the door behind him.

Three pairs of worried eyes inspected him closely. Roy didn't smile. He sat quietly, watching them. He let the silence linger on for a few seconds, aware his audience was getting nervous. Eventually, he spoke.

'My name is DCI Roy of the major investigations team of south Yorkshire police.' He held up his warrant card for them to see. The teenagers looked too worried to take much notice of the card, apart from the taller boy, who looked like their leader. He examined the card then glanced at Roy. The girl was leaning against him, and Roy guessed they might be a couple. The other boy was shorter, but stocky around the chest and neck.

'This is now a murder investigation, as you know. You found the victim, is that correct?'

Hesitantly, all three nodded. Roy asked, 'Were all three of you together when you found the body? Or did one of you come across it before the others?'

The girl flicked her eyes towards the taller boy. 'What's your name?' Roy asked. He had taken down the names from Jonty already, just to be sure.

'Marcus Fairbanks,' the boy said, in a composed tone. He kept eye contact, but his nervousness was apparent in the way his legs moved, and his left hand gripped his knee.

'Do you mind if I call you Marcus?'

The boy agreed, and Roy murmured his thanks.

'Tell us what happened, Marcus.'

After a pause, the teenager said, 'I went upstairs and saw this man. He was sitting on top of the woman. When the torchlight fell on him and I shouted, he got up and ran. He jumped through the window and grabbed the branch of a tree. He shinned down it very quickly, we couldn't stop him.'

'I'm glad you didn't,' Roy observed. 'What happened after that?'

'By that time, my friends had come up the stairs. We saw the girl was in a bad way. There was a lot of blood. It came from the wound in her abdomen.' Marcus stopped, and his eyes flicked down to the floor.

'You're doing well,' Roy encouraged him. 'Take your time.'

'I felt for the pulse,' Marcus licked his lips. 'It was really fast. I've done first aid, and I know that means major blood loss. I think she was still breathing, because I saw the chest rise and fall. I called an ambulance. It took a while for the ambulance crew to arrive. By that time, she'd stopped breathing.'

'What did you do while you waited for the ambulance?'

The girl stirred, and sat up straighter. Marcus glanced at her. 'What's your name?' Roy asked.

'Lucy Albright,' the girl said, clearing her throat. 'We didn't know what to do, to be honest. Marcus wanted to give her CPR. He said that might save her.'

Roy glanced at Marcus. 'Did you?'

Marcus shook his head. 'I wanted to, but there wasn't any point. We needed to stop the blood loss, and we didn't know what to do. I try to press on the wound, but it kept welling up between my hands.'

'It was pointless,' Lucy's voice trembled. Her eyes glistened with tears. Mascara had smudged around her eyes, and she wiped away fresh tears. 'It was horrible. Our hands were full of blood, but we couldn't stop it pouring out.'

Marcus put a hand around Lucy's shoulders, and she leant into him. They were quiet for a while.

'I'm sorry,' Roy said softly. 'You did the right thing, by the way. Did she stop breathing shortly after that?'

In silence, the couple nodded. Roy shifted his focus to the other boy, who sat the watching him, his face the colour of a white sheet. He was breathing fast, and it seemed like he was going to vomit. Roy shuffled to the ambulance door and opened both of them. A gust of fresh air came in, relieving the close atmosphere. Roy took a seat again, and gave the teenagers a few seconds.

'What's your name?' he asked the boy.

'Derby Johnson.'

'Do you have anything else to add, Derby?'

Derby shook his head. He looked at the floor, then blurted out suddenly. 'I didn't want to go in there. I knew this was a bad idea.'

Roy saw Lucy and Marcus stiffen. Marcus shot Derby a warning look, but the boy wasn't paying attention.

'What was a bad idea?' Roy asked. Marcus interrupted before Derby could speak.

'The rave we arranged. We thought this hunting lodge might be a good location, but it's actually very unsafe.'

Roy let his eyes linger on Marcus for a while. When the silence grew uncomfortable, he spoke. 'If you were organising a rave, where's all the equipment?'

Marcus swallowed, his Adam's apple bobbing up and down. 'We were scoping it out, actually. I thought this might be the right location, but it turned out that wasn't so. That's why we went inside to have a look.'

'Are you sure that's the reason you came here?'

Marcus nodded, and Lucy and Derby looked to the floor. Roy kept his attention on Marcus, who was fighting for composure. Roy blew out his cheeks.

'As I already said, this is now a murder investigation, Son. Which means you need to give a statement. You found the body, so your statements will be used in a court of law. Do you understand that?'

Marcus didn't speak, but his eyes flickered to the floor, and a muscle twitched in his jaw.

'If you don't tell us the truth now, and it comes out later on, then we have to consider your role in this crime.'

It was Derby who spoke. His foot stamped on ambulance floor, making it shake.

'Just tell him, damn it!' he shouted. 'Just tell him, okay?' He glared at Marcus, his eyes wild and red-rimmed. Marcus closed his eyes and sighed softly. Roy waited.

'All right. We came here to buy some hash. Weed, I mean. Cannabis. This guy I know could sell us nine bars for half the price. He didn't turn up, as it happens.'

'Are you sure?' Roy asked. 'What if he was the guy who attacked that girl upstairs?'

The question stunned the teenagers. Their spines seemed to jerk straight in unison. Even Marcus showed fear on his face for the first time. Colour drained from his cheeks, and his mouth opened.

'We have to consider that option,' Roy said. 'Your dealer might have come up here, with someone that he intended to kill. He was going to kill her, and then wait for you. But you chanced upon him while the matter was still in progress.'

The teenagers had nothing to say. Roy continued. 'What's the name of your dealer?'

'Naz,' Marcus said slowly. 'That's all I know. He's a friend of the guy I score from usually. I've never met Naz before, but I spoke to him. I've got his number.' Marcus shrugged.

'I need that. And the contact details of your usual dealer.'

'It's on my phone and I had to hand it to your lot outside.'

'OK. What did this guy Naz sound like? Was he young, old? What sort of accent? When you spoke to him, could you hear sounds in the background?'

Marcus frowned as he thought. 'He had an accent from around here, no doubt. He coughed once, I remember that. And he was on a street, I could hear cars. But then he went through a door, and it was quieter.'

'When did you speak to him?'

'Eight o clock, last night. Around that time, anyway.'

'Did you hear any other voices? Maybe a woman, or a child?' Roy pressed.

Marcus concentrated, staring at the floor. Then he shook his head. 'No.'

Lucy spoke up. 'Our phones. When do we get them back?'

'Your phones will be examined by the forensic department. You will need to come into the station to give a statement. You can have a lawyer present if you want to. Are all of you under eighteen?'

The teenagers nodded. Roy said, 'In that case there will be a safeguarding officer with you at all times, to talk you through the process. Your parents can attend if they want to, but if you're over sixteen, it's not compulsory.'

'Thank you for being honest with me,' Roy said to Marcus. 'Is there anything else I need to know?'

'I've told you everything.'

Roy pressed his lips together. 'Your torchlight showed the man's back, is that correct? And he was sitting astride

74

the woman on the floor?' Marcus nodded.

'Did you see his hands on neck, or any exposed part of his body?'

Marcus thought hard. Patches of colour were returning to his cheeks. 'No, I didn't. His hair was black, I think. Dark brown. I didn't get a look at his hands, sorry.'

'What was he wearing? What type of shoes?'

'A black jacket up to his waist. Dark trousers, I couldn't tell what colour. It happened so quickly. He went through the window, and down the tree.'

'Can you guess his age?'

Marcus shrugged. 'He's not old, clearly. I can't say for sure.'

Roy looked at the other two teenagers. 'Did you see anything else?' Lucy and Derby shook their heads.

Roy nodded. 'Your parents have been informed. They should be here soon.'

CHAPTER 13

Roy came out of the ambulance, and spoke to Inspector Jonty Adams briefly.

'Where are the phones?'

Jonty took Roy to one of the sergeants, who had them stashed in specimen bags in his car. Roy took the phones back to the ambulance, and Marcus logged into his. Roy got the number of the two drug dealers, then took the phones away again.

He faced Jonty after he had inserted the numbers in his own phone.

Roy asked, 'Has Justin arrived yet? Justin Dobson was the head of Scene of Crime, or the forensics department.

'Not yet,' Jonty said. 'He didn't answer his phone. I've left a text, and will try again.'

'What about Dr Patel?' Sheila Patel was the veteran

pathologist for Yorkshire police, and Roy respected her opinion. She had a sharp tongue, and a tough exterior, but he suspected her heart was in the right place.

'She's on her way,' Jonty said. 'To be honest, she always picks up a phone, no matter how late, or early.'

Roy thanked him, and made his way to the gates of the large building. The old stone fence was crumbling, with many of its blocks missing. The entire structure was leaning to one side, and looked dangerous. He took a few seconds to appraise what he could see of the building. There was a faint glow at the edges of the horizon, and the light was improving slowly. The derelict building had once been grandiose, and it was now in a sad, sorry state. Given the way in which sections of the roof had caved in, he didn't think it would be safe inside. The huge windows didn't tilt to one side, and there weren't any big cracks that were visible, which meant there wasn't any subsidence.

He lifted the blue-and-white tape, and his boots crunched gravel as he went up the drive overgrown with weeds and vegetation. The stench hit him immediately; rotting leaves, and putrid animal waste. A uniformed constable was standing guard at the entrance. Roy gave him his name and rank, and put on shoe coverings. He snapped nitrile gloves on his hands, and also a mask, which he pulled down to his chin.

Uniform had cleared a path inside, and laid down plastic boards. He stepped on them, and walked in slowly, flashing his torchlight around. Years of dust and rubble lay scattered on the floor. As he went through the massive reception lobby, he saw a pile of bricks and powdery plasterboard and timber where the ceiling had caved in.

He went through the double doors, and into the wide hallway with the floor-to-ceiling windows on his right. The sun wasn't visible, but between the hills, a pink iridescence was making its presence felt, banishing the dark blues from the sky. In its heyday, this place must have been beautiful. Roy wondered what happened to leave it in such dereliction. It was a shame.

He stepped carefully on the sterile boards placed on the stairs, and went up to the now well-lit room. Bay windows looked out to the rolling countryside down the hill. Marcus had been right, a couple of trees almost leant their branches inside the window. Shards of sharp glass remained attached to the windowsill. Bright lights stood in tripods in four corners, casting long shadows.

A uniformed sergeant and constable were looking out the window. They had established a perimeter, with white paint around the central crime scene, where the body lay. The woman was on her back, fully clothed. She had black trainers on her feet, and blue jeans. She wore a light-blue denim jacket, and a blouse underneath.

Blood had seeped out and formed a halo around her midriff. Her entire chest and abdomen was bathed in dark blood, slowly turning to black. Her eyes were wide and staring, fixed into a never-ending distance. She had long black hair. Her skin tone suggested the initial reports were right, she was IC4, or South Asian. Indian, Roy thought from her facial features, rather than Pakistani.

He didn't get closer to the body. He looked around the place first. Somehow, the ceiling joists had held in this room. Damp had claimed all the walls, and the plasterboard lay in dusty heap on the floor.

Wooden beams were exposed on the walls, but some parts of the wall remained. He could see the elaborate carvings on the corners. Someone had spent a lot of money on this place a long time ago. He noticed two doors. He'd entered through one, and next to where the uniforms stood there was another door on the left. He turned to the uniformed sergeant, and flashed his torchlight at the rear door.

'What's through there?'

'I wouldn't advise going there, guv. The floor's caved in, and gone right through the ceiling of the lounge below.'

Roy went and had a look in any case. The sergeant was right. His torch beam picked up a gaping hole in the middle of the floor, through which the ground floor room was visible. The floorboards creaked and dipped alarmingly, as he took a couple of steps inside.

He went back to the crime scene. He was glad that Forensics hadn't arrived as yet. It gave him a fresh, first view. A bit like a painter looking at her macabre canvas that hadn't been touched as yet. The woman's body in the middle was the centrepiece, but the rest of the room was just as important. He went to the windows, and examined the floor around carefully.

His torch beam picked up boot prints on the floor. He pointed the prints out to the uniforms, who confirmed they hadn't walked in that direction.

Roy took out a marker pencil from his coat pocket and circled the boot prints with black ink. Not perfect, but they would attract Justin Dobson's attention when he finally arrived.

'Keep this area clear,' Roy instructed the uniforms.

He saw half a boot print on the window ledge as well. The killer had to be young, fit and agile, he thought to himself. The branches that were less than six feet away from the windowsill, and could hold a man's weight, but this wasn't the job of an old bloke.

The shards of glass on the windowsill didn't have any marks of blood. But he did see a piece of black cloth. He took out a specimen bag from his coat pocket, and, with a gloved finger, removed the fragment of cloth. He held it up to the halogen lights. It looked like a piece of leather, which, with any luck, was from a leather coat the killer was wearing.

Small scraps of clothing could yield valuable clues. He folded the specimen bag inside his pocket, and shook out a new one. He continued his surveillance around the room. The rest of the floor was clean. He stopped when he came to the large patch of blood around the body's midriff.

He didn't have to use the torch beam any more. The woman was in her early twenties, or even younger, he thought. She had dark eyes, and light-brown skin. He noted the necklace around her neck. She had marks on her throat, but he knew the killer probably wore gloves. In any case, Justin would check for fingerprints all over the body.

The clothes were cheap, and well worn. The fingernails were painted, but they were fading. Carefully, he stepped closer and crouched by the hands. With a gloved finger, he pulled the mask up to cover his nose. Gently, he prised the fingers open, and looked at the palm. The hand was rough and calloused, a working woman's hands. He saw some yellowish stains around the nails, which could be due to nicotine. The rest of the body was unremarkable.

Steps came up the stairs, and Dr Patel appeared. She saw Roy crouching close to the body.

'Hope you haven't messed up the crime scene, DCI Roy,' she said, her sharp features blank. Short black hair was combed down the middle, and, despite the early hour, she looked ready for a business meeting in her neat navy-blue skirt suit and tights. She even had some make-up on. Roy wondered if she went to sleep like that, but wisely refrained from making any comment.

'Just looking after it for you.' He straightened, grimacing as his knee joints popped. 'Cometh the hour, cometh the pathologist,' he said.

'Flattery will get you everywhere,' Dr Patel said, stepping inside the circle.

CHAPTER 14

Roy watched as Dr Patel put her briefcase on the floor, then took out a sterile sheet. She placed on it swab sticks, specimen bags, and a rectal thermometer to measure core temperature.

She had already put on a sterile plastic apron gloves mask and shoe covers. Roy let her get on with the work. He went back down the stairs, and through the double doors, into the corridor.

The tall windows were letting in the first rays of sunlight. Three rooms lay to his right, and when he pushed the broken doors open, he saw the same rubble on the floor, and gaping holes in the ceiling. The last door led to a staircase that went downstairs.

He took out his torch and pointed the beam down. Immediately, he saw the boot prints on the dusty steps. He bent down to take a closer look, then took some photos. He put rings around the prints with the white marker. Then he looked at his watch. Justin should be here soon. He went down the steps, carefully avoiding the boot prints. The prints looked similar to the ones had found upstairs, and hopefully the forensic gait analyst would be able to match them.

The basement was dark and dingy. Rodents scurried in the far corners, hiding from the beam of the torchlight as it surged across the floor. Old furniture lay stacked in one corner, next to some rusty garden spades. It was a large basement, one where he could just about stand to full height, and walk around. The floor had caved in several places, exposing the black earth underneath.

The footprints on the steps meant someone had come down here. It might well have been the killer. Did he come here and hide, waiting for his victim? It was certainly possible.

The teenagers watched the woman die, so she wasn't killed somewhere else and brought here. Which meant the murderer and the victim met here for a specific purpose. Why meet in this remote place, where the roof could fall on your head? Because no one else would come here.

Roy stood there, and it seemed his torchlight was trying to scythe through the darkness in his mind. He looked around the basement for a while longer, but found nothing apart from the detritus of dereliction. He went back upstairs.

He heard voices, and steps coming in from his right, the direction of the main entrance. The familiar figure of Justin Dobson appeared, resplendent in his blue Tyvekcoated Michelin man forensic suit. Even the suit couldn't hide his bulging belly. His eyes were red-rimmed, and he glared at Roy.

Roy tapped his watch. 'What time do you call this?'

'Bloody awful time, that's what,' Justin said morosely. Roy pointed at his belly, which had grown considerably in the three months he had known Justin.

'Too much beer, that's your problem. Five pints last night?'

'No,' Justin said, at tad defensively. 'It's a weekday night.' Roy got closer, and Justin flinched. Roy could smell the alcohol on his breath. He shook his head.

'You stink like a brewery. Hope you had some company as well.' He raised his eyebrows at the last statement. Justin was a confirmed bachelor. He had never been married, and his long-term relationships didn't last. Justin's drinking had gone through the roof recently. He remained tight-lipped about it, but this wouldn't be the first time he had turned up to work looking like a wreck.

Justin remained silent, and Roy knew the answer.

'I better get started,' Justin said, moving away. He had a bulky bag in his hand, and Roy knew it was the first of a few. His other equipment was in the van.

'Where are your helpers?'

Justin pulled a face. 'It's like trying to rouse the dead. Tony should be here in a couple of hours.'

Roy left Justin, and walked outside. A couple of cars had arrived, and he saw a group of men and women speaking to Jonty Adams. The parents were here.

Roy knew that Jonty was more than capable of handling the preliminaries. He left them to it, and walked across the fence, and to the rear of the property. There was an outhouse to the side, a stone structure whose roof had collapsed completely, and tall weeds grew all around it.

He went up to one of the broken windows and flashed his torchlight inside. Nothing but the usual rubble met his eyes. He picked his way through the knee-high vegetation and had a look at the garden. It was a jungle really, that sloped down the hill and disappeared into a bank of trees at the rear.

The light was improving and he looked around for a while, searching for boot prints, a scrap of paper, anything. He couldn't see anything obvious.

The rear of the house was in similar shape to the front. The huge roof was in tatters, and the elements had eroded most of the walls. Large double door wooden glass patio doors led into what had once been a sculpted topiary garden. Now the hedges were twisted into weird, macabre shapes.

Roy walked down the stone steps laid in the garden. He went in through one of the rear entrances. The floors had collapsed, exposing rotten timbers and earth. He skirted around the edges of the room, and emerged into a corridor that linked up with one of the front rooms. He heard a creak above his head, and looked up to find a lose timber joist, barely held in place at one end. This place was a death trap.

He went out, and circled back around to the front. The ambulance and one of the squad cars had gone. So had the parents. Jonty came up to him.

'The parents will take the teenagers home first, and then bring them back to the nick. Do you want me to stick around?'

'No need. The parameters have been set, and your men will be here. If you're heading back to the nick, would you mind asking Traffic to look for CCTV footage on the A57 last night? I want to log the cars that turned into Mortimer Road last evening. That's the only road route up here.'

'No worries, guv.'

Roy watched Jonty go, his mind churning. He went back inside, and made his way up to the crime scene. Justin had set up two cameras and tripods, and was taking photos. Dr Patel was taking swabs from the victim's hand. Roy crouched on the floor and the pathologist looked up at him.

'I guess this is one case where you won't be asking me the time of death,' Dr Patel said, going back to her task.

'No. Just after midnight, according to the teenagers. Half past, they said.'

'Well the body certainly very fresh. The colour changes just starting, and no sign of rigor mortis as yet. Death was recent, no more than four to five hours.'

'What else did you find?'

Dr Patel pointed at the hands. 'Take a closer look at the stains on her fingers.'

Roy did so, as Dr Patel held the lifeless hand up to the light. At first, he wasn't sure what he was looking at, but then he saw the traces of colour on the fingertips.

'What on earth is that?'

'Different types of nail polish. I could use the technical terms, but you wouldn't understand.' Dr Patel suppressed a smile, then became serious. 'I think she worked at a nail bar.'

'There's plenty of those in town,' Roy said.

'Yes,' Dr Patel agreed. 'And also, she's in her late teens to early twenties, at the very oldest. She could be a student at the university.'

'Good point.' Sheffield University was one of the biggest in England, and the city had a large student population. The victim could be a student during day, and work at a nail bar in the evenings.

'Her hair is also greasy,' the pathologist said. 'She's probably not washed it for a while. There's also some bruising in the arms, like she's been in a fight. They're old bruises, so a few days old at least. She's got fresh bruises on her face and neck – that's from last night.'

Roy pondered that. 'She got into some scraps before? As a student she doesn't quite fit that mould. Unless someone hit her.'

'Yes. I can see old bruising on her cheek as well. This woman has been hit in the recent past.'

'Her clothes are cheap,' Roy observed. 'Primark would be my guess, or even second hand. Not that I know much about women's clothes,' he admitted. His experience consisted of taking Anna shopping. He was the odd one out in Urban Outfitters, the solitary male trying to look inconspicuous as Anna tried on new clothes. Bags of fun.

'The trainers are also scuffed and old,' Roy continued. His eyes rested on the terrible wound in her abdomen. 'Pretty deep knife wound?'

'Certainly.' Dr Patel nodded. 'Her attacker wasn't a novice. He knew how to hit the aorta, which is quite deep in the abdominal cavity. That's the main trunk of blood supply to the lower half of the body. Once that's severed, death happens quickly.'

'And why would a student know a man like that?' Roy murmured to himself.

CHAPTER 15

Dr Patel's work was done, so she packed up her stuff. Justin was working away, taking swabs from the ground. Roy went up to him.

'Be careful around here. No place to go roaming. The roof might just fall on your head.' Roy grimaced. 'What a shame that would be.'

'You can forget a quick forensic report, for starters,' Justin said, pulling his mask down. 'And I might just need more booze to get rid of the pain.'

'Not much change to your current plans, then. And yes, I do want a report by later today.'

'See? You better wish nothing falls on my head.'

Justin indicated the body. 'Young girl. Never nice.'

'Nope. I bet you we don't find anything on IDENT-1. But stranger things have happened.' IDENT-1 was the national database for fingerprints.

Roy waved goodbye. 'I'd better get back to the nick. I meant what I said about this place being a deathtrap. Be careful.'

'I'd watch what you say,' Justin said. 'Sounds like you care about me.'

'Fat chance,' Roy said, grinning to take the sting out of his words. 'See you later.'

'Alligator,' Justin called out as he walked down the stairs with Dr Patel.

'Not heard that one since primary school,' Roy called back. He went downstairs, and found Dr Patel gingerly picking her way on the sterile boards. Roy joined her, and she gasped when she heard him.

'Sorry, didn't meant to startle you.'

'Oh dear.' Dr Patel had a hand on her chest. She looked at the horrible mess of the room, the once-lovely ceiling now caved in with damp and rot. 'This place really does give me the creeps.'

Roy nodded his agreement. 'There had to be a reason why they came here. The youngsters were foolish, but the killer and victim had an agenda. It didn't seem like she was forced to come here. She didn't expect to be killed.'

Their voices echoed around the room. They came out into the large reception, and then outside. Dawn was now painting itself into a grey-blue sky, broad brushstrokes of gold and pink giving way to celestial blue. The green hills seemed to shrug and rise out of their dark slumber, as if saying hello to the universe. A cool, pristine wind gathered pace across the valley, bringing with it the scent of heather and bracken. An invigorating sight and smell, particularly refreshing after the sad decay inside. Man had nothing on nature, Roy had to admit.

'The killer couldn't have gone far,' Dr Patel remarked. She knew what the teenagers had seen. 'If I were you, I'd focus in the villages around here.'

'There's only two as we're not far from Sheffield. Wyming Brook Nature Reserve is only thirty miles from here. Uniform squads have already been sent for a door to door. Now that we have light, time to get the drones up there.'

'Good. I'll get the post mortem done later today. Ask Sarah to give me a call.'

Sarah and Dr Patel were good friends. Roy didn't know why exactly, but then again Sarah had friends everywhere in the force, it seemed.

'She's a little preoccupied, but I'll tell her.'

Dr Patel stopped and turned. Her normally stern face was changed, touched with concern. 'Why? What happened?'

Roy struggled with the need to tell Dr Patel. In the end, he realised she would hear anyway. News like your ex-partner and son's father turning out to be a serial killer didn't happen every day. Dr Patel's face fell when he finished talking.

'Keep it to yourself, please. Apart from us, no one else knows.'

'I'll see her at the hospital, now. Thanks for letting me

know. I wondered why she didn't return my call this morning.'

'I think she needs to—'

'Rest, I know. I know the medical consultants at Northern General. I want to speak to them as well, about her.'

She nodded, and walked off, heels clicking on the stones. Roy started towards his car. He wondered about how he was going to resolve the current crisis, and deal with this new case. Without Sarah. That was a significant factor. Unconsciously, he had learnt to rely on her, and he would miss her while she took some time off. Knowing her, she would be raring to come back. But he wouldn't let her. She needed to be there for Matt right now. That poor boy needed a lot of support. Thank goodness Sarah had her mother, Catherine.

He waved goodbye to the uniforms. As he drove down the dirt track, he knew he had to find Jayden, and Lydia, without delay. After him, someone else had visited Jayden's flat and searched it top to bottom. There must be a reason. Who could be looking for Jayden? And what for?

All of a sudden, a worry stung his mind like a spear. He pulled out his phone and thumbed Anna's number. It rang out. He cursed, and called her again. It was still early morning and, like all teenagers, Anna loathed rising early. Roy pulled over, but there were no hard shoulders on this country road. He put his hazards on, and checked the security video cam footage around his house. The garden and front was quiet. Nothing to see in the ground-floor rooms either. But the anxiety continued to churn in his mind.

If Jayden was indeed his long-lost brother, then Lydia would know about him as well. Was she behind Jayden running away? And what about Anna?

Roy indicated, and started driving. He called Switchboard, and asked to speak to Jonty Adams.

'Send a squad car to my address, now. It's my daughter. She might be in danger.'

CHAPTER 16

Lydia Moran and Kevin Rawlinson were leaning against a car, on a hilltop. From here, they had the perfect view of the street where DCI Rohan Roy and his daughter lived. Kevin had his binoculars out and focused on the house Lydia had pointed out to him. From here, he could see the rear garden, and the golf course behind it. Wooded land encircled the golf course.

'You sure he lives at number 64?' Kevin asked. Lydia nodded.

'I've seen his daughter come out of the house. She's got a friend there, three houses down, at number 61.'

Kevin observed for a while longer, then put his binoculars away. 'And this Jayden Budden. You say he's Inspector Roy's brother?'

'Yes. My partner found him when the boy was lost. He

kept him, and raised him. But the boy went off the rails, and ran away.'

'Lost?' Kevin lowered his eyebrows, and his eyes danced with a morbid curiosity. 'Well, if he was lost, and then found, why didn't your partner just return him to Roy's parents?'

Lydia shrugged. 'I don't know. They didn't want him back. Or whatever. I'm not sure of the details.'

Kevin kept his eyes on Lydia, and he could tell she was hiding something. Lydia raised her chin in the air and sniffed.

'Get back in the car,' Kevin said. When they were seated, he put his hand on the steering wheel, and stroked the scar on his cheek.

'How do you know for certain Jayden is Roy's brother? I've just got your word for it.'

'Believe me, it's the truth. Roy's looking for him as well now. We both want to get Roy, don't we?'

'He's interfering with my business. I want to get rid of him. But why do you hate him so much? Apart from the fact he put your partner behind bars.'

'Wouldn't you hate someone for that?' Lydia faced him. 'What if someone did that to your wife?'

Kevin thought about Karen, and had to agree. But there was something more here, and he couldn't quite figure it out. He didn't like it when he couldn't see all the angles. He didn't buy the story of Lydia's partner picking up Roy's brother from the street. Stephen Burns. The name rung a bell somewhere, but his associates didn't know. He wasn't a gang member, nor a runner.

Kevin suspected Burns had abused Roy's brother, and maybe that's what he did, hence he was now behind bars. A bloody kiddy-fiddler. That was despicable, and Kevin didn't want to know Burns – but if he could use Lydia against Roy, then job done. He needed to get rid of Roy – he was hurting business, all over the North. From Liverpool to Sheffield narcotic supply chains had been disrupted, thanks to Roy's shenanigans. The top boys in the Liverpool and Manchester gangs wanted business to return as normal. That put a price on Roy's head. Kevin was more than happy to say he'd do it.

Lydia said, 'Just trust me on this. If we get Jayden, we can do anything we want with Roy. And we know where his daughter is.'

'Abducting the daughter will be like chucking a rock in a wasp's nest,' Kevin said thoughtfully. 'One of your lot tried that already, right?'

Lydia nodded. 'Yes. That's why getting Jayden makes more sense. We can make Roy do what we want.'

'Can we though? How do we know he really thinks that's his brother?'

Lydia glanced at him. 'Again, you have to trust me on that.' In the library, Lydia had seen Jayden approach Anna. Lydia had recognised Jayden, and although she couldn't hear what they were saying, it wasn't hard to put two and two together.

'I've been staying in touch with Roy.' A thin smile crept across Lydia's face. 'Dropping him clues that his brother might be around. I know how much he cares.'

Kevin nodded slowly. Lydia was a crafty woman. He would have to watch her. He wanted to use her to get Roy, but then he didn't know. He might have to get rid of her. For now, Lydia wouldn't grass him up because she was under his protection, and she also was on the run. Roy was hunting for her.

Kevin tapped a fat finger on the steering wheel. 'Our search of Jayden's flat didn't reveal much. Where do you think he might be?'

'Oh, I think it did. I went through the pockets of his clothes. Funny how men don't do that when they search a flat.' Lydia grinned and her hand dipped into her handbag. She pulled out a few receipts, and straightened them on her lap.

'Here, look. These are receipts from the Grey Goose pub in Sculthorpe. He goes there often. And he bought drink from this off licence, also in Sculthorpe. It's just outside Meadowhall. I think he's got a friend there.'

'You're one useful woman,' Kevin smiled.

CHAPTER 17

Roy stormed in through the front door and roared his daughter's name. He had called her again on the drive down, and she hadn't responded. His heart rate was nuclear, and his chest felt tight. Try as he might, he couldn't stop thinking of the worst. *Not again.*

'Anna!' He dashed into the kitchen, and didn't find her there. She wasn't answering, which wasn't good. His feet thumped up the stairs, and he called for her again. The bathroom door opened and Anna stood there with a towel around her hair, and a bathrobe on. Steam poured out from behind her.

'What? I'm washing my hair!'

Roy felt so weak with relief he could've sagged to his knees. He rested a hand on the banister and sighed.

'Why didn't you answer your phone?'

'I didn't have it on me.' Anna frowned, and came forward. 'What's the matter? Anything happened?'

'No. Don't worry. Just take your phone into the bathroom next time.'

Anna nodded, her expressive, beautiful black eyes searching his face. He felt that serene calmness when he knew his little girl was safe and sound.

He also knew it was time for Anna to head back down south. School was starting next week. It wasn't just that. He had his hands full all of a sudden. Lydia was still out and about, and Jayden was missing. Now he had this murder case on his hands, Anna was better off back in London. She had mentioned her mother's current partner being a little odd, and Roy suspected Anna was staying in Sheffield longer for that reason. He needed to speak to his ex about that, today.

'I've got to head back to work. What're you doing today?'

'I'll probably be around here. Pearl messaged me. She and her friend are meeting up here for lunch. There's a cafe on the high street.'

'OK, please let me know where you are.'

'And don't go anywhere alone. Yes, I know.'

'What time is the train tomorrow?' Last week, they had booked Anna's return trip back to London.

'Ten am. Will you drop me off?'

'No, you can walk.' He smiled and Anna pulled a face.

Roy blew her a kiss, and went downstairs. He was

famished, but he also had to get back to the nick. Traffic was heavy in the morning rush hour. He decided to call his ex-wife from the car. She might be at work, but she worked from home a lot these days, according to Anna. Melissa didn't answer often, so he was surprised when she did.

'What do you want?' Melissa asked. No hello. No warmth, but that had been a constant feature of their ten-year long marriage.

'Your boyfriend. Anna's not too sure about him. I don't know why. She won't tell me much. But I get the feeling she's wary of him.'

He could tell this was already going down the wrong track. Maybe this'd been a mistake. He didn't want an argument.

'I didn't know she had a problem with him. I'll talk to her.'

'If you don't mind me asking, who is he? What's his name?'

'I do mind you asking, as a matter of fact. What will you do, put his name through a criminal database?'

In fairness to Melissa, that's exactly what Roy had done in the past, not that he ever told her. He wanted to be sure the man she was with wasn't dodgy. Melissa could do what she wanted, his only concern was Anna. But he also knew Melissa wouldn't bring home anyone who was unsafe.

'I just want to know that Anna will be alright.'

'Like I said, I'll speak to her, and find out.'

'What's his name?'

'None of your concern, Rohan. I suggest you mind your own business.'

'It's not—'

'Goodbye.'

Melissa hung up. Roy shook his head, and put the phone down. As usual, a waste of time. He was better off speaking to Anna. She told him the bloke's name was Paul, but she didn't know his last name. It had been more than six years since they broke up. Melissa had had a couple of relationships since then, but Roy didn't know anything about those men. Anna hadn't mentioned them much either, which meant she wasn't bothered by them. But Paul was clearly different, and that worried Roy.

He had to go down to London, in any case. He had to see his mentor, Arla Baker. It was Arla who had sent him up to Sheffield. It had only been four months, but it seemed like a lifetime. He'd had to get his official clearance from the Met, and become a permanent member of Yorkshire Police. Since Anna liked it here, his last doubt had disappeared. Yes, Anna was down in London, but in two years she was off to university, and she could be anywhere in England. With any luck, she might end up in a northern university, and then he'd be closer to her.

Roy parked in the rear car park of the station, his car belching a burst of black smoke as the engine shuddered, then died. Springs popped in the seat as he heaved himself out of the cramped driver's side. He stretched, then waved at a couple of the uniforms strolling into the nick. He stopped at the canteen and picked up a coffee and some biscuits. Biscuits remained his only vice. He had given up on everything else sweet. Well, apart from the occasional dessert when he went out for dinner, which was hardly ever. And the small chocolates left in the office reception.

The two DCs were at their desk, and so was Melanie. She was the first to speak when she saw him.

'We heard. IC4 female in her twenties, right?'

'Correct.' Roy took his coat off and draped it around his chair. He put the coffee and biscuits on the table, but didn't sit. His back was still stiff from sitting in his car.

'Knife wound to the abdomen. She died of blood loss. Did you hear about the three teenagers.'

Melanie waved a sheet of paper. 'Just read their statement. Pretty horrific for the youngsters to have to face that.'

Rizwan cleared his throat. 'And they're lying about organising a rave there. Stupidest thing I ever heard. That place is literally falling down.'

'Almost fell on my head when I walked around,' Roy agreed. 'Blooming deathtrap.'

'Aye,' Oliver said. 'It was built in 1833 for William Glossop, the Sheffield Steel tycoon. It was a hunting lodge from him and his rich mates. Just imagine the number of deer and foxes they killed. Shame.'

Everyone looked at him. Rizwan said, 'Never knew you to be an environmentalist. You eat meat like it's going out of fashion.'

'As long as it's sustainable, I don't mind.'

'Give over. You mean you only buy that expensive organic stuff?'

'Sometimes, yes.'

'Like once a year.' Riz snorted. 'And hang on, doesn't your mum do the cooking anyway?'

'So does yours.'

'Nope,' Riz said with evident self satisfaction. 'I moved out, remember? Sharon does the cooking now.'

'That's enough,' Roy said. 'Did you find anything else about Thornseat Lodge?'

'Yes,' Oliver glared at a widely grinning Rizwan, then looked back at his screen. 'It was sold to developers in the nineties. As Mortimer Road goes close to it, they had plans to build it up as a block of houses, and make a new, connecting road. The plans are still on the council website, but it fell through.'

'Recently though,' Oliver continued, 'Another developer has become interested. The council owns the land now, and they're in talks to sell it to a leisure centre builder.'

'Leisure centre?' Melanie frowned. 'Out there?'

Oliver was staring at his screen. 'More like an activity centre, with rides, toy trains, swimming pools. For all ages, apparently. Here, have a look.'

'Send me the link, please,' Melanie said. 'That sounds better than what it's used for now, which is nowt. Or for worse things.'

'Yes.' Roy sipped from his coffee, and stretched one last time. 'I spoke to the teenagers, and their leader, Marcus, was there for a drug deal.' Roy told them what Marcus had said. Then he took out his phone and sent the number of the drug dealer to Oliver and Rizwan.

'Naz is his name, that's all I know. He could be the man who attacked the victim. Triangulate any calls from that number. Naz is Marcus's new dealer. He was introduced to Marcus by Damien, his usual dealer.'

'Got his number here too,' Riz said, his phone checking Roy's message. 'We'll call them, and then start tracking.'

Roy sat down and took his notebook out, where he had scribbled his thoughts.

'Right, our victim.' He rose, and went to the whiteboard. He took a black marker pen and wrote number 1.

'She was in her late teens to early twenties. Dr Patel said she might be a uni student, and I agree. Can we please check that first. We don't have a name, so use her description, and e-fit image, and circulate it at Sheffield Uni campus. Put up posters if necessary. Ask the student office if any student has gone missing recently.'

'She was of Indian origin, I think. Pakistani would be a close second. Can we ask in their communities if there's any missing person.'

Rizwan said, 'I'll do that, guv. I know some mosque leaders, and will reach out to the Citizen Advice Bureau. They will know who to contact.'

Melanie said, 'There're lots of South Indians who are Roman Catholics. Almost everyone from Goa, for instance.

104

So we should ask in the Catholic churches as well. I'll do that.'

'Good point,' Roy said. 'I'm not sure if there's a big south Indian community in Sheffield, most of the south Asian population here are Muslims. But worth a try.'

Roy wrote number 2. 'The victim had marks on her fingers in keeping with working at a nail bar. We need to ask around in them.' He took his phone out and showed Melissa the photo he'd taken of the victim's hand. Melissa inspected it closely.

'Makes sense,' she agreed. 'There's a row of them in town. I think first we ask the ones on the street, rather than the posh ones in Meadowhall shopping mall.'

'Yes. From her clothing and appearance, I'd say she had seen some hard times.'

Roy looked at the two DCs. 'I asked Jonty to check with Traffic to see what cars went up Mortimer Road last night. Can one of you please chase it?'

'On it,' Oliver said, lifting up his phone.

Roy looked back at his notebook, then the white board. He counted off on his fingers.

'So, for an ID, we're looking at the nail bars in town, university, the Asian community. Anything else you can think of?'

Melanie said, 'Anything from the soil samples under her shoes? That could give us a clue. Or under her nails.'

'Have to wait for Justin to get back to us. She did wear a necklace though. A pendant with a gold chain. She also had a golden ring with a green stone on her left forefinger. It's in custody now. Let Justin and his crew look through it first. I took photos.'

He took his phone out and passed it around the team. Roy said, 'Both the necklace and ring look very Indian to me. As in, they were made in India. The ring is large, and the green stone is too. Women here would wear a much smaller and subtle ring on their fingers.'

Rizwan said, 'Don't Indians wear birth stones on their fingers? It's what the astrologers tell them to do. Then they can control the movement of planets and stuff.'

Roy smiled. 'That's right. Load of hogwash if you ask me, but some people swear by it, especially in India. That's why I think this ring was made in India. Her necklace is similar, the chain is too heavy to be fashionable here.' He gave his phone to Melissa. 'What do you think?'

'Definitely. The jewellery designs are very ethnic. To be honest, I thought the same of her shoes. Those type of flats are rare here. They're too open by the toes.'

Oliver said, 'We should tell Justin. He might find it useful.'

'Call him and let him know,' Roy said. 'This is good work. I feel like we're getting somewhere. Chances are this girl was a recent immigrant to UK. She worked in a nail bar. She might still be an overseas student. That narrows the field considerably. There won't be that many overseas students from India at Sheffield – India has thousands of universities.'

'If she's at Sheffield,' Melanie said. 'We should ask in Leeds and Manchester as well.'

Oliver said, 'If she is a recent immigrant, there are tight visa controls. To get in she needs to be a highly skilled migrant worker, or that twelve-point visa or whatever they do these days. We should check with the Home Office for recent arrivals to Sheffield, maybe?'

'Brownie points for that, Detective Constable,' Roy said. 'Please check.'

Oliver tried to hide the flush of pleasure at the commendation, and failed. With a smile on his face, he got busy on his laptop.

Roy turned to Melanie. 'Any news of Lydia Moran or Jayden Budden?'

'Nothing from the APB. Which means neither of them have gone through a major transport hub. Which means they could be local, or anywhere in the UK.'

'Jayden doesn't have a car,' Roy said. 'According to the DVLA there's none registered in his name. And we have Lydia's car. No train tickets purchased in their name? National Express coach?'

'Nothing as yet, guv.'

Roy sat down and rubbed his chin. 'I think,' he said, darkly, 'they're close by.'

CHAPTER 18

Jayden parted the net curtains and had a look outside. The sky was several shades of grey, and a light drizzle had started. He was living in a tiny two-up, two-down, terraced house. A woman with a pram hurried down the road. Another man walked on the opposite side, and Jayden let the curtain fall and withdrew, but kept watching the man. He walked past without a glance in his direction.

Jayden relaxed. He had another three days here before his friend returned from his holiday. Then he had to move, and he wondered what he should do. After meeting with Anna, he had panicked. He thought Lydia might be questioned by the police, and she might get arrested. But then so might he. As time had passed, he had realised that he might have overthought the situation.

He hadn't done anything wrong. His past had messed up his whole life, and his evil stepfather was responsible for that. Why would the police want him? He had met that detective – Rohan Roy. He didn't seem like a man who would put two and two together and come up with five. Perhaps…perhaps going to see Rohan Roy might be the best thing. Then he could actually explain his situation, and make him understand what no one had, all his life.

Jayden knew he needed help. The terrible trauma of his days with Burns had destroyed his memory. He had blocked out so much, he barely knew who he was. A man without any idea of where he came from was destined to be a rootless vagabond. He would drift along, not knowing what had really happened to him. All he knew was the nightmare of his time with Burns, and running away from home.

Maybe it was time to bring that to an end. It was time to tell someone who might actually pay attention to what he had to say. Despite his brief talk with Anna, he knew she had listened to him. And she was disturbingly familiar – like he'd seen her somewhere before. And yet, no matter how much he searched his mind, he came up with a blank. Her father, Rohan Roy, was also vaguely familiar, for some reason.

In any case, Anna had presumably spoken to her dad, and hence Roy might be willing to listen to him. And if he did, would he search for Jerry? Find out where he was now?

The thought made hair stand up on his neck, and goose pimples spread down his arms. If he could confront that bastard once again…

Jayden paced the room, then went out into the small garden. It was well kept, with a central lawn and a small shed on the side. It was gloomy, and the rain kept falling, so he stood under the rear porch. In a way, getting out of Sheffield had helped. His mind was now clearer. He would go to the police and ask for Inspector Roy. He would tell Roy everything. What's the worst that could happen? Roy wouldn't arrest him for warning Anna to stay away from Lydia, would he?

Jayden shut the garden door, locked up the place, and put his anorak on. He had to do some shopping. As he walked, he heard a car door open and shut behind him. He didn't pay any attention, it must be one of the neighbours. Two men walked past him, then stopped. They were tall and big, and one of them was a skinhead, with a long black leather coat. Both men turned towards him. Fear spiked in Jayden's spine. He didn't know who these men were, but he knew he was in trouble.

'Jayden Budden?' One of the men said, getting closer. He had a face like a cancerous bulldog, some disease had eaten away half his right cheek, and it had been patched up with cheap cosmetic surgery. Jayden took a step back, not responding. He had to make a run for it. He whirled around, only to find another two men, both the size of nightclub bouncers, standing behind him.

Jayden ran to the side, and jumped on the bonnet of a car, then slide down the side. One of the men grabbed the end of his anorak, but couldn't keep hold of it. Jayden heard the rush of running steps behind him as he crossed the road at full tilt. The men were coming on either side in a pincer movement. He couldn't run down either side of the road. He was trapped. His only option was the fence of the house in front of him, on the opposite side of the road. It was low, and he could scale it easily.

He flung himself past another car, and grabbed the top of the wooden fence with his hands. He hauled himself over before the men could stop him. He landed on the other side, and crashed into a woman. She screamed, and Jayden fell, with the woman landing on top. She got off him, and shouted for help. Jayden got to his feet, and spread his hands.

'I'm sorry, I didn't meant to hurt you.' He looked over the fence. The goons had stayed away, for now. Then a pair of meaty hands hooked over the fence, and a red face appeared. The man clocked Jayden, then dropped out of sight. Jayden didn't waste any time. He heard a dog barking from the other side of the fence. He scrambled on a tree that bordered the neighbour's, and immediately saw the dog. It was a poodle, and was wagging its tail and barking furiously. Jayden jumped down to the other side, and the dog rushed up to him. It recognised him as an intruder, and tried to bite his ankles. Jayden fended him off, and ran to the next fence. He heard another woman shout, but didn't turn to look. At this rate, he was going to wake up the neighbourhood. But what choice did he have? If he kept going like this, he would end up on the other side of the high street, from where he could escape into the park.

After the third fence, and another dog, Jayden had enough. He scrambled on the shed of the garden, and looked down at a path that ran down the rear all the houses. The goons were nowhere in sight. He jumped down, and a bolt of pain shot up his left ankle. He grunted, then hobbled a few steps. It hurt like mad, but he could still step. He half ran, half hobbled away from the barking dogs and screaming women as fast as he could.

CHAPTER 19

R oy had collected a few clothes from Jayden's flat, and submitted them to Forensics. From the underwear, Forensics could definitely get hold of DNA. He opened the door to the lab and walked in. Justin was still at the crime scene, but Darren, one of the technicians, was present. He was standing, looking into the eyepiece of a microscope the size of a water cooler. He turned as Roy came to stand behind him.

'The DNA samples of Jayden Budden. Did you get any results?'

Darren picked up his glasses from the white counter and put them on. He blinked a couple of times. 'Yes, we did. Jayden is the man who's on the run, correct?'

'Yes. And did you get a match with the other sample?'

Roy had also done a cheek swab on himself for DNA.

He had submitted them as an anonymous sample.

'Let me have a look.'

He followed Darren into another room that was dark except the faint blue glow from several machines on white table tops. Darren sat down at his desk and fired up a laptop. He went to the website of the National DNA Database and pulled down some results.

Darren scrolled down to the bottom of the results, which consisted of graphs, lines and numbers, none of which Roy understood in the slightest.

'Bloody hell,' Darren said softly. 'This anonymous sample has almost 4,000 centimorgans matching with the index sample. Index being Jayden Budden.'

'What does that mean?'

Darren turned to look at Roy. 'We get fifty percent of our DNA from each parent. But they get mixed up in random genetic combinations. So I could have fifty percent of the same genes as my sibling, but they will never be an identical match. Does that make sense?'

'Yes.'

'All our genes are on chromosomes, and a centimorgan is basically a map unit that gives us the distance between two genes on a chromosome. The more centimorgans match between two samples, the more are the chances the genes comes from the same place, that's why they are close together.'

'I kind of follow,' Roy said slowly. 'So what does it mean in relation to this sample?'

'Right,' Darren pointed to the screen. 'A match of 4,000 centimorgans means half the genes come from the same source. That can only happen with first blood siblings. This anonymous sample has to be Jayden's brother.'

Roy's hands clenched together. He swallowed the heavy weight at the back of his throat. His heart cannon balled against his ribs, the sound distant, but loud, like a train moving inside a tunnel. His voice was hoarse.

'How can you be sure?'

'Probability. You cannot get this high a match without the genes coming from the same source. For example, if these two samples were half siblings, then we would see a match of about 1500–2000 centimorgans, no more. And in first cousins, a quarter of that. In second or third cousins, an eight. You get the picture.'

Roy nodded, his mind trying to keep pace with Darren's reasoning, and almost failing. Darren mistook his silence for either confusion, or disbelief.

'There's another thing to show here that puts it beyond all doubt.' He smiled like a magician about to pull a rabbit out of a hat.

Roy could barely speak. He simply stared at Darren. 'There's one type of DNA we only get from our mothers. Only women can pass it on to their offspring. It's called Mitochondrial DNA, or mDNA. And in this case,' Darren's smile got wider, 'both samples of the mDNA are matching. These two DNA samples came from the mother.'

Roy sagged against the chair, breath wheezing out of his chest. For the first time, Darren seemed to notice something was up with him.

'Are you alright, guv?'

Roy felt dizzy. One side of Darren's face was lit from the laptop screen, the other almost in darkness. Roy had trouble focusing. He cleared his throat.

'Yes. Fine, thanks. Can you please print me out a copy of the results?'

Darren did so, and handed Roy the papers. 'Whoever the brother is, I hope you find him quickly. Does Jayden know about his brother?'

Roy looked at Darren for a while without speaking. 'No. I don't think he does.'

CHAPTER 20

Detective Sergeant Melanie Sparkes, and Detective Constable Oliver Walmsley were walking down the parade of shops in Fargate, one of Sheffield's premier shopping centres. There were a number of nail bars here, more than in the other shopping precincts. They had already been to three, and another seven were on their list.

Oliver glanced at Melanie. 'I'm glad you're here, but, to be honest, I'm also a little surprised. Riz and I could've handled it.'

'It's better if Riz rings up the mosques and such. Besides, I fancied stretching my legs. Not cramping your style, am I?' She looked quizzically at Oliver, whose mouth fell open.

'Oh god, no. It's okay, like, of course. I meant you're senior to us, so we could've done the grunt work.'

'No bother,' Melanie grinned. 'When is Sarah coming back to work? Poor lass. Can't imagine what she's been through.'

'Aye. That'll take her a while to get over. Not sure when she's back.'

'I called her today but she didn't answer. I'll try later.'

They were quiet for a while, each wondering about the horrific events of the last three days. Thank goodness Sarah and Matt were alright.

Melanie pushed open the glass door of another nail bar. 'Right, here goes nothing,' she said under her breath. Oliver was getting the same disappointing feeling. Chances were they would draw a blank again.

The nail bar had a row of tables on both sides, where women wearing masks tended to their client's nails. All the clients were women, and a couple of them were on chairs, getting their toenails done. Oliver couldn't help but notice all the working women looked like they were from the Far East. He was not good at spotting different ethnicities. But the women looked similar to those in the other nail bars they had so far visited. They could be from the Philippines or Malaysia, even China. He couldn't be sure. One thing he was confident of. Hardly any of them looked Indian or Pakistani. Sheffield had a sizeable Pakistani community, and his mate and colleague, Rizwan, was from the Punjab.

So far, Oliver had seen two, maybe three women workers of Indian origin. He followed Melanie, his eyes scanning, then finally noting the solitary female worker at the end. He could only see her profile, and she wasn't aware of them. Melanie went up to the counter and showed her warrant card to the Asian woman in charge.

'We are looking for a missing woman.' Melanie showed the victim's e-fit photo. It had been magnified to make recognition easier. The woman brought the photo closer to her face. She put it down, and went to the Indian woman who was busy with her client. She tapped the younger woman on the shoulder, then whispered in her ear. The woman stopped working and turned around, noticing Mel and Oliver for the first time.

'Please give her five minutes while she finishes up,' the manager said, coming back. 'I think this photo is of a girl who was friends with Layla here. She worked for about a week. Her name was Noor. Layla will be able to confirm.'

Layla turned to look at them for a few seconds, then quickly turned her head down. Oliver couldn't help noticing how pretty she was. Her large, expressive brown eyes lingered on him for the briefest moment in time, then they were gone, like the glimpse of an exotic bird in a forest. She wore a brown t-shirt that stretched over her shapely torso, which he could only see from behind. He admonished himself to keep his mind on the job.

They didn't have to wait for long. Layla's client came and paid, then left. The manager ushered them into the back office, and Layla followed. The manager shut the door, and left them alone.

Layla had jet-black hair tied up in a ponytail. Her nose was small, tapering to full lips and a soft chin. Her eyes were troubled as they flicked between Oliver and Melanie. Oliver introduced them, and they showed their warrant cards.

'We found a woman's body last night, and your manager recognised her. She said she was your friend.' Oliver took out the e-fit image on his phone and showed it to the girl. Her neck constricted, and fear rippled across her face, like a chainsaw running through a beautiful canvas. Her body shuddered once, and her fingers gripped her jeans. Oliver and Mel exchanged a glance. The proof was in the pudding, already.

'She's your friend, isn't she?' Melanie asked softly. 'Is her name Noor?'

Layla was still looking at the photo like she was transfixed. Oliver stretched out an arm and prised the phone gently off her hand. Her eyes followed the phone like she was handing over a precious object reluctantly.

'Layla,' Melanie said firmly. 'Was that your friend, Noor?'

Slowly, Layla's neck moved to the left. She looked at Mel like she was seeing her for the first time. Her face was deathly pale.

'No.'

Oliver felt Melanie stiffen. He glanced at her sideways and she caught his eyes, then stared back at Layla.

'Are you sure? Look again.'

Oliver held out the phone, and Layla glanced then averted her eyes. She shook her head, then picked a thread on her jeans.

'Layla, your manager recognises her. She's your friend, Noor. How can *you* not recognise her?'

'I don't know.'

'Okay.' Melanie took her own phone out, and scrolled to the photos of the victim at the crime scene. Roy had sent it to her. She showed them to Layla, who looked shocked again. This time, she squeezed her eyes shut and got out of her chair. She moved backwards, her eyes wide, like the two police officers were going to hurt her.

'Take it easy,' Melanie said, raising her hand. 'We can protect you, Layla. The girl in the photo, you know her, right?'

Layla breathed heavily, then a mask seemed to slip from her face. The fear was replaced by a crestfallen look of resignation. With it, came an eerie calm that seemed to envelope her, like she'd made her mind up about something. Oliver watched her closely.

'Yes. That's Noor. She worked here.'

'You knew her from before,' Melanie said. It was a statement, not a question. 'How did you know her?'

'I met her once in the park. We talked for a while. I told her I worked here. That was it.' Layla had an Indian accent.

'Really? She worked here after you spoke to her just once?'

Layla was more evasive than a politician facing journalists. Unlike a politician, she looked at her nails, and picked at them.

'Yes.'

'Where do you live?'

'Netheredge.'

'Do you live with your family?'

'Yes.'

Oliver wondered how long these monosyllabic replies would continue. Layla was clearly uncomfortable, and clearly lying. It was time to cut to the chase. He glanced at Mel, and leant forward.

Oliver said, 'Layla, you're afraid of something, or someone, aren't you?'

Layla was still standing, her hands gripping the chair. 'No.'

'No? Then what are you so scared of?'

'I'm… I'm just sad to see Noor like that. She's dead, isn't she?'

'I'm afraid so, yes.'

'How did she die?'

Oliver glanced at Melanie, and she nodded. 'She was killed,' Oliver said quietly.

The patches of colour that were appearing on Layla's face vanished like a piece of blotting paper was wrapped around her face.

'Why don't you sit down?' Oliver suggested. Layla did so.

'How long have you known Noor for?'

'We met in the park, like I said. Look, can I go now?'

Melanie said, 'Is there anything else you can tell us

about Noor?'

'Don't be afraid. If you know anything, you can tell us. You're not in any sort of trouble.'

Layla shook her head. Melanie sighed and sat back in her seat. It was clear they wouldn't get much more out of Layla.

Oliver said, 'We need your contact details. What's your phone number?'

Layla gave him a strange look, like she wanted to say something, but couldn't. 'I don't have a phone.'

Oliver frowned. 'OK. What's your address?'

Layla gave them an address. The postcode seemed familiar to Oliver, who knew Rizwan's address in Netheredge.

'Do you know if Noor had any friends?'

'No. I didn't know her that much.'

'You just spoke to her once in the park and that was enough for her to start working here,' Melanie said.

The jibe registered with Layla, who looked away. Oliver felt a little sorry for her, and Melanie spoke gently.

'You can talk to us, Layla. Nothing will happen to you. Alright?'

Without speaking, Layla nodded. Her watchful gaze moved between the two of them. 'Can I go now?'

Melanie sighed. 'Yes, but don't leave Sheffield. We will want to speak to you again.'

CHAPTER 21

Oliver lit a cigarette and took a deep drag. He exhaled smoke, and spoke on his phone. It was Rizwan, who was back at the nick. He gave Riz Layla's details, and hung up.

'What was that about?' Melanie asked, rhetorically asking about Layla. They were standing opposite the row of nail bars, under the shade of a tree.

'She lied, then backtracked. I think she realised how dodgy it looked,' Oliver said. 'She had to acknowledge that she knew the victim, but she's still lying.'

'She's scared. We need to watch her. Does her address look genuine to you?'

'Yes, I looked it up. The house exists. Shall we take a look?'

'Yes. I want Layla under surveillance as well, but that

might not be possible right now.' Police surveillance had to go through a series of checks. Only individuals who were highly suspicious could be put under surveillance. So far, Layla was only lying.

'She doesn't have a phone. What does that say?'

'She could be lying. How can she not have a phone?'

Oliver stubbed out his cigarette. They had spoken to the manager of the nail bar. She had seen Noor a few times, but never spoken to her. The girls were paid in cash, and there was no job contract. Like Layla, Noor didn't have a phone number. She had an address, and it was in the Victoria Quays area of Sheffield.

Melanie said, 'Let's visit Noor's house first. See what her family have to say.'

Noor lived in the corner of Victoria Quay that was run down, with boarded-up shops on the street, and the sort of grimy, small terraced houses that were maintained by the city council. The address led them to a block of apartments. The colour had long leached off the walls, and the shabby, nondescript block was covered in graffiti. A group of youths lounged in the corner, watching the detectives park. They wore the black tops and tracksuit bottoms beloved of the street gangs, and they looked young enough to be in school.

Oliver and Melanie walked towards the main entrance of the flat complex, and the youths watched them in sullen silence. A couple of them pulled up ski masks to cover their faces.

One of them called out as they walked past. 'You lot Feds?'

The detectives ignored them, and went through the gates. A few snotty-nosed children ran around in the enclosed playground. The complex consisted of three long, needle-like concrete filaments, each with numerous windows. They housed Sheffield's needy and destitute, and hundreds of them were scattered across the city.

They took the lift up to the fifth floor. A knock on number 514 didn't elicit a response. Oliver banged on the door, then announced his name through the letterbox. Nothing happened. They didn't have a number to ring, nor did they have a last name. But they did have Riz. Oliver rang him.

'Flat is registered to a Daniel Jones,' Riz said, 'According to council records. They have a number here. I've called him, but he's not responding.'

'Doesn't sound like an Indian name,' Oliver said. 'Maybe he's the landlord. But the tenants should be registered to pay the council tax.'

'It's only his name on the records, and he pays it every month.'

'Dirty buggers,' a voice said behind them.

'Keep trying. And see if this Daniel Jones has a police record.'

Oliver hung up and joined Melanie as she walked across the landing to face the man who spoke. He was in his thirties, thin, with a long face. He had a light, scruffy beard that was salt and pepper. He had short, dark hair. He wore a t-shirt with the cross of St George on it. A cigarette glowed in his right hand, the smoke tendrils crawling up his muscular right arm.

Melanie asked, 'Do you know who lives in 514?'

'Aye. That's what I just said. Filthy scum, the lot of them.'

Now that he was closer, Oliver could see the tattoo on the man's left forearm. It was a Nazi swastika, with the words NF, or National Front, on it. Oliver exhaled. An enlightened man, clearly.

Melanie said, 'They're your neighbours. Do you know their names?'

The man took a toke on his cigarette and grimaced. 'Weird ones. That's all I can say. Can't be bothered to remember.'

'And what's your name?'

The man looked Melanie and Oliver up and down. 'Who's asking, like?'

Melanie showed her warrant card. The man's face changed. He stood up straighter. 'What's going on?'

'Can you please answer the question? What's the name of the family who live in 514?'

'I don't bloody know. I see them around, but don't mix with that lot. They're better off where they came from.'

There was a noise behind him, and a woman appeared. She looked younger. Her red hair was frizzy, and she wore a dressing gown. She looked at them inquisitively.

'What's going on 'ere, like?' she asked, her voice high-pitched.

'They want to know about that lot.' The man jerked a

thumb in the direction of 514.

'What for?'

Melanie tapped her foot on the floor, and Oliver could tell she was losing patience. She glanced at him and beckoned him forward. Oliver knew what she wanted. He took out the e-fit photo and showed it to the couple. They leant in for a look.

Melanie said, 'Your name is…'

'Martin Donald,' the man said in a gruff voice, then coughed. He dropped the cigarette on the floor, stubbed it out with his shoe, then picked it up and went inside without another word. His wife stood there, starting at the e-fit photo.

'I'm Amanda,' the woman said. 'Yeah, I recognise that girl. She lived there. A few of them did, like. They used to come and go.'

'What do you mean by a few?'

'About four or five girls. They used to have a bloke with them. All Asians. I saw different girls, and I remember seeing this one. She spoke to me a few times.'

'Can you remember her name?'

'Nooz or summat, I think.'

'Do you mean Noor?'

'Aye, that's it.' Curiosity danced in Amanda's brown eyes. 'What's she done, like?'

Martin had come back, and he leant against the door, behind his wife. He caught the end of their conversation.

'Bloody pakis,' he muttered. 'Always up to no good.'

Oliver grit his teeth. He hated men like Martin. Melanie said, 'Actually, she's dead.'

Amanda's mouth fell open. Behind her, Martin's face blanched white, which Oliver thought was interesting, given his hatred of Noor's *type*.

'Chuffin' 'eck,' Amanda whispered. ''ow did that 'appen, like?'

'That's what we're trying to find out,' Melanie said patiently. 'Now, when did you last speak to Noor?'

'Last week I think. Yes, that's right. She was in the lift with me and a few others. We just said hello, that's all. '

'Was she on her own?'

'No, there was a bloke with her. I've seen him before. He comes and goes. Asian guy. Tall, with a light beard. I think he lives there, not sure.'

'Did you speak to Noor that day, or before?'

'She was very quiet, just looked at me once, that's all. And before...' Amanda lowered her head, thinking. 'Couple of weeks earlier I seen her downstairs. She was with another girl, and they were going to the shops. We stopped and said hello. She wanted to talk to me, like. Just asked how I was and that, and then moved on. I don't know much about her, to be honest. Only said hello the first time I saw her here, as she was our neighbour.'

'Can you describe the girl with her?'

'Pretty Asian girl. Wore a brown top, long black hair. They were about the same height as me.'

That sounded like Layla, Oliver thought. He asked, 'Do you know where she worked? Or what she did?'

Amanda shrugged. Oliver noted Martin was quiet, and listening to his wife.

'She worked at a nail bar, she said once. Before that, she was in a restaurant. Her friend worked in the restaurant as well.'

'Do you know the restaurant's name?'

Amanda turned to her husband. 'We got a takeaway from there once. Do you remember?'

Martin scowled, and shook his head. 'No. They're all the same, anyway. Greasy, horrible food.'

Oliver said, 'If you ordered a takeaway, maybe you have the menu somewhere in the house?'

Martin stood in Amanda's way. 'Look, we have stuff to do. Can you not come back later?'

Melanie said, 'Not really. This is a murder investigation, and we have to make enquiries.' She looked at Amanda. 'Can you please search for the menu?'

Amanda brushed past her husband, and went inside. Martin was getting annoyed now. His cheeks were mottling red. 'Now look 'ere. We don't care about that lot. All they do is bring trouble. Why don't you ask around, instead of bothering us?'

Melanie ignored him. 'Your wife spoke to Noor, and they lived opposite you, but you never spoke to them?'

'I said no, didn't I?'

'And you never saw the man who was with them?'

Martin rolled his eyes. 'Bloody hell. Like Amanda said, tall Indian guy with a beard. They all look the same if you ask me.'

Melanie looked at Oliver and shook her head slightly. This man was getting on their nerves. Luckily, Amanda returned. She had a small menu in her hand, the type that gets dropped through the letterbox often. She gave it to Melanie who accepted with thanks. The restaurant was called Mumtaz, and the address was in Hillsborough, a northern suburb of Sheffield.

'We might return if we need to,' Melanie said, giving Amanda her card. She eyed Martin. 'If you think of anything in relation to the women there, please give us a call.'

CHAPTER 22

The drive to Hillsborough didn't take long. Traffic was light in the late morning. The restaurant was situated in the Hillsborough Corner, the main high street of the area.

As Oliver drove, Melanie called Riz and informed him of the situation.

'Where's DCI Roy?'

'He went upstairs to the crime lab. Should be down soon. Do you want me to ask a uniform squad to attend where Noor lived?'

'Yes please. And tell them to stay there. I want a team patrolling the council estate. I want a door to door. Drop in the e-fit image with her name through the letterbox if people don't respond. We knocked on the doors of her immediate neighbours, but no one else was in.'

Riz was clicking on his keyboard as Melanie spoke.

'Shall I do a PCN check for Martin Donald as well?'

'Definitely. Let me know if you find anything.'

'Copy that, guv.'

Oliver parked his car on a road called Holme Lane, and they got out. Mumtaz restaurant was in the middle of a parade of shops, and sandwiched between a nail bar and hair salon. The long windows were tinted, and the red brick building was two storey. Two more windows with normal glass face the road from upstairs. Oliver knocked on the door, and after a while, a young man opened it. He was Asian, and dressed in a tee shirt and jeans. He looked them up and down. Oliver introduced himself and Melanie, then showed his warrant card. The man looked worried, and he gaped at them.

'Can we speak to your manager? It's about someone who used to work here.'

The man, who looked very young, was unsure. His eyes darted around. 'Stay here, I'll see if he's in.' He tried to close the door but Oliver put his foot forward, stopping him.

'I'm afraid we need to come in. This is a serious matter, and we need to question the staff.'

'The staff aren't here till the evening.'

'Whoever is here needs to be questioned now.' Oliver moved forward, and the man opened the door, and retreated. He walked off quickly, and disappeared through a side door. They were in a standard restaurant space, with comfortable chairs arranged around tables. There was a bar area at the end, with a door that was probably the kitchen. The air was musty, and smelt of old leather and spices.

The side door opened and a man emerged. He was in his late thirties to early forties and his hair was getting sparse, which made him look older. The pot belly straining at his shirt buttons didn't help. He had a cropped black beard, and was tall, north of six feet. His sharp, dark eyes were inquisitive, with a hint of anxiety as he scanned their faces. Melanie wondered if he was the man Amanda Donald had seen outside Noor's flat.

'I'm Sunil Ambani, the proprietor. What's this about?'

Oliver introduced them, and showed his warrant card again.

Melanie handled the questions. 'Did a girl called Noor work here?'

Sunil frowned. 'No, that doesn't ring a bell. Why do you ask?'

'We have reason to believe that she worked here. Are you sure that she didn't?' Melanie was suspicious at how quickly the denial came. There was something odd about Sunil. His expression was fixed, wooden, like he'd been preparing for this. She didn't trust him.

'Yes, positive.'

Melanie glanced at Oliver and he understood. He took out his phone and showed Sunil the e-fit images. Sunil shook his head.

'Nope, never seen her before.' Sunil hid his insincerity like a leopard trying to hide its spots. He gave the photo no more than a cursory glance. Melanie thrust the phone at him once again.

'Please have a look again. Are you sure?'

Sunil glanced down. 'Yes, positive. Why do you ask?' He had a northern accent.

'This woman was found dead this morning. She was killed. Her contacts have said she used to work here. Do you understand?'

Sunil frowned. 'Are you sure you have the right restaurant? There's more than one Mumtaz in Sheffield.'

'But it's the only one in Hillsborough,' Melanie said. 'So I don't think there's a mistake.'

Sunil spread his hands. 'Look, I'm sorry this woman has died. But she didn't work here.'

Melanie indicated to Oliver, who showed Sunil the crime scene photo. Sunil cringed, and looked away.

'Horrible. I can understand why you're chasing this up. But I'm sorry, she didn't work here.'

Melanie was confused now and not sure if Sunil was acting. If he was, it was very good. She stared at him. If this was acting, then he deserved an Oscar. But earlier, she was sure he was hiding something. She indicated behind Sunil.

'Can we speak to the man who opened the door? And anyone else who's here?'

'There's only Rahul and me here at the moment. And he won't know who this woman was. I can guarantee that.'

'Regardless, we still need to speak to him.'

Sunil was clearly unhappy, but he backed down eventually. He left, and went out the side door, closing it.

Melanie noted the kitchen door was still shut. She glanced at Oliver, and together, they walked up. The bar was darkened, and the smell of old spices was stronger as they walked past the assorted tables. There was a glass panel on the door, at eye level. The door was locked. Lights were off in the kitchen, but Melanie could make out rows of counters, and gas hobs on either side. The place was empty. She looked around the walls of the restaurant. There was a map of India, and photos of half naked holy men, and some shots of nature – birds and a tiger.

The side door opened and the young they had seen previously entered. Melanie went up to him, and pulled up a chair. He remained standing till Melanie asked him to sit. He fidgeted like he was sitting on a bed of pins, and couldn't wait to get up.

'What's your name?'

'Rahul Tripathi.'

'Do you mind if I call you Rahul?'

'No.'

Oliver showed Rahul the e-fit image. Like Sunil, Rahul didn't look at it for very long. His face remained blank, but there was a subtle shift in his attitude. He seemed more restless than before. His feet tapped on the ground.

'Do you know her?'

Rahul shook his head. 'Are you sure? Look at the photo again?'

He did so, and still denied knowing the woman. 'Her name was Noor,' Melanie said. She took the phone back and scrolled to the crime scene photos. This time, Rahul's eyes bulged, and panic blossomed in his face. He looked up at Melanie, his breathing harsh.

'No,' he whispered. 'I've never seen her.'

Melanie and Oliver exchanged a glance. Oliver said, 'If we find out later that you did, then this looks bad on you. You could be arrested for lying, if we have suspicions about why you lied. This is a murder investigation.'

Rahul rose shakily to his feet. He wiped a hand across the film of sweat on his forehead. 'I've got nothing else to say. Goodbye.'

CHAPTER 23

'Shall we arrest him?' Oliver asked, once they were outside. Melanie was deep in thought, and she kicked the pavement with her shoe.

'No point. If he keeps denying, a duty solicitor will take get him free within a few hours. Just a waste of time.'

Oliver indicated the nail bar next to the restaurant, which was already half full. 'We should ask in there.'

They walked to the shop entrance of Paradise Nail Bar and Beauty Lounge and looked through the large glass front. A number of women wearing masks were diligently at work making their clients nails beautiful.

'I'm wondering if we're going to get much joy if we go in all guns blazing,' Melanie said, a glint in her eye. 'Perhaps time to go undercover.' Oliver raised his eyebrows, confused. She pulled on his arm and dragged him to one side. She took off her coat and handed it to him.

'I'll go in there and act as a client to make some, shall we say discreet, enquiries.'

'Good idea,' Oliver enthused. 'I'll come as well.'

Melanie stared at him for a few seconds. 'That kind of defeats the purpose, don't you think?'

Oliver opened and closed his mouth. 'Uh, I could be a gay or trans man, looking to do his nails?'

Melanie shook her head in disbelief. 'Olly, you don't…anyway, just trust me on this. It's best if I go alone.'

'Really? I could be-

'Looking like a police officer in his suit,' Melanie interrupted, raising a hand. 'Just stay here. I'll be back soon. Here, hold my jacket. And don't look in through the windows. Stand on the opposite pavement.'

'What if you get into trouble?'

'I won't, so don't worry. I'll call if anything happens.'

Leaving a sad faced, dejected Oliver behind, Melanie made some adjustments to her clothes, and pushed the door and went inside. A bell chimed somewhere, and an Oriental woman at the reception looked up. The women working didn't raise a head, all kept on working as normal.

'Hello, I want an appointment to get my nails done,' Melanie smiled at the woman.

'Mani and pedi, or just mani?' The woman asked, in a strong Chinese accent. It took Mel a few seconds to understand her accent, and what she meant.

'Yes, both please.' She looked around. 'Nice place you have here. Is it always this full?'

'Yes, gets busier as the day goes on. Have you been here before?' The woman opened up a book, pen in hand.

'Oh no, sorry, I haven't. My name's Alice Cooper.' Melanie waited while the woman took down some details that she made up on the spot. Fake phone number and address.

'Is this your place?' She asked.

'Yes.'

'What's your name?'

'Liyan.'

'Oh, that's a lovely name. I hope you don't mind me asking, but are you from China?'

Liyan looked at Melanie cautiously, appraising her in silence. 'Yes.'

'My friends went to Shanghai last year, and really enjoyed it. They went to a town that was built on a river, and it's called the Venice of the East. Suzo or something like that. Sorry, excuse my pronunciation.'

'Suzhou in the Jiangsu province, north of Shangai,' Liyan smiled for the first time. She said it like *Sooz How,* and Melanie tried it out, much to Liyan's amusement.

'They loved it,' Melanie gushed. 'They went on trips down the canals and ate in floating restaurants.'

'Oh, nice.'

Melanie leant forward. 'I don't live far from here. This

restaurant next door, what's it like?'

Liyan looked to her left, then nodded. 'It's alright. Gets rowdy at night, I've been told. Lots of drunk men. When we finish late I sometimes get the girls a takeaway from there.'

'Good that you look after your employees. The restaurant isn't expensive, is it?'

'Oh no, it's fine. Standard prices. The women bring the food over and we get a discount.'

'Do you mean the female waitresses?'

'Yes, that's right.'

'One of my friends daughter's used to work there. A girl called Noor. Did you meet her?'

Liyan frowned, and pressed her lips together. 'Yes. Noor, that's her name. She used to bring the food over. I remember her name.'

Bingo.

'Nice girl.'

'Yes, she was,' Liyan agreed. She asked me once if she could work here. I don't think she was very happy in the restaurant.'

'Oh really, why?'

'They work long hours in the evening and at night. They don't get paid much.'

Melanie expressed her best sympathetic look. 'I think she'd been there for a few months.'

'Longer, I think. Almost a year. Sometimes, her friend

used to come with her. She also wanted to leave. Her name was Lila or something.'

'Layla?'

'Yes, that's it.'

'They were friends,' Melanie agreed solemnly. 'Do you know if they still work there?'

Liyan shrugged. 'No idea.'

Melanie thanked her, and took an appointment for next week. When she walked out, she saw Oliver standing right opposite, on the other side of the road. He waved at her, and she ignored him and walked to the left. She went down the alley where she'd taken her coat off, and Oliver hurried after.

Melanie took her coat from Oliver with a murmur of thanks. 'We need to keep an eye on the restaurant,' she said. 'And on Sunil Ambani. He's up to no good.'

CHAPTER 24

As Oliver drove, Melanie read out the names she had written on a piece of paper.

'Daniel Jones, the man to whom the flat is registered. That's where Noor lived. Sunil Ambani, the restaurant's proprietor. Martin Donald and his wife, Amanda. Oh, and the waiter, Rahul Tripathi.'

Rizwan wrote the names down, and promised to search up. But he had something on Martin Donald already.

'He was arrested twice for petty vandalism when he was younger in his twenties, and a third time for GBH. He didn't do much, just got into scraps. Mostly with the police trying to maintain order during National Front marches. He's an active member of the party, and heads up the local chapter in East Sheffield. Even calls himself a political activist.'

Melanie grimaced. 'What political party would have him as the activist? He didn't seem very active when we saw him. If you have any photos of him on record, can you please send them to me?'

'Will do, guv. Checking on the others now and will keep you posted. Where are you off to?'

'To your neck of the woods, as it happens. Layla Patil lived in Netheredge.' Melanie bent closer to the satnav display on the dashboard as she read off the address.

'Aye, I know where that is. Bunch of council estates there, not the best of Netheredge, must admit. By the way, that reminds me. Layla Patil and Noor Jehan both entered the UK with student visas. Noor came before Layla, about eighteen months ago. Layla has been here for nine months. They came to study accounting at Don Valley College, according to their visa documentation from the Home Office. Not sure if they ever attended. I think we need to speak to the college to see if they actually admitted these students. The admissions tutor is called Tim Ludlow. I'll call him.'

'Good idea, and well done. We won't be long. Let the boss know what's happening.'

Melanie hung up. They were in Netheredge now, the aptly named place in the south of Sheffield's southern suburbs. Oliver drove through a network of narrow streets till he came to Surbiton Road, a depressing row of terraced brown-brick houses. A couple of cars had their windows smashed in, a dustbin was overturned, and foxes had feasted on the rubbish.

Melanie went up to number 13 and opened the rusty

iron gate that was leaning to one side. It creaked noisily, and almost fell off its hinges. The garden was overgrown with weeds, and one panel of the ground-floor bay window was boarded up.

Melanie knocked on the door, and waited. They soon heard the shuffle of steps. The letterbox flap lifted, and a pair of invisible eyes observed them in silence.

'Detective Sergeant Melanie Sparkes of South Yorkshire Police. Can you please open the door?'

The flap snapped shut and there was no sound, or response. Melanie knocked on the door again. Oliver stepped to the side and backwards. He craned his head up. One of the windows upstairs had opened a fraction. The curtains were still drawn and he couldn't see anything. That window was shut when they arrived.

'I'll go around the back, on the street behind. See if there's a side alley between the houses. Someone's watching from up above.' He pointed upwards, and Melanie followed his line of vision.

'Okay.'

Oliver sprinted to his car, and took off with speed. Melanie thumped her fist on the door, and shouted this time. The shuffle of steps appeared again. A key turned, and slowly the door opened. A young Asian man stood there. His skin was fair, and he had a light-black beard. His eyes were brown, and they had a hint of fear in them.

Melanie put her foot on the step. 'Can I come in? It's about Layla Patil, who lives here.'

The man was skinny, his white t-shirt sticking to him

like a second skin. He was sweating. His ribs appeared against the shirt as he breathed. Melanie's hand rested on the baton on her waistline. She had used it many times in the past, and her senses were suddenly tingling, on red alert.

'She…she's not here right now.'

'What's your name?'

'Akbar Sharif.'

'OK, Akbar. We know Layla lives here. So do you, right?'

'Yes. I'm busy right now, can you please come back later?'

Akbar had a strong accent. He was either from India, or Pakistan. Melanie went inside. The door remained open behind her. Akbar stepped back till his back hit the stairs. The carpet was threadbare thin, and the floorboards creaked under their steps.

Melanie scanned the ground floor. Two doors opened up to her right, and straight ahead, there was a kitchen. The kitchen was empty, and she heard no sound from the rooms. She glanced upstairs, and her ears didn't pick up any sounds.

'Why are you sweating?' Melanie asked.

'Oh, uh, I was working in the garden.' Akbar pulled at his collar and his eyes darted around. Beads of sweat rolled down his temples, and he wiped them with his sleeves.

'Look, can you come back later? Layla's not here.'

'Is there anyone else here?'

'No.'

'Are you sure?'

Akbar nodded. Melanie watched him for a few seconds. He was barely a man, as young as Rahul, the waiter at the restaurant. A boy just growing into manhood.

'Where do you study?'

Akbar's Adam's apple bobbed in his thin, reedy throat. 'Don Valley College.'

'Same as Layla then. And Noor as well. Do you know Noor?'

Akbar's eyes widened a fraction, then returned to normal. 'No. No, I don't.'

'Are you sure? She's also enrolled at Don Valley, and she knew Layla.'

Akbar shook his head, blinking. There was no conviction in his actions. Melanie heard a sound and looked behind quickly to see Oliver at the doorway.

'Layla used to go to Noor's house. You sure you don't know Noor?'

'No, I don't.'

Melanie's eyes lingered on Akbar, and his discomfort grew. Melanie raised a hand and waved it briefly. 'You and Layla rent this place? Or is it university accommodation?'

'We rent.'

'Who's your landlord?'

'Uh, I don't know his name. Layla does. Look, what's this about? Has something happened to Layla?'

'No. Something's happened to Noor.'

Again, that veil passed over Akbar's face, like a shadow obscuring his expression. He seemed in two minds whether to ask the next question, but eventually he did.

'What happened to her?'

'She's dead. She was killed by a man in the early hours of this morning.'

Akbar's eyes bulged, and a vein appeared in the middle of his forehead. His cheeks mottled red, and his nostrils flared. He swallowed, then his lips parted as he gasped.

'What's the matter?' Melanie asked. Akbar shook his head. Melanie stepped forward again, till she was almost eye to eye with the young man.

'See Akbar, I think you're lying. You knew Noor. You knew something was going to happen to her. And now that it's happened, you don't know what to do. Isn't that right?'

Although Akbar fit the description of the killer, Melanie wasn't too worried. If he had killed Noor, he wouldn't be here. He would've left Sheffield as soon as possible. But stranger things had happened. Noor's death could be a crime of passion, and young men like Akbar had done it before.

'Tell us the truth, Akbar. Layla, you and Noor, were close, right?'

'No.'

'No? Then why are you so scared? What happened to Noor?'

Akbar shook his head. Melanie glanced behind her and Oliver stepped forward. He said, 'You're not in any trouble. But you might be if you're hiding anything from us. Tell us what happened, Akbar.'

The youth's wild eyes flicked from Melanie, to Oliver. Then he grabbed the stair banister, turned, and ran up the stairs.

'Stop!' Oliver shouted, running after him.

CHAPTER 25

Roy was walking when he heard his phone beep. He had two messages from Rizwan and Oliver. He stopped in his tracks as he read about Layla and Noor coming here on student visas. Rizwan had tracked down Mr Ludlow, the admissions officer at Don Valley College. Roy called Riz as he got into his car.

'DCI Roy,' he said when Riz answered. 'Did you speak to Mr Ludlow?'

'Yes. He says he had no idea about the admissions documents, nor the fact Noor or Layla were students here. He claims they're forgeries.'

'Hmm, I think we need to go and see him. The Home Office has records of the paperwork from the college?'

'Yes. That's what I sent him. To be honest, guv, you won't believe it. It's just a one-page letter saying she's been accepted, that's all. So easy to fake.'

Roy put Riz on loudspeaker and drove. 'The Home Office doesn't care much as she's admitted as an overseas student and brings money into the college. I wouldn't be surprised if the college had no idea what's going on.'

'I'll set up an appointment with Mr Ludlow for later today?'

'Yes, do that. When you see him, make sure you get a list of all the overseas students the college has.' Roy's radio chattered loudly. 'I better go. See you at the nick.'

He hung up, then reached into his jacket's left breast pocket and turned the black knob of the radio. The metallic voice of the duty traffic sergeant came on the line.

'All units alert. IC4 man seen intruding in multiple properties in Sculthorpe.'

There was a buzz of static and other voices spoke on the line. 'Suspect seen wearing tan jacket, dark jeans and white trainers. Clean-shaven.'

Roy frowned. Sheffield had no dearth of men fitting that description, but the memory of one man wearing those clothes was stuck in his mind. Jayden, the day he saw him, and when he dropped by at the station to give his statement.

He logged into the channel. 'DCI Roy speaking. Can I please have coordinates for last sighting of suspect.'

When he got the location, he fed them into his phone, then followed the satnav. Traffic was building up, the rush just prior to school break-time. He put his siren on, and ploughed through. Sculthorpe was to the south of the urban sprawl that occupied Sheffield's eastern reaches. These inner-city areas had large complexes of council flats, with their teeming masses. It was also close to Meadowhall, the giant temple of retail therapy, Yorkshire's largest shopping mall.

Roy drove down the ring road, and took the exit for Sculthorpe. It was one of those villages that had reluctantly sagged into the net of city life. It's narrow streets, red-brick terraced houses were built for the steel-workers in the Victorian age, when Sheffield was a leader in the global steel industry, thanks to the raw iron ore mined in the colonies.

Roy drove to the street in question, and parked up. He let the silence flow in. Sculthorpe was a forgettable small town, nothing much happened here. No one walked down the road. All the small parked cars had seen better days. So had many of the houses on the street. Roy flicked his radio on, and asked which door number the complaint had come from.

He got out of the car and knocked on the door. A young woman opened the door. Her white vest was stained with food, and she had a toddler in her arms. The baby twisted in his mother's hold to stare at Roy.

'Sorry to bother you. My name's DCI Roy.' He showed her his warrant card, but the woman was looking directly at him. 'I understand an intruder came into your garden about an hour ago. Is that correct?'

'It is an' all. Bloody 'eck, it were right mardy. My baby and I were in the back, like. He come out of nowhere, over the fence. I fookin', sorry, I mean I got well scared, and shouted an' that. He took off to next door, and gave the old lady a right scare.' She shook her head. Then she squinted at Roy. 'I'll tell you what tho'.'

Roy raised his eyebrows, aware the woman was staring at him with a concentration he found rather strange.

'I hope you don't mind me sayin' this, and' I know you're a copper an' that, but he looked a bit like you.'

'What do you mean?'

'I mean, his height and appearance an' that. I didn't get that close a look at him, obviously. But something about you is similar, like.'

Breath was suddenly stuck in Roy's chest, and he couldn't breathe. The woman could be mistaken, of course. But an inner voice told him she might also be right.

'You gave us his description. Did you notice anything else about him? Was he wearing a cap? Did he have glasses?'

'Nowt like that. He 'ad this tan leather jacket, and black jeans on. White pumps on his feet. He saw me and ran. That were all I saw.'

'And he went into the next door's garden?'

'Yes. He jumped over, and vanished, I heard her dog barking, and she told me he went over her rear fence. There's some woods down there.'

'Thank you.' Roy held her eyes for a couple of seconds. He wondered what was so obvious to a stranger had so long eluded him. Maybe he was still looking for a lost little boy. But Robin had grown into Jayden, and he needed to find him.

He'd turned to leave when the woman called him. 'Sorry, I forgot to tell you summat.' Roy looked at her questioningly.

'Two men came to look for him right after he took off. Big and buff they were, like nightclub bouncers. Looked dodgy to me.'

'Did you tell this to the police when you rang?'

'No. Sorry. It slipped my mind, like. The little one was screaming and it were doin' me head in, like.'

'No problem,' Roy said gently. 'Thank you,' he repeated, and meant it more than the woman would ever understand. 'What's your name?'

'Cathy Bairstow.'

'The man jumped over your neighbour's rear fence, is that right?'

'Yes. He went into the woods.'

Roy thanked her again, and set off running. He circled around the rear of the terraces, and came upon the path that separated the houses from the woodland behind. Behind Cathy's house, and all along the path, he saw a number of boot prints. They could belong to anyone. He went down the path, and into the woods. The shrubs and undergrowth caught in his trousers, and ripped at his hands as he ran through them. Pretty soon the going got harder as the trees thickened. Waist-deep in vegetation, Roy looked around him. He realised if Jayden had run down here, he would've been caught by the men chasing him. The two big blokes who came calling at Cathy's door. Who sent them? Who was after Jayden…and why?

They had to be the same men who trashed his flat. Roy could only think of one person who might be behind this. Lydia Moran.

He searched for a while longer, till his shoes sank into muddy waters. No way would anyone come down here, unless it was to hide. He didn't give up, and spent the next half hour looking around. Then he wiped sweat from his brow, and stomped his feet in frustration, then punched a tree trunk, which hurt like hell. He bit into his bruised knuckle, tasting metallic blood.

His phone rang, distracting him from his meltdown.

'DCI Roy,' he growled.

'It's Dr Patel,' the familiar female voice said. ' I've done the post mortem. You need to come down to the morgue ASAP.'

CHAPTER 26

Sheffield was a university town and the evidence was everywhere. Large buildings near the city centre were dedicated to learning and research. Apart from the main university campus, student accommodation was scattered all over the city. But the University dominated Sheffield, one of its main sources of revenue. It had a medical school, and the massive Royal Hallamshire Teaching Hospital, which is where Roy was headed.

He parked in the visitors' car park, and put a sign on the dashboard that identified his vehicle as belonging to Yorkshire Police. He had to admit anyone noticing that sign would wonder how his decrepit rust bucket of a car would belong to the police force. But that was their problem, not his.

He followed the signs to the morgue, which, as expected, was in the basement. His hunch that it would be close to the medical students' dissecting room also turned out to be correct. His experience of morgues in England was rather good as a result of his job.

When he emerged from the lift at level minus two, the familiar whitewashed walls and silent corridor seemed to be the same he had encountered up and down the country. A group of white-coated medical students – they were far too young to be doctors – walked past him. They queued up outside a blue door, and went in single file. That would be where they learnt anatomy in detail, picking their way around numerous cadavers, already cut open to show them important structures.

His mentor and previous guvnor, Detective Superintendent Arla Baker, had taken him to a dissecting room when he was a rookie detective. He had cringed when he saw all the cadavers laid out in rows of gurneys.

'Learn the surface anatomy,' she said, with perfect seriousness. 'Where a killer can stab to puncture the lungs, and where the major arteries appear on the skin. Check behind the ears and in the hairline for needle pricks. Learn to think like a murderer.'

That day he spent in the dissecting room had stayed with him for the rest of his life. Every time he looked at a dead victim now, he automatically checked the surface anatomy. Thinking about Arla Baker made him realise he had to get back to London sooner rather than later. Although he was now on the payroll of Yorkshire Police, he wasn't a permanent member of the force. He had to get his formal leave from the Met.

He walked past the group of students and came up to

the tall white double doors of the morgue. He pressed the buzzer, and the door opened from inside. Ese, the short and sparkling African woman who worked for Sheila Patel, opened the door. Ese's hair was in dreadlocks, and she had gold, red and yellow beads in them. She was dressed in the traditional surgical blues of the morgue, and had Crocs on her feet.

'Inspector Roy, how nice of you to come,' Ese said in her posh accent. 'We've been expecting you.'

'And my reputation precedes me, clearly,' Roy said, shutting the door behind him. The smell of formaldehyde and disinfectant was heavy in the air, like an invisible cloud that cloaked his skin.

'I wouldn't go that far,' Ese said, clearly not amused. 'You're not Dr Livingstone. Not that I think much of those so-called explorers in Africa. The world has changed, thankfully.'

Roy smiled and a knowing look appeared in Ese's eyes. She waved him to the changing rooms. 'See you in a jiffy.'

Roy went in, and took off his jacket and shoes. He put on a pair of Crock, and tied a plastic apron around his midriff. He pulled on a blue surgical mask and re-emerged into the land of the dead. Dr Patel was leaning against a standing desk, watching the screen. She didn't turn when Roy approached.

He looked to his left, where Ese was taking the covers off a gurney. He saw Noor's black hair, tucked in under her head. He could see the stitches across her skull where the saw had cut through.

'Shall we?' Dr Patel said.

'What did you find?' Roy asked. From the stony expression on her face, he knew it wasn't good news. She pulled out a pair of gloves from the packet on a desk, and Roy followed her to the gurney. Dr Patel pointed at the head.

'Small bruises on the scalp where her head banged against the floor, but nothing else. The grease on her hair is cooking oil. It's heavier than what we can expect from daily cooking. I'd say she worked in a restaurant as well.'

'That's what I've heard. Although the restaurant owner is denying it apparently.'

Dr Patel glanced at him and nodded. She looked down at the body again. There was something amiss about her today, a loss of her usual sharpness. She was lacking the normal no-nonsense attitude that he'd got used to. She seemed under a cloud.

'Some bruise marks on the neck where she was briefly strangled. I couldn't find any fingerprints, and neither did Justin, by the way. The killer was wearing gloves.' Dr Patel trailed down the gurney like she was being pushed along.

'Skin samples under the nails. I have sent them off for DNA testing. If there're any matches on the database we will know by tomorrow.'

She pointed to the wound in the abdomen, which had been cleaned, and then left open. She talked mechanically, like a robot, without looking at Roy.

'As you know, death was by extravasation, low-volume shock causing multi-organ failure. It happened within a couple of hours.' Dr Patel's eyes remained fixed on the abdomen for a few seconds, then she slowly lifted them to meet Roy's. Her eyes were dead and flat. She stared at him without speaking, and, in that instant, he knew. The skin tightened on his face, and his heart shrivelled.

'Was she pregnant?'

Dr Patel's face was carved in stone. Only her lips moved and that too with reluctance, it seemed.

'Yes. The uterus is a deep structure in the pelvis. The knife wounds were extensive, and they caused damage to multiple organs, but not to the uterus.' She paused, and Roy knew then she had opened up the womb.

'The uterus was gravid, which means it was larger than the normal size, and thicker. She was about ten weeks pregnant, I'd say.'

Dr Patel looked away, and moved further down. It seemed she was shrinking in size as she went along the gurney.

'There were signs of recent sexual activity. I found sperm in the vaginal vault. Again, DNA samples are awaited. If you have any DNA from suspects, please send them to me ASAP.'

'I will.'

'Nothing much to report on the legs. She was wearing jeans, so not many lacerations there. Did you get any feedback from Justin on the jewellery?'

Roy shook his head. 'I'll speak to him now.'

'The blood samples don't show much. Toxicology for

drugs is awaited, maybe in a few days time. That's all then,' Dr Patel said. She looked tired all of a sudden, like the explanation had exhausted her. She trudged back to her desk, and Roy followed. He didn't know what to say, and he knew there was nothing that would help.

'I'll get along, then,' he said, taking the plastic apron off. He put it in the bin.

Dr Patel had sat down at her table, and was clicking on her keyboard. 'I went to see Sarah, by the way. She's doing alright.'

'Good. Thanks for checking on her.' Roy turned to leave. Dr Patel's words stopped him.

'Find who did this, Rohan. Find him now.'

He half turned to her. That old glint was back in her eyes. 'I will,' he said.

CHAPTER 27

Oliver raced up the stairs, and stumbled on the landing as his foot caught on a rug on the floor. He went sprawling, the floorboards banging into his ribs. He grunted with pain, but got to his feet swiftly. There was a bathroom to his right, and two bedrooms. The bathroom door was open but the other two were shut. To his left, across the landing, there was a sash window and it was open. A curtain fluttered in the breeze. He rushed to it, and found himself looking down at a small garden. The familiar figure of Melanie was visible, checking the back fence. Like the experienced detective she was, Melanie had tried to block Akbar's exit from the rear.

But there was no sign of Akbar. The rear fence was covered with creeping vine, and it was about two metres high. If Akbar had climbed over it, he would've landed in a path between the next row of houses. He could've gone in any direction, but Oliver didn't see any of the neighbours' gardens getting disturbed. A woman was putting out clothes on a line, directly opposite. She might've heard something.

He checked the two bedrooms, which had a mattress on the floor, and a single wardrobe. He took the two toothbrushes and shaving kit in separate specimen bags. In the first bedroom, he found women's clothes hanging from the wardrobe, and some shoes. This must be Layla's room. He went into the second bedroom, which was similar, but with clothes strewn all over the floor, competing with an Xbox and a knot of cables that snaked up to a flat-screen TV. Pizza boxes and cans of pop mingled with the clothes, and there was a stench in the room from food that had gone off. This had to be Akbar's room then.

He heard Melanie's radio as she came up the stairs. She'd already alerted the local uniform teams about Akbar. The chatter on her radio was drowned out by the sound of fast-approaching sirens.

'They're going around the back and sides to see if they can cut him off,' Melanie said. 'You alright? I heard a crash.'

Oliver rubbed his chest where his ribs were a little sore. 'Nothing I can't handle, guv. He was quick though. Went out that window before I could even get up the stairs.'

Melanie shook her head. 'We should've been expecting that. Don't know why I didn't arrest him. He might've lawyered up and given us nothing. I was seeing how much I could get out of him. Silly of me.'

'Not your fault, guv. He looked scared out of his wits, like he had a smashed egg under his flat cap.'

The front door opened and a uniformed sergeant called

out. 'Not seen him yet. Any chance he might be in one of these houses?'

'Start a door to door,' Melanie suggested. 'We need to do one anyway.'

With Oliver she went into the bedrooms. They searched carefully, not disturbing too much as SOC, or scene of crime, would be here soon. They didn't find a laptop, but the Xbox would come in handy.

They searched the tiny kitchen and the lounge. Nothing unusual anywhere; the place did look like a couple of poor students lived here. Oliver opened the understairs cupboard and found a stack of single mattresses. He pointed them out to Melanie.

'Maybe more people lived here at some stage.'

Melanie was looking at her phone. She had received the PCNs and photos of Martin Donald. Riz had sent over passport photos of Sunil Ambani and Rahul Tripathi as well.

'More so-called students, eh?' Melanie sighed. 'God knows how long this has been going on for. If we're done here, let's head back to the nick, but I want to swing past Noor's flat once again. She didn't live alone, according to the Donalds. Someone should be back by now.'

They left the uniforms in charge, who were setting up a perimeter. This was a crime scene now, and SOC would be arriving later. But the most pressing thing, Oliver thought as he started driving, was to find Akbar. He even fit the killer's description.

They drove back through the serpentine roads of

Netheredge, and cut across east to reach Victoria Quay. As they walked up to the block of flats in the estate, Oliver nudged Melanie. He indicated the group of youths who were lounging at one side under a pillar, some of them sitting on the railings, watching them. All of them wore black tracksuits, and hoodies.

'We should ask them if they saw Noor.'

'Good idea, but I get the feeling they won't say owt to us.' Melanie grimaced. 'But worth a try.'

The young men stopped talking and looked away as they approached. Some of them swore softly, and pulled ski masks up their faces. One of them spoke, his face covered by a mask.

'You lot are the Feds, right?'

'Yes,' Oliver said. They showed their warrant cards. 'We want to ask you about a girl called Noor, who lived in flat 514 of this block.' He took out his phone, and showed them her passport photo that Riz had now sent over. Several of the gang members leant into have a look. The majority of them were only teenagers.

A couple of them looked at each other, and went silent. Oliver focused on them. 'You know her?'

'What if I did? What you want?' One of them asked belligerently.

'She's dead. She was killed in the early hours of this morning. We need to find out who lived with her, and who she hung around with.'

There was silence. Melanie spoke up. 'We spoke to Mr Martin Donald, her neighbour on the fifth floor. Noor was seen with one of her friends called Layla, walking in the compound.'

There was a palpable shift in the air. Oliver didn't know what caused it. But all of the boys and men around them seemed to snarl in unison. Some of them leant closer, and swore loudly.

'Martin Donald? Why you talkin' to him for?' The man who spoke let forth a string of choice cuss words. Oliver looked at them. Five men circled him, all of them were black. He assumed, Martin Donald, due to his political affiliations, was no friend of this lot.

'Like I said, we spoke to him. His wife said Noor and Layla walked here together. Did you see them?'

The men looked at each other. Oliver could tell they knew something. Melanie glanced at him, and she nodded. Oliver said, 'None of you are in any trouble. What you tell us remains confidential.'

The man who was speaking earlier cursed loudly. 'We don't give a fuck about that. Man like that idiot deserves what he gets. He's a lying bastard, that's what he is. Shags around with coloured women, but then rants all his racist crap.'

Oliver frowned. 'Really?'

'Yes, mate. This Noor girl, he shagged her as well. We seen them, lurking around. There's empty flats in the estate, where man and girl dem go for a shag, you seen?'

Oliver knew enough of the Caribbean lingo to understand what they were saying, but he could scarcely believe his ears. Mr National Front man had a fondness for dark-skinned women?

Melanie said, 'When did you last see them together?'

'Yo listen,' the man said, adjusting his face mask up. All of them had masks on, and just their eyes were visible under the hoodies.

'You didn't hear this from us, alright? But there's flats here where girl dem can go to earn some extra cash. You get me? It's safe for the girls, they got protection. Man dem just pay, do their business and leave.'

One of the other men butted in. 'But for that Indian girl it was different. That racist pig liked her. They kept it hidden, but we could see.'

'Enough, bro,' one of the men said quietly. 'Say nuttin more.'

They fell silent. They turned their backs, and walked off. Oliver knew it was pointless to ask them any more questions.

Melanie said, 'Well, well. Looks like we need to pay Mr Donald another visit.'

CHAPTER 28

Roy walked into the office to find Melanie, Rizwan and Oliver busy at their desks. Rizwan saw him first.

'Now then, boss. We were wondering what happened to you, like.'

'I got a call from Dr Patel and went to see her at the morgue,' Roy sighed, taking his jacket off.

Melanie angled an eyebrow at him. 'Not good news?'

'You could say that. I need some tea, first.'

All heads turned to look at Riz, who frowned. 'Why me?'

'You've been sitting on your arse all day, doing sod all, that's why,' Oliver said, helpfully.

'Without my intel you'd still be running around like a blue-arsed tit.'

'Enough,' Roy said. 'Both of you, get some tea and biscuits. Please.'

'I'm famished, to be honest,' Melanie said. 'I could do with some nosh.'

Roy dug into his pocket and took out a twenty. He waved it at the two DCs. 'Get me a BLT. And whatever anyone else wants.'

Melanie ordered a chicken Caesar salad, and the men went off to the canteen.

'Now tell me,' Melanie said. 'What turned up in the post mortem? Sheila managed to get it done quickly.'

'She did, and no, it's not good news. Noor was about ten weeks pregnant.' Roy lapsed into silence. There wasn't a great deal more to say. They both knew they didn't have any suspects, but Melanie's eyes danced with a sudden light.

'Listen to this, guv.' She told Roy about Martin Donald and Noor. 'And he lives right next door to her. We went up to arrest him, but he's done a runner. His wife said he works in the packing factory in the Burngreave Industrial Estate. We swung by there as well, but he's not around.'

Roy frowned. 'So there's a chance that he was the father of Noor's baby. Now, why would he want to kill her? Because it looks bad if it gets known, given his so-called political activism?'

'Yes, I guess so. Amanda, his wife, said he was out last night. He went to the pub to see his mates, and he came home after she'd gone to bed. He didn't say which pub.'

'Does he have a local pub that he frequents? What

about the National Front office?'

'Good idea, I need to check. They might know. I'll check.'

'So, Martin had the motive, as he didn't want his political friends to find out he was going to be the father of a mixed-race child. He also had the opportunity, as no one knows where he was. He could have planned to meet up with Noor at Thorndean Lodge with the purpose of killing her. As for means, he has a history of violence, right? He was arrested for GBH and D and D?' Drunk and disorderly was a common cause for arrest after the pubs shut.

'Yes, he beat up a couple of police volunteers during a march of the BNP.' The British National Party was a modern version of the National Front, both extreme right wing parties.

'We need to find him. He couldn't have gone far. Any car records on the DVLA?'

'He's got a driving licence, and owns a car, which is parked at the estate's car park. So he's not escaped that way. But he's not around, and we only saw him this morning.'

The DCs came back with food and drinks. They put them on their desks, and Roy accepted his change with a murmur of thanks. Not until he saw his BLT sandwich did he realise how hungry he'd been. His stomach rumbled loudly. The bacon in Sheffield tasted fresher, juicer than in London, and he unwrapped the sandwich hungrily.

There was a lull in the conversation as they tucked in. Roy wiped his mouth with a tissue, and went to the white board at the far corner. He brought it closer, and made notes with a black marker pen.

He wrote number 1 and then Martin Donald's name. 'He seems to be our number one suspect right now, but we need to keep an open mind.'

'He doesn't have an open mind,' Oliver smirked. 'That's for sure.'

Roy shrugged, and wrote number 2, Sunil Ambani. 'The restaurant manager is lying to us, and we need to find out why. So is the waiter, Rahul.'

'And her friend, Layla,' Melanie said. 'Which for me is the strangest part. Layla is keeping her silence, when she could be helping us. She's clearly afraid of something.'

'And so is Akbar. Otherwise he wouldn't have run,' Oliver added.

Roy wrote down all the names, then inspected the board. He added Mr Ludlow as number five.

'Layla and Akbar could be in danger,' Roy said. 'If we stay with Martin as number one suspect, he could be after them as they might have known about his relationship with Noor.'

Rizwan glanced at Oliver. 'Uniforms are staying on scene at Noor's flat?'

'Yes, but they can't be there 24/7. It makes more sense if we speak to Layla again after she finishes work.' He looked at his watch. 'It's past four p.m. We should head there now.'

Roy agreed. 'Yes. Bring her in. Arrest her if you have to, it might well be for her own good. We need to consider the fact these young people were living here under duress. They came on a student visa, but never attended college. It seems they worked in menial job for less than the national wage, if they got anything at all. The fact that Layla can't even have a phone is suspicious.'

He glanced at Melanie and Oliver. 'Any sign of Akbar?'

'The door to door hasn't revealed anything,' Melanie said. 'Akbar doesn't have a car registered under his name, but it's possible someone was waiting for him, and gave him a ride.'

'He can't be far,' Roy mused. 'It's possible he's hiding somewhere local. Have we checked if he worked in the Mumtaz restaurant?'

'I rang and asked,' Oliver said. 'The answer was no, like the responses to our previous questions. Lying sods.'

'I'd say we bring in Sunil Ambani, the restaurant owner,' Rizwan said. 'The restaurants are known to employ people from India, Bangladesh and Pakistan who come here illegally. It's nothing new. By the way, I rang up the local mosques in Netheredge, and described Noor, Akbar and Layla to them. They didn't know of them, and Layla's last name is Patil which means she's Hindu. I called the two temples in that area, but they've never heard of her.'

'Which only means they weren't religious,' Melanie said.

Roy went back to his desk and took another bite of his BLT. He had lost his appetite. He needed to find Jayden, and he kept getting distracted, which wasn't helping. He squeezed the sides of his temples, only too well aware of the growing headache.

'Right. This is getting worse, so I want to call the Modern Slavery Unit of the Yorkshire Police. As long as they have one, that is. If not, I'll think of another similar unit. I suspect there's an organised network at work here, and we need to get to the bottom of it.' Roy stood, and pointed at Rizwan.

'You and Ollie, go and get Layla, and don't come back empty-handed. Got it?'

Both young men nodded solemnly, their attention fixed on Roy. He turned to Melanie. 'Let's go and see what Mr Ambani has to say for himself.'

CHAPTER 29

It was close to five p.m. by the time Roy and Melanie knocked on the door of Mumtaz restaurant in Hillsborough. The street around them was busy in the early evening. Shoppers were loading their cars to go home. The nail bar next to the restaurant was still almost half full. Roy knocked for the second time on the glass door of the restaurant. He didn't want to hammer his fist on it, in case it wobbled. The dark-tinted windows now had curtains drawn, but a light was on inside.

'Shall I have a look around the back?' Melanie suggested.

'Someone's here.' Roy tried to peer through the curtains. 'I can see a shape moving.' As he watched, the light inside went off, and he was denied any further visibility. 'That's odd. They should be opening up for the evening now.' He looked back at Melanie. 'We might have to try another entrance. They must have a rear door for supplies and rubbish.'

He knocked on the door again, more forcefully this time. Melanie was on the phone as well.

'It's ringing,' she said, 'But no answer.'

They heard steps and a figure appeared. It was a young man in a white shirt and black trousers, the de facto uniform for waiters. He opened the door and stared at them nervously.

'That's Rahul Tripathi, guv,' Melanie whispered to Roy.

'Can we come in?' Roy said, putting a foot on the doorstep, making it clear he wasn't taking no for an answer.

Rahul moved backwards, and they stepped in. Roy smelt the familiar aromas of frying onions and spices. The tables were empty but a light glowed in the kitchen at the back, visible through the round glass panel on the door at the back of the room. But the light in the restaurant was now turned off. They stood there for a while, Roy watching Rahul, who seemed to squirm under his gaze.

'Is the restaurant always this dark?' Roy demanded.

'No, sir,' Rahul stuttered. 'We're just getting ready.'

'Turn the light on. Now,' Roy said. Rahul hurried to the wall, and a dull yellow glow filled the room. Melanie and Roy walked towards him. Rahul gaped at them, fear in his eyes.

'Where is your boss, Sunil Ambani?' Roy asked. 'And before you say anything, just remember that we know Noor worked here, and Layla still does. Don't lie to us anymore.'

Rahul stared at them, then his lips trembled. He seemed to be held prisoner by an invisible force, but his eyes were almost pleading to be released. He couldn't utter the words on his tongue, and he shook his head.

'I don't know,' he whispered, then looked down at his feet.

Roy indicated the side door at the rear, which was shut. It said Staff Only. 'Mr Ambani has his office upstairs, correct?'

'Yes, but he's not in.'

'We can still have a look,' Roy said, brushing past Rahul. Melanie went for the kitchen. Roy had taken Rahul with him upstairs. The narrow, creaky flight of stairs went up one floor and ended in a small landing with three doors open in front of them. One of them was a bathroom, and Roy checked it quickly to find it empty. As he turned in the landing, facing a nervous Rahul, he heard a thud from one of the other rooms. He pressed on the door handle, and the door was locked. He kicked it with his foot, and it wasn't locked anymore. The door frame cracked as the hinges came flying off, and Roy barged inside. He was in a small office, enough for a desk and three chairs. He saw a tall man with his legs astride the window ledge. The sash window was raised, and the only reason the man had not jumped was because of his size. He was busy lowering his head below the upper sash when Roy grabbed his collar and pulled him backwards. It wasn't easy, as the man had a pot belly, and he was heavy. But once his centre of gravity turned, he collapsed like a sack of spuds on the floor, raising a cloud of dust from the carpet.

Roy grabbed his meaty hands and folded them behind his back. The man fought, but Roy put a knee on his back, and kept him face down. He handcuffed the man, then sat him up against the wall.

'Sunil Ambani,' Roy said, meeting the man's hateful eyes. 'You're under arrest.'

CHAPTER 30

Oliver and Rizwan stood in front of the Asian lady who owned the nail bar where Layla worked. The owner's name was Nikki, and she remembered Oliver from the morning.

'She...she gone home now. I don't know where she gone,' Nikki said, in her broken English.

'You don't know where her home is, you mean?' Oliver asked, trying to be helpful. Nikki nodded.

'What time did she leave?'

'She said she no feeling well. She leave after you come this morning.'

Oliver frowned. 'What time was that?' He glanced at Rizwan, who also had a troubled expression on his face, and their eyes met briefly.

'I no remember,' Nikki said. 'Just after lunch. Maybe

two pm. She tell me she want go home.'

Rizwan said, 'And you're sure she left by herself. She didn't go with anyone? There wasn't anyone waiting for her outside the shop?'

Nikki's smooth forehead crinkled as she thought, then she shook her head. 'No. She went alone. She said going home.' Nikki shrugged to indicate she didn't have a clue where Layla was.

The detective constables thanked her, and left. Outside, Rizwan rang switchboard and asked to be put through to the uniforms team in Netheredge, guarding the property where Akbar and Layla stayed. They hadn't seen anyone go inside the property.

'Chuffin' heck,' Oliver muttered. 'Don't tell me we got another missing person on our hands.'

'First Akbar, and now Layla. But safe to say Akbar is a suspect as he matches the killer's description. We should look for Layla on CCTV, eh, mate?' Rizwan pointed to the cameras on the high street. 'They should be able to pick her up around two p.m.'

'Definitely.'

Rizwan made the call to the traffic department, and conveyed Layla's description and her online case file number, linked to Noor's case.

'Now what?' Oliver asked.

'We need to find Martin Donald, eh? Shall we swing by his home, then his workplace?'

'I've got his wife's number. Let's give her a call, like.'

They had arrived by the car, and Oliver lit a cigarette, then spoke on the phone. Amanda Donald answered, and thought her husband was still at work.

'She's not lying, is she?' Rizwan mused, as they got in the car. 'She must know her husband's been in trouble with the police before. She could be trying to protect him.'

Oliver shrugged. Rizwan started to drive, and Oliver glanced at his friend.

'If she is trying to protect him, then there's no better way than to let her know what he's really been up to.'

Riz nodded slowly. 'Aye, I can see that. But don't forget we're taking the word of some gang members. I'm not saying they're lying, but we need more proof I think. A DNA match with the semen sample found on the victim would be the best way. But we could ask around in the estate.'

Oliver's eyes came alive. 'I've got an idea.'

When Rizwan heard what Oliver's bright spark was, he shook his head firmly. 'Absolutely no bloody way. Have you lost your marbles? Sorry, you never had them in the first place.'

'Come on, Riz,' Oliver threw his head back. 'It'll be alright.'

'Nope. No friggin' way.'

'You know it makes sense.'

'To an imbecile, or an idiot maybe. I mean, have you considered the consequences of this going wrong?'

'It won't go wrong though, will it? It's foolproof.'

'Foolhardy, more like. Just shut it, will yer?'

'Come on, mate.'

'No bloody way.'

Fifteen minutes later, a cross-looking Riz was sitting with his arms folded in the car. Their car was an unmarked major investigations team car, so it could be parked anywhere. Riz was on the high street of Attercliffe, and there was a parade of second-hand and pound stores opposite. From an Army Salvation clothes shop, Oliver emerged. He was wearing 1970s-style big sunglasses, a blue and white shell suit that popstars wore in the eighties, and baggy tracksuit bottoms. He had white trainers on his feet. His usual suit and black shoes were presumably in the bag he was carrying, unless he had sold them for his new outfit.

Riz could only gape at his friend. Oliver walked with a swagger, shoulders rolling, knees slightly bent. He got in the passenger side, and lowered his sunglasses, then winked at Riz.

''ey up, chuck. You alright, like?'

Riz could hardly get the words out of his mouth. 'What the hell are you doing, you pillock?'

'I'm going undercover.'

'You call this...' Words failed Riz. 'You look like a porn star from our dad's age.'

Oliver waggled a finger. 'Exactly. That's the look I was goin' for. Now they'll believe me.'

Riz closed his eyes. 'Oh god.'

'Come on, chuck, let's go. No point in wasting time. For all we know, Martin's in the estate, shagging some other bird.'

Riz let out a deep sigh, and started the car. He had a sinking feeling in his chest. 'I can't believe you talked me into this.'

'You'll be sorry if we don't.'

Riz drove down the high street slowly. He looked at Oliver, who was grinning like a Cheshire cat. 'You're enjoying this, aren't you?'

'Lighten up, mate. Like I said, you'll be sorry if we don't do this.'

'I'm already sorry.'

CHAPTER 31

A few minutes later, Oliver was walking through the estate in his 70's retro outfit. He thought he looked rather good, despite what Riz thought. He got a few looks from people who walked past him, he thought they were admiring glances. He walked towards the group of teenagers and young men loitering by one of the staircases at the base of a block of flats. He kept his sunglasses on so his eyes were hidden. His radio was also switched for two-way transmission, but only on the frequency he shared with Riz. Riz could hear the conversation.

''ey up,' Oliver called out as he approached the group. The men turned to look at him.

'Who are yer, Jimmy Savile?' One of them cackled, and the others burst into laughter. Oliver ignored them.

'I'm new here,' he said, getting closer, dropping his voice. 'I heard there's a place where you can get some birds, like. You know.' He wiggled his eyebrows, and made a lewd gesture with his hands.

The men had disbelieving looks on their faces, which Oliver mistook for admiration. He whispered, 'My mate told me. There's some birds who do that round 'ere. Eh?'

One of the men folded his arms across his chest and frowned. 'Who are yer? Not seen you before.'

'Cos I'm new. My name's Brian. I live at number 274, in that block. Moved in last week.'

'Where you from?'

'Scunthorpe. Sunny Scunny.' Oliver grinned.

'Do they dress like that in Scunny? Not goin' to work 'ere, mate.'

'Aye, I know. Been getting' odd looks an' that. I used to DJ in a pub see, seventies throwback music. Kind of got used to wearing these clothes.' He was getting a little nervous, and let out a fake laugh. 'Anyway. You lads know the place I'm talking about?'

There was a change in the group's attitude. Several of the men looked at each other. The one with a shaven head, who seemed to be the leader, stared at Oliver unblinkingly.

'Who told yer about them?'

'My mate Paddy. Irish lad from Loxley. He comes here for that stuff, you know.'

The man stared at Oliver for a while, then shrugged. '620, in block eight. No skin off my back, like. Now bugger off, Jimmy Savile.'

Mission accomplished, and the dodgy compliment ringing in his ears, Oliver walked off. When he was out of earshot, and under the cover of a pillar, he turned up the knob on his radio.

'Did you hear that? Job done.'

'Stop talking to me, you moron,' Riz hissed. 'Find out what you can and get the hell out. I ain't comin' after you if you get stuck.'

'Oh yes you are.' Oliver hung up. He squared his shoulders and smiled. Riz was just jealous he didn't think of it himself.

He took his sunglasses off and followed signs to the block. He took the stairs up as he didn't want to see anyone in the lifts. He was perspiring by the time he got to the sixth floor. The shell suit didn't breathe very well. Huffing, and wiping sweat from his brow, Oliver knocked on door number 620. Footsteps approached, and he was observed in silence through the eyepiece. Then the door opened a crack. Behind it, a disembodied voice spoke.

'What do you want?'

'I'm here from one of them girls.'

'Who sent you?'

'Martin Donald. He lives in number 518.'

There was a period of silence, then the chain rattled, and the door opened more. Oliver took his glasses off to get used to the darkness inside. He saw a short and wiry middle-aged man, whose eyes were sweeping all over him. Oliver stepped inside the narrow lobby, and the man shut the door, then faced him.

185

'Martin sent you?'

'Yes. He said he used to meet some girls here. One of them was called Noor.'

The man's eyes narrowed. Then he rubbed his cheek, and relaxed. 'You got money?'

'Yes. But I came to see if this place was still going. Martin said that was a good idea.'

The man nodded. 'Fifty for half hour, one hundred for one hour. You need to come in the evening after seven. OK?'

'Will Noor be here?' Oliver saw a funny look skim across the man's face and he changed his question quickly. 'I mean, Martin said she was good. But if you've got someone else, that's also OK.'

'All the girls are good,' the man said. 'Yes, Martin sees Noor, but she's not the only one here.'

The man spoke as if Noor was still alive, Oliver thought. He wondered if he should press further, but decided against it.

'Alright then. I'll come back after seven tonight.' He made for the door, and the man opened it for him. Just as Oliver was about to leave, the man stopped him.

'Have I seen you somewhere before?'

Oliver shrugged, acting casual. 'Don't think so. I'm new here. Best be going.'

The man didn't move. His eyes remained on Oliver like he was memorising his face. Then he tugged on the door. Oliver stepped out, and heaved a sigh of relief.

CHAPTER 32

'See?' Oliver gloated. 'I told you it would be fine. Now we know for a fact Martin was sleeping with Noor. He went to that brothel. Now gimme a fag.'

They were leaning against the car. Riz handed Oliver a cigarette, and lit one himself. 'That could've gone wrong in so many different ways.'

'But it didn't, did it, chuck? And we now know where it happens, so we can shut the place down.'

'That's a good thing,' Riz conceded. 'And you got more evidence about Noor and Martin now. We better find him quickly.' From the corner of his eyes, Riz noted two Afro-Caribbean men staring at him across the road. As he watched, they crossed and stood a distance away, but still observing them. Concern unfurled inside him.

'Get in the car,' he hissed. 'We've been spotted. You

should've taken your outfit off as soon as you came out.'

Oliver said something, but his words were drowned out by a shout from one of the men watching them. 'Hey you. Jimmy Savile!' The two men got closer, and they shouted again.

'You a fed? That looks like a fed car.' The man swore loudly. Riz looked around, and saw another knot of men heading their way. Bystanders were alert now, and staring at them.

'Get in the bloody car,' Riz hissed, making for the door. Footsteps came running, and Oliver just managed to slam his door shut, and put the window up. A fist hammered on the glass, and a grimacing face glared at him. Another appeared on Riz's side. Then two men stood in front of the car, and planted their feet wide apart. Riz was trying to get out of his parking spot, but he couldn't do so without hitting the men. He flashed his lights at them, then honked his horn. One of the men put a hand on the bonnet, and thumped it loudly. Riz turned the wheel, and tickled the accelerator, making the car jump forward.

The men cursed. They kicked the car, and a brick landed on the windscreen, shattering it with brown fragments. Another brick landed on the side-view mirror, smashing it. Riz twisted the wheel, and moved forward, and the men scattered finally. Another brick landed on the car's ceiling, making it shudder. Riz floored the gas, and the car surged forward. He didn't relax till he got to the end of the road, and took the right turn.

'Happy now?' Riz panted, as they joined the main traffic on the high street. Both of them kept looking for men chasing them. 'We're not going back there in a rush. Your stupid act just made our lives more difficult.'

'Hey,' Oliver protested. 'At least I got more intel.'

'I'm thinking about the uniforms who patrol there. They're more visible than us, and vulnerable. We don't want to start a riot in there.'

Oliver wiped his forehead with his sleeve. 'They'll be outside the victim's flat. It should be alright.'

'Speaking of which.' Riz frowned. 'We've heard nowt about the others who live there.'

'The man who owns the flat isn't replying. Daniel Jones. We should pay him a visit as well. Let me give the uniforms a call.' Oliver called switchboard and asked them to connect him to the team inside the estate.

'Any sign of activity outside flat 514?'

'Dead as a doornail here,' the sergeant in charge said. 'We're doing the door to door in this block. There's an old lady on the ground floor who says she saw Noor with Martin Donald a couple of times. They never walked out together in the open. She sits on her balcony and watches the front yard. She saw Noor getting into Martin's car.'

'Good. Please take her details, and a statement. We might have to go inside the flat soon if no one turns up.'

Oliver closed the call and looked at Riz. 'Bloody hell. Martin was hanging around with Noor a fair bit.'

'We should stop by the warehouse where Martin Donald works. As long as you get out of that ridiculous outfit. Jimmy Savile...' He shook his head. 'That should be your new name.'

A look of alarm flickered over Oliver's face. 'Don't you dare.'

Riz grinned. 'I can see it catching on.'

They stopped for a quick takeaway coffee, then raced on to Burnsgreaves Industrial Estate, which had a collection of huge warehouses. Riz parked the car outside an office where the sign on the wall said Skipton Distributors. He got out and stretched. Next to the normal car park, there was a big area where all the lorries and trucks stood in rows. A stack of pallets was arranged in one corner, a forklift truck emerged from the warehouse, and the driver lifted one from the stack, and drove back inside. They went inside and stood at the reception where a middle-aged woman looked up at them expectantly. Her eyes went to Oliver, who was still in his white and blue shell suit. Mercifully, he had taken off the sunglasses.

Riz showed his warrant card and introduced himself. 'Can my friend here get changed in those toilets?' He pointed to a door that bore the sign of a loo. The woman looked confused, and her gaze shifted from Riz back to Oliver. The hint of a smile gathered at the corner of her lips.

'Are you a copper as well? Or is this some kind of joke?'

'I am a police detective.' Oliver sighed. He took out his warrant card and showed it to the woman. She put a hand to her mouth and smothered a smile. Oliver shook his head.

'Yes, sure. Use that one, like.' She pointed to the loo. Oliver clutched his bag and went to get changed. Riz turned to the woman, a steely look on his face.

'We're here to see Martin Donald, and it's urgent.'

The woman peered at her screen, then stood. 'He was at work earlier today. Let me check inside.'

Riz stepped forward. 'Do you mind if we come with you? It's urgent. Please wait till my colleague comes back.'

The woman, whose name badge said Rosie, frowned. 'What's this about?'

'Martin is wanted in connection with an ongoing case. I can't tell you much more, but we need to speak to him ASAP.'

Oliver emerged from the bathroom in his black suit. 'Right,' Riz said, and glanced at Rosie. 'Shall we?'

They went through a door behind Rosie's desk, and stepped inside a vast warehouse. Most of it was taken up by vast shelves that rose like steel trees to the ceiling. There was a hubbub of voices and machines on the floor as men in high-vis jackets moved around, and forklift trucks shifted around. Rosie stopped in front of a tall man who was speaking to a group. She whispered in his ear. The man turned around and acknowledged Oliver and Riz.

'I'm David, the foreman here. I saw Martin this morning, but he turned up late. Not seen him since his lunchbreak. What's this about?'

'It's an urgent enquiry, and we need to speak to him. Does he have any friends here, who might know he is? He's not at home, we checked.'

David swivelled his head, looking around. 'I need to

ask others. Have you checked the canteen? Here, I'll come with you.' David spoke to the group, asking them to look for Martin, and they dispersed.

They followed David to the canteen, which was practically empty at this hour. One man stood by the lockers, stuffing his hi-vis jacket inside, and pulling out his backpack. David went and spoke to him.

'Martin?' the other man said. 'I saw him go out for a fag break. Not seen him since.'

'Do you have CCTV here?' Oliver asked. 'Inside and outside, for the perimeter?'

'We do,' David said. 'I can ask our security guys for today's footage if you want.'

'Do you know if Martin drives here?' Riz asked.

David shook his head. 'I don't think so. He normally takes the bus. I've seen him on the bus a few times as I take it myself.'

'It's unusual for him to be absent like this, right?' Oliver asked. 'He should be at work now.'

'Yes. Let's go outside and I can take you to Security. With any luck, the others should've found Martin.'

On the main floor, David asked a few men, and stopped a fork-lift truck driver. No one had seen Martin. They went into an office on the ground floor and David knocked, then entered a door marked Security. He introduced Oliver and Rizwan to the two men who sat in front of a bank of black-and-white TV screens, arranged as two rows of four screens. David spoke to them, and they got busy, replaying the day's reels.

'Needle in a haystack though,' one of them grumbled. 'He could be any one of these lads inside.'

'Look outside,' Riz suggested. 'Check it from this afternoon.'

The guards did as told. Then one of them pointed at the screen, and stopped the scroll. 'Is that him?'

David leant closer, as did Oliver, who had seen Martin. 'Yes,' David said. 'That looks like him.'

They saw the back of a man who walked quickly across the courtyard, hands stuffed in his pocket. He looked back as if to make sure no one was following him. He ducked behind a green truck and vanished from view. The guard switched the view to another screen. Martin was visible again, running between the trucks, till he came to a gate in the fence. It was locked, and he was alone. He climbed the gate, then jumped over and disappeared again.

'We don't have any more footage,' the guard said, turning to Oliver and Riz.

'When did this happen?'

The time stamp said 15:40, which was two hours ago. 'We need to go,' Riz said. 'Thanks for your help. If Martin turns up, make sure you tell us.'

Oliver was already on the radio, calling for back-up as he headed out into the corridor. Riz ran after him.

CHAPTER 33

Layla looked at her phone and stiffened. She had a message from Afzal, who worked with Paresh and Ambani. Afzal wanted to meet her as soon as she finished work. It wasn't unusual for Afzal to meet her. He was one of the men who controlled her life. Layla knew her routine well. She had to finish at the nail bar and then go to the restaurant. She finished early, because that's when the brothels opened. She had an exhausting day, and the nights stretched on for longer than she could bear thinking of. The brothels were in various flats across the city, the busiest one being in the estate where Noor lived.

Had lived.

Noor was dead, and Layla still couldn't believe it. Her fingers trembled over the phone's keypad, wondering if she should call Akbar. He had betrayed Noor and herself. She had thought Akbar would help Noor get in touch with her family in Punjab. But Akbar was a spy, keeping an eye on the girls. Layla felt sick when she thought she lived with Akbar. The house was paid for by the men, and every other week, new people arrived. They kept four girls in each bedroom, and it was cramped and horrible. Some of the girls stayed, but mostly they moved on to other parts of the country. For the bastards who did this to her, business was brisk.

No, she couldn't get in touch with Akbar. She wanted to know where he was, and if the police had reached him already. And… She shuddered when the thought hit her. Could Akbar have killed Noor?

Shaking, Layla stood. She went to the locker room at the back of the nail bar and got her stuff. The woman who ran the bar paid rent to Ambani, and although she was decent enough, Layla would never trust her. She couldn't trust anyone, anymore. She walked out of the shop, and through the high street. She knew where she had to meet Afzal. Her mind was in turmoil.

With Noor, she had hatched a plan. If they couldn't go to the police, they could visit the Citizen's Advice Bureau. Someone there could put them in touch with a lawyer. The girls had also decided to call their families. Although the men had threatened to kill their family members if they got in touch, Layla had decided to call their bluff. Videos of them having sex would be circulated in their hometowns, and their families would be shamed. That was another threat, but was that worse than what they faced now?

Layla was exhausted every day, her body sore, bruised and abused. Her life was a nightmare without end, every day the same Hell as the previous one. The men kept a close look on everything the girls did – where they went, who they spoke to. Noor had gone to the hospital once, and Afzal had gone with her. Noor had terrible abdominal pains, for which she had a scan that showed an ovarian cyst. For the follow up, Layla had gone with Noor, and the girls had travelled alone. oA health problemwas the only way they could go anywhere not connected with the business the traffickers had forced them into.

Now, with Noor's death, Layla felt her time could also be up. Had Paresh, Ambani and Afzal found out what she and Noor had been up to? Is that why they had killed Noor? Layla had been careful. She'd told Noor not to tell Akbar. But Noor might've done.

Layla knew better than to try and escape. The men would find her. She didn't have access to a car, and with the pennies she had to her name – where would she go by bus or train? Her English was limited, and she needed a few hundred pounds to go on the run. She was paid in cash at the end of the week, and it was next to nothing. She had asked for more than thirty pounds, and got a slap in the face for it. A good week got her fifty pounds, and a lot of that went on food shopping. She was a slave, and she received slave wages.

She knew what happened to the girls who tried to flee. They ended up sleeping rough, and were inevitably caught. Afzal had taken them to a building site one day. Concrete was getting poured on the foundations, and on the body of a dead woman. Layla and Noor stared in shock.

'Try to escape, and this is what happens,' Afzal had said.

As Layla got closer to the car, she remembered that day, and her spine trembled. She didn't want to end up like that woman, but is that what happened to Noor?

Afzal was inside the car. Layla got in and shut the door behind her. Afzal's cold, dark eyes bore into hers.

'Did the police come to the nail bar? Did you speak to them?'

She knew there was no point in lying. She nodded. 'Yes. Two detectives in plain clothes, a man and a woman. They asked me if I knew Noor. I said no. They wanted to know where I lived. I had no choice, I had to tell them. If I lied, they could come back.'

Afzal stared at her unblinkingly, and she looked away. She hated his presence, the faint odour of his body smell. He had raped her twice, after beating her up. She had dared to complain, and ask for more money. That was in the beginning, when Afzal took her from Paresh's flat. She had learnt to say nothing in his presence.

'What did they tell you about Noor?'

'They told me she was dead. They showed me photos.' Layla's hands twisted on her lap. She found the courage to look up at Afzal. She found him distracted, staring out the window, fingers tapping on the steering wheel.

'What happened to Noor?'

Afzal's head slowly turned and his eyes fixed on her. He backhanded her, his rough hand striking her across the face. Pain blossomed in her head, and she felt the metallic taste of blood on her lips.

'Don't ask questions. Otherwise, you'll end up like

her. Got that?'

Layla suppressed her tears, and bitter anger. She nodded in silence.

'Where's Akbar?'

Layla shook her head. 'I don't know.'

Afzal swore under his breath. He started the car, and they drove away. Layla watched the city slipping past, and panic stabbed inside her. She braved another assault, and asked the question.

'Where are we going?'

Afzal silenced her with a look, and kept driving.

CHAPTER 34

Roy stifled a yawn with a cupped hand, then rubbed his eyes. It was past six p.m. The morning had started early, and his stomach rumbled in anticipation of dinner. That was still a while away, because Sunil Ambani was in custody and had to be interviewed, along with Rahul Tripathi. So far, Ambani had refused to make a statement. His phone rang, and he answered.

'DCI Roy.'

'It's me, guv,' Riz answered. 'We're checking out the woods behind the warehouse where Martin Donald worked. He jumped the gates over here earlier today. I pulled in the uniform team from Noor's flat, hope that's OK. A constable's remained on duty there.'

'Good work, and that's fine. Did you find anything more about Martin?'

'Yes, Jimmy Savile did some undercover work.' Riz chortled, mystifying Roy. 'I'll explain when we come back. Won't we, Jimmy?' Riz spoke to someone offline, and Roy heard a faint, whining voice. It belonged to Oliver. He wondered what was going on.

'Come back with Martin, if you can,' Roy said. 'We've got the restaurant owner downstairs, as well as one of the waiters. Hopefully we can get something out of them.' He hung up, and Melanie came in and put a steaming mug on his table.

'Thanks,' Roy said gratefully. It was nice cuppa, with two builder's tea bags to make it stronger. Milky, but no sugar, just as he liked it. Melanie sat on her desk, and waved a packet of cream custard biscuits at him.

'Didn't offer you these as I know you're watching your carb intake.' She grinned as she bit into one.

'That's just cruel,' Roy said. 'Here, give us one.' He leant over and grabbed a couple of biscuits from her.

'Ambani's got the duty solicitor,' Mel said. 'I doubt we'll get much out of him. Worth a try though.'

They were in the open-plan office, and it was starting to get empty. A couple of detectives from the financial crimes unit were at their desk, but the others had left. A woman in a charcoal skirt suit walked in, holding a slim leather briefcase in her right hand. She had black hair, cut short. Her make-up was minimal, but effective – she was an attractive woman. Roy was half turned to the door, and she caught his eye. She walked up to him, and smiled.

'I'm Natalie Scarrow from the Modern Slavery Unit of Yorkshire Police. We spoke earlier today. Are you DCI

Roy?'

'The same.' Roy rose and shook hands with Natalie. She was tall, coming up to his shoulder height. Almost six feet, and without any heels. Roy introduced Melanie and they sat down. Roy offered Natalie a cup of tea, but she refused.

'Just had a coffee in the car. I drove down from Leeds where I've got another case going.'

'Thanks for making the time. I've got some concerns about our current case. It involves the victim, who's a IC4 female in her twenties, and she worked in a nail bar and restaurant but came here illegally with a fake student visa, it seems. We're still establishing that fact with the college, but the visa is more than likely to be fake. She's not the only one. At least two of her friends also came like that, and both are now missing.'

Natalie had opened a red notebook and was jotting things down. She tucked a loose strand behind her right ear and looked up.

'That's a common tactic for human traffickers. They promise the trafficked person and their families a great future here. But when they arrive there's nothing. Often, the trafficked person is fleeing persecution, or is in trouble with law enforcement in their native land. They're also easy targets. The more desperate their situation is, the better it is for the traffickers. They go for the most vulnerable.'

'Despicable bastards,' Melanie spat. 'All criminals are bad, but these people actually deal in human lives.'

Roy nodded slowly. 'There's money in it, which sounds awful, but that's why the gangs do it. Some of these girls, including our victim and possibly her friend, were also into prostitution, it seems. We're gathering evidence on that. We need to stop them.'

Natalie jotted down something more on her notebook. 'Agreed. It seems you have stumbled across a major international gang here. If what you're saying is true, they must have a big network here and abroad.'

'I thought so too,' Roy said. 'The restaurant owner where the victim worked has denied her existence thus far. We caught him today trying to escape from his office. We're going down to take his statement now.'

'OK.' Natalie said. 'Do you mind if I go through the victim's case file and make some notes? Then I can cross-reference with my team to see if there's any matches with the individuals concerned.'

Melanie said, 'Yes of course. Here, just use my table and laptop. Do you know where the canteen is?'

'Yes.' Natalie smiled. 'Thank you.'

They left Natalie to it, and went downstairs. The custody sergeant was waiting for them.

'He's in interview room four, guv. Dickinson's the lawyer.'

Melanie rolled her eyes, and Roy waited for the explanation. 'He's a pain in the rear,' Mel muttered as they made their way to the interview room. 'I know all lawyers are, but this one you have to watch. He's young and out to make a name for himself with the criminals. He wants their business. I'm not joking,' she said, noting the sceptical look on Roy's face. 'Ambani is paying this guy, he's not just the duty solicitor.'

Roy didn't like the sound of that. Only hardened criminals had their own lawyer.

'And Rahul, the waiter?'

'He's also got a duty solicitor, a woman called Rebecca Aisling. She's new, don't know much about her.'

Ambani and Dickinson had done their briefing, and were waiting inside.

'Wait,' Roy said. He rubbed his chin as he thought about the suspects, and how they were arrested.

'I want to see Rahul first. Then we do Ambani. That's better. Is Rahul ready?'

'Yes. Do you want me to tell Dickinson to wait because he's less important?'

Roy grinned. 'Go ahead.'

Melanie went in and did the honours, and came back in a few minutes. Roy was leaning against the wall in the outer room, sipping a glass of water. Melanie had a gleam in her eyes.

'Dickinson hated that. Made a fuss about having to reorganise his diary. I told him to shove it up his backside.'

'No you didn't.'

'OK, I didn't, but I really, really wanted to.' Lawyers who protected criminals were widely hated by the police. Especially those who acted high and mighty.

They walked to interview room six, where Rahul was waiting with the duty solicitor. Melanie went in to ask them if they were okay to start. Roy waited outside. Melanie leant out the door and waved him inside.

Rahul was fidgeting in his seat, but his feet stopped tapping when he saw Roy. His eyes widened with alarm, before he looked away, and licked his lips once. Roy liked that. He was anxious already, and hopefully would sing like a canary under pressure.

Roy let Melanie do the questioning. He spoke into the machine, introducing everyone. Rebecca Aisling, the duty solicitor, was dressed simply in a blue vest and trouser suit. Her jet-black hair was pulled back in a tight ponytail. She looked over at her client often in a reassuring manner.

Melanie said, 'Rahul, can you please confirm where you work, and how long have you worked there for.'

'Mumtaz Restaurant. I've been there for…for six months.'

'Are you sure it's not been longer?'

'No.'

'How did you get the job? Tell us about your interview, and any contract you have.'

Rahul looked at Rebecca, who indicated for him to answer the question. Roy observed Rahul. His feet was tapping again, hands moving in his lap. He had a northern accent, more north Yorkshire than south.

'I…saw the job advertised in a newspaper and called the number. I had an interview with Mr Ambani. Then I got the job. It was cash in hand. There was no contract.'

'Which newspaper?'

Rahul stared at Melanie like she just spoke a new language. 'What?'

'The job advertisement, which newspaper was it in?'

Rahul swivelled his eyes around like he was searching for a way out of the room. 'I-I can't remember.'

'Are you sure?'

Rahul nodded. Melanie watched him squirm for a few seconds, which Roy approved of.

'Tell us about Noor Jehan. She worked in Mumtaz restaurant, didn't she?'

Rahul went quiet. His eyes still roved around, then settled on the floor. 'I don't know. I mean, no comment.'

'You just denied knowing Noor. This is being recorded, Rahul. If we end up going to court to find out who killed Noor, and you're brought in as a witness, will this still be your answer?'

Rebecca said, 'This is hypothetical, detective, and you know it.'

'It's a simple question, that your client just answered. He didn't know Noor. I just want to clarify that would remain his answer if we went to court.'

The silence seemed to weigh down on Rahul like a lead balloon. His sharp nostrils flared, and his sunken cheeks became paler still.

Roy nudged Melanie, and indicated the A4 envelope on the desk. She nodded, and took out the photos of Noor, lying at the crime scene. She spread them out for Rahul to see, and the effect was immediate.

He shrank back in his chair like he'd been shoved. His dilated eyes were fixed on the photos, then his lips quivered.

'Tell us the truth,' Melanie said softly. 'Nothing will happen to you. We can protect you.'

Rebecca glanced at her client, who now remained slouched on his chair, head lowered.

'Rahul?' Melanie said.

He took a while to respond. When he spoke his voice seemed to drag up from somewhere deep inside him.

'Yes. I knew Noor. She worked in the restaurant. I didn't know her well. She joined after I did. She was a quiet girl who didn't say much.' He looked up at Melanie. 'That's all I know.'

'You must have spoken to her some time. Was she friends with anyone else?'

'Yes, a girl called Layla. Both of them worked in a nail bar as well. They mostly talked to each other and didn't really talk to me or the other waiters.'

Melanie said, 'Where are you from?'

'Doncaster. A suburb of it, called Bessacarr.'

'How long have you been in Sheffield for, then?'

'Two years now. Thought I might get a better job here. Turns out I was wrong. No jobs anywhere, unless I work for minimal wage.'

'Noor, where was she from? Did you ask anyone about her, if you didn't speak to her that much.'

Rahul seemed more at ease now. 'Not really, but I could tell from her accent she weren't from round here, like. She and the other girl, Layla, they were off the boat, like. Freshies.'

'Why did you lie to us in the beginning?'

Rahul chewed his lower lip, and squirmed in his seat. 'I was told not to say owt about them to anyone.'

'Did your boss Mr Ambani say that to you?'

Rahul was evasive again, his eyes on the floor, feet shuffling. 'Yes, kind of.'

'Can you speak up please. Was it Mr Ambani who told you not to speak to us about the girls?'

'Well, actually, it were this fella who came around sometimes. He spent time with the boss upstairs.'

'Who was he?'

'A guy called Afzal. Look, you didn't hear this from me, alright?'

'What did this Afzal say to you?'

'He told all of us to keep quiet if the cops ever came around. He said we'd lose our jobs if we said owt.'

'What did Afzal look like?'

'About six feet tall, wears a dark baseball cap and has a beard. He was scary, like. Not sure what he did, but he…yeah, he was scary.'

CHAPTER 35

Roy held the door open for Melanie, and they stepped inside. Interview room four was the same as the others: green lino floors, a metal desk and chairs with the legs screwed to the floor, a drinking water machine. The familiar round white face, black armed clock ticked on the wall.

Ambani was wearing the white shirt he'd been wearing, and dark trousers. Dickinson had a smart blue suit on, the type that looked at home in a court house. He stood out here, and that was the point, Roy thought. He had seen enough of lawyers to know which ones were here to do their job, and the ones who had a grudge against the police for whatever reason. Dickinson belonged to the latter. It was obvious in the superior smirk that appeared on his face when he said hello to him and Melanie. He was in his late twenties to early thirties, like Melanie said.

Ambani, on the other hand, was in his late forties. His brown skin was darker than Roy's, and a pot belly rested against the table. His shoulders were meaty, and arms thick. He was a strong, tough man, and his facial expression was that of mild inquisitiveness. He didn't look intimidated in the slightest, and that wasn't good. It was important to keep an open mind, but Roy knew a criminal when he saw one. Ambani's police record was non-existent, but he wasn't pure as the driven snow. Far from it.

Melanie introduced everyone for the machine, and they took their seats. They had agreed that Roy would lead with the questions. He had nabbed Ambani, and he might be able to ruffle his feathers more.

Roy started by showing the photos of Noor at the crime scene. He didn't say a word, just put them across the table. Ambani stiffened, and his jaws clamped tight together. Roy let the silence linger before he spoke.

'Evidence 001 exhibited for the attention of Sunil Ambani. They show the deceased victim Noor Jehan, at the scene. Mr Ambani,' Roy made sure he had the man's attention. 'Can you confirm that Noor worked at your restaurant?'

'No comment.'

That would be the benefit of the lawyer's advice, Roy thought. 'You previously denied that Noor worked at your restaurant. Is that correct?'

'No comment.'

'What about Layla Patil?'

A light flickered in Ambani's eyes before dying out

swiftly. 'No comment.'

'How about Akbar Maqbool?'

Again, that brief light flared to life. 'No comment.'

'Do you know the nail bar next to your restaurant? And the sandwich bar on the right?'

Ambani's face had gone back to blank. Roy said, 'What about the taxi rank opposite your restaurant?'

Ambani shrugged. 'What about them?'

'People there have seen a woman matching Noor's description going in and out of your restaurant. She also delivered them food on occasion. Layla was also seen.'

Ambani glanced at Dickinson, who cleared his throat.

'Do you have any evidence, DCI Roy, or is this just hearsay?'

Roy ignored him, aware that would get on Dickinson's nerves. He remained focused on Ambani.

'Can you answer the question please.'

Ambani and Dickinson exchanged a glance, and a quick whisper followed.

'No comment.'

'So you are denying knowledge of the same people who were seen to enter and exit your restaurant, and worked there as waiters. I want to make you aware that the business owners who gave us evidence can be brought to court as witnesses.'

Dickinson piped up immediately. 'There is no charge, never mind a date for a court case. Hence, there is no point in these baseless accusations.'

Roy felt his eyes on him, but again ignored him pointedly. He could feel the hatred radiate from Dickinson, which was good. Dickinson was too good to lose his cool, but Roy could try and get under his skin.

'Why were you trying to escape this morning?' Roy asked Ambani.

'I was having a cigarette from outside the window. I had dropped my lighter on the fire escape stairs, and was bending to pick them up.' A well-prepared statement, if he'd ever heard one, Roy thought.

'Then why did you resist when I asked you to get back inside the room?'

'I didn't.' Ambani had a smug smile on his face. He was winning this one, and he knew it.

Roy changed tactic. 'Rahul Tripathi is a waiter at your restaurant. Is that correct?'

The smile slipped away from Ambani's face. 'Yes.'

'It's clear that he knew Noor and Layla, maybe also Akbar. Can you answer how he knew Noor, but you, the owner, didn't?'

'How is it clear, Inspector?' Dickinson asked. 'Has Mr Tripathi given a statement?'

Moving his neck a quarter of an inch to the left, as if he was being forced to pay Dickinson attention, Roy looked at the lawyer. He smiled, and watched Dickinson's face fall.

'Yes. We have his statement. Noor worked in the restaurant, as did Layla. You need to tell your client to stop lying.'

'It's the waiter's word against my client's.' Dickinson was trying to act brave, but even he now knew it was a losing battle.

Roy looked at Ambani. 'Well? Are you still going to deny you didn't know the victim? You know what a judge is going to say. This looks bad on you.'

Dickinson said, 'Even if the victim worked at my client's restaurant, it's possible that my client wasn't aware, as he has to run a large establishment. Can you now please release my client, as he has answered all your questions.'

'We can retain him for twenty-four hours,' Melanie spoke up. 'He's a suspect in a murder inquiry. That means he will stay overnight till tomorrow, five p.m.'

Ambani closed his eyes briefly and his shoulders sagged. Roy said, 'We are making contact with Noor Jehan's family in India. Also for Layla and Akbar. Interpol has been informed, as we believe these persons were trafficked into the UK by an international gang. As their employer, you were aware they were trafficked. Didn't you, Mr Ambani?'

Ambani's jaws were tight, and a muscle ticked in his forehead. Dickinson said, 'Inspector Roy. Haven't we had enough of this? Please stop harassing my client.'

Roy didn't like the smile that appeared on Ambani's lips for a second, then vanished. He leant forward.

'Who's Afzal?'

Something changed in Ambani's attitude. He went still for a moment. A shadow seemed to pass over his face.

'He was your business partner,' Roy said. 'Or are you going to deny that as well?'

Ambani's eyes glinted, and a low snarl spread across his lips. He didn't reply.

Dickinson said, 'I urge you to let my client go today. He's done nothing wrong, and you have no grounds to keep him.'

Roy ignored him and kept his eyes on Ambani. He asked him about Afzal once again.

'No comment.'

'We'll see you tomorrow,' Roy said. 'We will have more evidence by then.'

CHAPTER 36

Natalie Scarrow was in the office when Melanie and Roy trudged upstairs. She was making notes, and didn't hear them till they got close. She turned her attractive face to them and smiled sympathetically.

'How did it go?'

'Ambani's not giving anything away,' Melanie said, as they sat down. 'But we got something out of the waiter, Rahul. He mentioned a man called Afzal. No last name as yet. Does the name ring a bell, by any chance?'

Natalie thought for a while, then shook her head. Melanie said, 'Long shot, I know. Just on the off chance you heard something in your cases.'

'Not so far, but I will ask my team. Did anything else turn up?'

Melanie looked at Roy, who shook his head. He said,

'We know about Noor working at the restaurant. That's now definite. Her friend, Layla, is missing, and so is Akbar. The last two lived together.'

'Can you find them?'

'CCTV should show something about Layla. She finished work at the nail bar and then vanished. She won't be that far, and neither will Akbar. I doubt either of them have the resources to get out of the country.'

Rizwan and Oliver trudged into the office, a dejected look on both their faces.

'Now then,' Melanie said. 'Cometh the hour, cometh the men.'

Roy knew something was wrong when he looked at the two detectives. Their body language was all wrong. Shoulders slumped, eyes hollow. They collapsed on their chairs. Roy introduced them to Natalie and the men murmured their greetings.

Rizwan spoke first. 'No sign of Martin Donald. He jumped over the security gates of the warehouse where he worked and he's gone. We scoured the woods behind the industrial estate, no joy. We called his wife again, no sign of him.'

'He left his car behind, right?' Roy asked.

'Yes.'

'And have we checked for any card transactions, in case he's tried to get a train ticket, or gone to the airport? If not, let's do that, and also alert the Home Office to put a block on his passport.'

'I'll do it,' Melanie offered. 'I'll also go and check if Traffic have any clues about Layla. You told them to check CCTV for her, right?'

Rizwan pointed at Oliver. 'Jimmy did it? Ain't that right, Jimmy boy?'

'I heard you calling him that on the phone,' Roy said. 'What's this about?'

'I took a photo,' Rizwan said, pulling his phone out. Oliver looked to the ceiling and rolled his eyes.

'Give over, ye mucker,' Oliver muttered. 'What you taken photos for, ye daft bugger.'

'I'm gonna make a poster and hang it on the wall over your desk, that's why.'

He showed Roy a photo of Oliver resplendent in his 80s retro outfit. Melanie had come round to look over Roy's shoulder, and she couldn't help but laugh with a hand over her mouth.

'Ollie! Is that you?'

Roy grimaced. 'Sinking to new depths here. What was this in aid of? Don't tell me you're doing some TV show.'

'Maybe a horror show, with him as Jimmy Savile,' Riz said.

Oliver seemed to be shrinking in his chair, his head disappearing between his shoulders, spine slumping.

'Honestly, what was this for?' Roy asked.

'You want to do the honours or me?' Riz asked.

Oliver glared at him, then spoke hesitatingly, like a

school boy just caught cheating in an exam. 'I thought it'd be a good idea to go undercover and ask about Martin Donald and Noor. In the estate, like.'

All heads turned to him, and silence ensued, along with shock. Oliver looked down at his hands, and his spine lowered further down the chair.

Roy gnashed his teeth together. 'You call this undercover? Jesus Christ, man, how the hell did you become a detective?'

'He wouldn't make it as a circus clown.' Riz chortled with glee. 'But he did get into the flat used as a brothel, and find out that Martin saw Noor there pretty often. But then we got chased by some of the lads that he spoke to.'

Roy growled. 'Got chased? You meant they realised who you were? If you had a brain cell between the two of you, surely you could've foreseen that. What happened?'

'Uh, they threw bricks at the car, but we managed to get out of there.'

Melanie shook her head and swore softly, while Roy closed his eyes. 'Whose idea was this?' Roy asked.

Rizwan looked at Oliver, but no explanation was necessary. Roy heaved a breath. 'Honestly, of all the stunts you've pulled, this is top drawer. I mean, a five-year-old would have more sense than you two.'

Rizwan protested. 'I didn't—'

'Shut up,' Roy said. 'You could've stopped him. Who drove him there? He wouldn't have done it without you. If this gets back to Nugent, I'm going to have do some explaining. Are the uniforms at the estate alright?'

'They joined us in the search for Martin Donald,' Riz said. 'Yes, they're fine.'

Melanie said, 'I guess we have to look at the funny side, guv.'

'I don't have a funny side,' Roy grumbled. 'Riz took photos, but what if the gang members at the estate did too? Can you imagine Jimmy Savile here splashed across the tabloid front pages – Detective in Disguise?'

Melanie laughed again, and Riz and Natalie joined in. Oliver looked like he wanted to vanish down a sink hole. He ran a hand over his hair. 'I'm going to get some coffee. Anyone want some?'

'You're on beverage duty for the rest of your life, Son. And extra time in the weekends. Yes, get me one, thanks.'

Natalie and Melanie asked for tea, and Natalie offered to help the men get the drinks. Melanie went upstairs to speak to Traffic. Roy took out his phone, and saw he had two text messages. They were from an unknown number. His heart shrivelled in his chest as he read them.

You had your chance and you blew it.

You'll never find your brother again.

CHAPTER 37

Roy stood, shaking. This had to be Lydia, it couldn't be anyone else. The number was disguised, and he couldn't call back. He gripped the phone in his palm and stalked out of the room. In the corridor he halted as Detective Superintendent Nugent's short but stocky form appeared around the corner. Nugent had the form of a dwarf bull, a man whose barrel chest and bulbous arms seemed to make up for the loss of height. Almost, but not quite. He had the look and feel of a Popeye cartoon character about to explode. He also had the mood to match. He stopped a few inches short of Roy and snorted.

'This new victim. I've not had a report on her as yet.'

Roy fought the urge to tell Nugent where to stick it. He always got the feeling Nugent was abrasive on purpose, itching to start a disciplinary process on him. He wouldn't give him the satisfaction. Besides, despite the roughness of their regular contact, they had moments of agreement. Nugent knew about Robin, and his situation.

'I'll do it before I go tonight, sir. We have two suspects in custody, and two more out there. We should bring them in tomorrow.'

'Good,' Nugent grunted. 'I heard about the men downstairs. The uniforms told me. You got nothing out of him?'

'You mean Sunil Ambani, the restaurant owner. He's bent as a teapot, and it will take time to straighten him. Hopefully we'll get something from digging into him. The waiter, Rahul, has started to sing. Don't think he's the killer though.'

'OK. Get me the report, in case I have to feed it back upstairs.'

'Will do, sir.'

Nugent walked past him, and his steps faded. Roy didn't relax till he was in his office and he heard the door slam shut. He hurried down the grey lino corridor, nodding absentmindedly to the couple of uniformed officers who went past him. Outside, he feverishly stabbed the phone's keypad, trying to get back to the person who sent him the text. As expected, the line wouldn't connect. He sent a text back, asking who it was, but the message failed to send.

His fists clenched, and he roared a bellow of frustration, then slammed his hands on the wall. He called David Bloomsdale of the traffic department, the sergeant who had helped him to track down Lydia's car. He explained the situation to David.

'I heard about this. You keep getting these anonymous texts from an unknown number, right?'

'Yes. Can you triangulate them with the signal alone?'

'Yes of course, but the problem we had last time was the caller used a GPS blocker right after they sent you the text.'

'What does that mean?' Roy fumed. 'I want to know this phone's location.'

'We use GPS triangulations these days, guv. Cell phone masts are not as precise. I'll try, but it's possible they're using the GPS blocker again. They probably also turn the phone off and take the battery off. I can try.'

'Please do.'

Roy hung up, and called Anna. He was relieved when she answered. 'Hello, Daddy. When are you home?'

'Soon, my love. You okay?'

'Yes, I went to see Pearl, but now back home and packing.' Anna was leaving tomorrow, back down to London as her school was starting next week.

'I won't be long. Call me if you need anything.'

'A Versace dress?'

'Keep dreaming.'

'Just the shoes then. Or athlewear from lululemon.'

'Maybe from Primark, and that's being generous.'

'What more could a girl want?'

'There you go,' Roy said approvingly, smiling down

221

the phone. 'I should be home soon, less than an hour.'

'Famous last words?'

'I hope not, but you never know.'

He hung up, and checked his phone once again. No further messages, which was both a relief and a pain. If the phone was active, he might get a GPS signal. He went back inside, his mind screaming round the bends of a tortuous racetrack. Where was Jayden? And Lydia? Maybe he should focus on finding Lydia first. Stephen Burns knew about Lydia despite his denials – Roy could tell from speaking to him. He was also the man Jayden knew as his stepfather – Jerry Budden.

Could Lydia know another of Stephen Burns' evil associates, a man or woman who was sheltering her? The despicable ring of paedophiles that Burns was a part of had now been dismantled, but what if some members remained, and bore a grudge against Roy?

It was very much possible. Lydia could've hooked up with them…and could she be searching for Jayden? Roy stopped abruptly. Is that why Jayden ran? He knew someone was after him. When Roy met Jayden, he had felt an odd flicker of recognition. He had ignored it, because that happened every now and then with a stranger. Now he regretted it. He should never have ignored his instinct. Jayden had seemed a mild-mannered person. There was a vulnerability to him as well, lurking just beneath the surface. Roy had sensed that, too.

He pulled out his phone again, and called his old mentor, Arla Baker. Arla had risen up the ranks to become a Detective Chief Superintendent in the Met. He wouldn't be surprised if she was busy, but she answered his call.

'Hello, stranger,' Arla said. 'Out of sight, out of mind?'

'No way, just not had the time.'

'Yes I heard you've been busy. Is Anna OK? She's still there with you?'

He had spoken to Arla last month, so she knew. 'Yes, but she's going back down tomorrow. I need to ask a favour.'

'Go on.'

'It's about Stephen Burns. Can you put some feelers out to see if any of his old gang still survive. I know they're jailed for life, but they might have friends doing their shite for them.'

'You took down the online grooming gang last month. Isn't the NCA keeping an eye on the remainder?' Roy had worked closely with the National Crime Agency to bring down Burns, Burgess and his followers. It was an international ring, and Interpol was also involved.

'They are, but I need ears on the ground. You see, I think I might've found my brother, Robin.' He sighed, and sat down on a slab of stone ringed around a tree. He had walked to the rear of the building, where it was quieter. He explained the situation with Jayden and Lydia.

'Dear god, Rohan. This is huge news. Why didn't you call me before? I'm so happy for you. Also worried. Are you coping okay?'

He could hear the emotion in Arla's voice as it wobbled slightly. It gave him a warm, fuzzy feeling. Arla had been through the same loss of losing a sibling. Her pain would never fade, it made her who she was. But at least she had made peace with the past. He was still struggling, and the end was now so close he could almost touch it.

'Yes, I'm fine. Busy with another homicide now, which is taking up time. Look, I just want to know if Burns or Burgess have other friends no one knows about. They could be anywhere in the country.'

'Leave it with me. It's late now, but I will send some feelers out first thing tomorrow.' Arla's voice dropped an octave. 'Look after yourself, Rohan. I know you've found Robin, which is immense. But take it easy. One step at a time. This is the finish line, make sure you get there.'

He knew what she meant. He had a habit of putting too much on his plate, then losing sleep to sort it all out. Then again, he couldn't do things any other way. Still, Arla's words cut through.

'I know. Thanks, talk to you soon.'

'I'll call as soon as I have some news. By the way, you need to come down here to get your official release. Hope you haven't forgotten that.'

'How could I? I'll be there soon as.'

'Don't make me come up to get you.'

He grinned. 'Terrifying thought. Say hello to Harry. How's Nicole?'

'Talking back to me, now that she's a teenager. She needs to meet Anna, I think.' Nicole was just turning thirteen, three years younger than Anna.

'I very much doubt Anna will be a help in that regard. But let's meet up when I'm down in London.' He said goodbye and hung up.

As he walked inside, he called Sergeant Bloomsdale in Traffic.

'Nothing, guv,' David sounded apologetic. 'He or she must be using a high-quality GPS blocker. I mean military grade. If I hear anything I will let you know.'

'Thanks. Can you please do me a favour? There's a uniform team patrolling the Sculthorpe neighbourhood for an IC4 man. Can you see if there's any updates?'

Roy had arrived at the open-plan office and he strode past the desks to the rear, where the major investigations team, his team, was based.

'Hello, guv.' David returned on the line. 'No sighting as yet. Shall I keep you posted in case anything shows up?'

'Yes, please do. Thanks.'

Natalie was still here, and so were the others. Melanie turned as he approached, and he saw the flush of excitement on her cheeks.

'We found CCTV footage of Layla.' She pointed to her laptop screen, and Oliver moved to make space. Roy saw a woman emerge from a shop and walk down the high street. She was facing the camera.

'That shop is the nail bar where Layla worked,' Melanie explained. Layla's figure was in a red circle, and the circle moved down the busy high street. The screen changed, and now showed Layla from behind, walking down the main street, then taking a left. She proceeded down a narrow alley, and walked till she came to a residential street of terraced houses. Here, she got into a car, and it drove off.

'Traffic checked the ANPR of that car. It belongs to a man called Afzal Hamid. We checked his records. He's got a colourful PCN list from burglaries to drug-dealing. Works as a cab driver as well.'

Roy held Melanie's eyes. 'Could that be the same Afzal that Rahul mentioned?'

'I think so, guv.'

CHAPTER 38

The little boy called Robin stood trembling. Tears rolled down his eyes. His thin, frail body shook like a leaf in a storm, the knife shuddering in his hand. In front of him lay a ghastly sight. His friend, Andy, tied up in a chair. A cold gust of wind blew in from the window and, with it, drops of rain. The man came up behind him, and slapped him on the back of the head.

'What are you waiting for? Do it, now.'

Terror had seized Robin's limbs. His fingers felt cold and lifeless, and the knife dropped from his hand, clanging on the cement floor. The man slapped him harder, and the pain made Robin whimper. Tears rolled down his cheeks.

The man crouched beside him. 'If you don't kill him, then you're next. Andy was a bad boy,' the man whispered, pointing to the chair, where the helpless boy squirmed. His eyes were popping out with fear, he knew what was coming his way. Both of them had seen it happen to another boy.

'And you know what happens to bad boys, don't you?' The man whispered. 'Eh, Jayden? That's your new name. I'll call you Jayden from now. My Jayden.' The man whispered the name again, and Robin shivered with a mixture of fear and panic. The man, who called himself Jerry, picked up the knife and gave it to Robin.

'Go on. Hold it.' Robin refused, and Jerry slapped him again, harder. The blow almost felled Robin, but somehow he stood straight.

'I want to see you do it,' Jerry whispered in his ears, then touched him all over. 'Go on.'

'I don't want to,' Robin whimpered. Jerry squeezed his neck till it started to hurt. 'Do you want to go on the chair? Eh?'

'No.' Robin wept, shaking.

'Then do it. Take the knife. Go stab him, or I'll make him stab you.'

Crying, Robin grabbed the knife. He walked up to the chair. For a second, Andy's terrified eyes met his. Andy squirmed, moaning against the gag in his mouth, but he couldn't scream. Robin cried out, and plunged the knife in Andy's chest.

Jayden woke with a start. His eyes took a while to get adjusted to the fading daylight. He had escaped into the woods, and the goons chasing him had given up after a while. He didn't dare go out on the streets, in case they were waiting for him. He also had to assume his friend's house in Sculthorpe was now compromised. He found a space under a tree, well covered by the undergrowth. He had rested on the ground, wrapping his coat tightly around him, and fallen asleep before he knew it.

He rubbed his eyes, and listened closely. He could hear some birds in the trees, but nothing else. He stood carefully, not straightening to full height. Dusk was falling swiftly, and with any luck, it would be dark soon.

He could only think of one option now. Go to the police station on Eccelshall Road, and ask for DCI Roy. There was no other way. How long could he be on the run for? He had escaped Jerry's clutches, and somehow eked out a life for himself. The nightmare visions remained, just like the horrible dream he just had. The same dreams kept recurring. He never knew peace. He didn't know when, or how, the monster would rise inside him, remind him of what he had to endure as a child. It had reduced him as a man, made him incapable of having a normal relationship. Not just with a woman. He didn't have any friends. He couldn't be open and trusting with other human beings like most people were.

The years of disgusting depravity he suffered at Jerry's hand had ensured that. He felt strangely helpless, like any power he once had to live a normal life had been taken for him. He felt angry, bitter, confused. The agony built inside his chest, till his eyes heated up, and tears rolled down his cheeks.

He sniffed, and dried his eyes, then carried on through the woods. He didn't know how long he trudged on for, but the sky got progressively darker. His phone was also running out of charge. He had deliberately not gone towards the main street of Sculthorpe, in fear of the men waiting for him. From there, Meadowhall was a short bus ride. But according to the map on his phone, he was going in the opposite direction. He could see an opening in the woods, which was crossed by a few roads. His aim was to flag down a car and hitch a ride.

As he got closer to the road, he heard the cars. A truck lumbered past, and he saw it's headlights, then the red and green body flash through the foliage. He cursed and increased his pace. A truck was the ideal vehicle to hitch a ride from. It reminded him of many years ago, when he escaped from Jerry's house. A truck driver had taken him from Leeds to Sheffield, and even given him a tenner to buy some food. Jayden never forgot that driver.

His feet were heavier now, and he had to drag them through the tangling knots by his feet. Panting, he leant against a tree and wiped his brow. He had taken his jacket off, but now he put it back on, as the road was right in front of him. He saw headlights approach from the left, the right lane was empty.

Jayden stepped out and waved at the car. It slowed down, and then came to a halt. Jayden ran towards it, but he heard another car behind him. He turned to see the other car was also stopping, which was a little weird.

He ran, then stopped as two men stepped out from the car that he had flagged down. Fear churned in his heart. These were the men who had attacked him in Sculthorpe. He whirled around, and panic lashed against his spine. Three men had spilled out from the car behind him, and were walking towards him. He was trapped, again.

'We've been looking for you, Jayden,' a voice behind

him said. Jayden turned. The man came forward slowly. He was big and beefy, and a scar ran down the left side of his face. The headlights of the cars were off now, but he could just about make out the man's features as he got closer.

'These woods only have three roads circling it. You had to come out of one of them, sooner or later. Come with us, someone wants to meet you.' The man smiled, and it looked like a wolf licking his lips at a stranded lamb.

'Who…who are you?' Jayden stammered.

'My name's Kevin. Now get in the bloody car.'

CHAPTER 39

Roy was having that same dream again – where his mother blamed him for wrecking their lives. Her white hair was like a tidal wave, and her teeth were bared in fury. She screamed at him as he cowered in the corner, hands over his ears. Mercifully, the alarm also screeched in his ears, drowning his mother's voice. His hands groped for the offending machine, and finally he slapped a hand over it, slapping it to the carpet. He lay there in the dawn darkness, blinking at the ceiling. He rubbed his face, then swung his legs down from the bed. He had slept alone now for more than two years. He had grown used to being alone, but if he was being honest with himself, he missed not having a partner. Such thoughts only occurred to him occasionally, and he made himself busy with work to forget them. That was always the antidote. Overthinking never helped anyone.

He read his emails and texts before he went to the

bathroom. Sarah had replied, reassuring him that she was OK, and back home. He had called her before turning in. It was a relief to know she was alright, and back home with Matt, and her mother, Cathy. He didn't see any emergencies cropping up overnight, which was a relief. He was getting used to the quieter life here.

As he brushed his teeth and got ready, his mind went back to the current case. They had to charge Ambani today, or let him go. He was lying through his back teeth, and his clever lawyer would get him out. Roy knew he couldn't charge him for lying, and his lawyer would have a hundred excuses as to why he lied. No, Ambani had to be scared some other way. He was worried, Roy knew that. Rahul Tripathi had done them a big favour, at least they had Afzal's name now. Layla had got into Afzal's car, and a man was driving it. CCTV had followed the car to Meersbrook in south Sheffield, where they lost it in a CCTV dark zone. Meersbrook wasn't far from Netheredge, but the uniforms team patrolling outside Layla's house hadn't reported anyone going in. They had knocked on the door, but no one seemed to be in.

Layla, Akbar, and most importantly, Martin Donald was still out there. They had slipped through their fingers, and they needed to be questioned.

Before Roy left, he listened with an ear on Anna's door. He couldn't hear anything, so assumed she was sleeping. He left a message on her phone to say he was leaving for work.

He got a coffee and yogurt pot from the canteen at the station. His eyes lingered on the fresh bacon and eggs, and his stomach rumbled. He paid and left quickly, before his belly made up its own mind. It was still early, and no one had turned up.

Roy pulled up the case files of Afzal Hamid. He was a young man, twenty-six years old. He was born and raised in Burnley, Lancashire. He was raised in foster care, and there was a file on his social care. His life of crime started when he was caught with drugs aged fourteen. He was released, but he later attended juvenile prison for repeat offending. He progressed to burglaries as an adult, and another stint in jail for possessing and distributing narcotics. He had last been in prison four years ago. But Roy couldn't see any link to human trafficking gangs.

He had no doubt Afzal was linked to them. It couldn't be a coincidence that Afzal was picking up Layla up after she'd been interviewed by the detectives. Could Layla be in a relationship with Afzal? Yes, she could, but what were the chances a man called Afzal also frequented the same restaurant where she worked, and had told the staff there not to speak to the police? Slim to none.

When Ambani was questioned about Afzal, he looked uncomfortable. He hadn't expected that. There was a link between the men, Roy was sure of it.

Could Martin Donald be linked with them, too? It seemed unlikely, thus far, but it was possible. Martin's political aspiration was obvious, and that meant he wouldn't be close to the other two suspects. But it was now crystal-clear Martin was a fish of deep waters and, despite his political beliefs, he had a fondness for dark-skinned women – Noor, in particular.

Roy looked at Martin's file. It had his phone number,

and the researchers had diligently got his call list. Martin hadn't made any calls or used the phone since yesterday morning, so locating the signal hadn't been possible. He could be using a burner phone.

Roy looked through Martin's call list. If the same number appeared more than once it was circled, and cross-matched with the numbers of the other suspects. Again, the researchers had already done this. Martin had called his wife a couple of times, but the other repeat numbers didn't have any matches – as yet. That ruled out Martin calling Ambani or Akbar, but he could've called Afzal. Roy checked Afzal's file to see if there was a number and found three. He manually checked them but didn't find a match. He went to Ambani's file and repeated the process.

On Martin's list, Roy noted one number that was called every day, at least twice. It didn't have any matches. Could this have been Noor's burner number?

None of the three students – Noor, Layla and Akbar, had any record of a phone. Voice data from the phone company took a few days to arrive, even with an urgent police request. From now on any calls the suspects made on their phones would be recorded by the police, but it was too late.

Natalie Scarrow, the Modern Slavery Unit detective, had left a message on his phone to say she would look into Noor and Layla's family. The problem was India's vastness. In a country of 1.4 billion people, he was sure there would be more than a few with same names.

He pulled up Noor and Layla's files and went through them. On their student visa applications, they had addresses and contact details in India. He imagined what it was like for a British Consulate officer to see these applications on his desk. Would he or she have time to ring up the families? Perhaps not. They would look at the letter from the Don Valley College, then interview the applicant and that was that.

Which meant no one checked if the applicant's contact details were fake. The name and DOB couldn't be fake because there would be a birth certificate and passport check. Roy knew how India worked. Anything could be faked with money. But not a passport, not easily anyway. For the human traffickers, a fake passport, when detected, would derail their plans at the start. Roy focused on the passports, and the letter from Don Valley College.

He noticed something new. On Layla's student visa application, her home address was different to the address on the letter from Mr Ludlow, the admissions secretary at Don Valley College. He put that letter to one side, and checked again. On the college letter, her address was in Ahmedabad, in the state of Gujrat. Yet on the visa application, it was an address in New Delhi.

Roy entered the address from the college letter into the internet, and did a search. After a few tries, he had a phone number. He rang the researchers, one of whom had arrived at work. Her name was Sally, and she promised to verify the number and get back to him ASAP.

Roy checked the files of Noor and Akbar, but found the same address in the college admission letter and their visa application. Somehow, everyone had missed the two different addresses on Layla's file.

236

While he was engrossed in the folders, Sally called back. She had confirmed the number and address belonged to a bona fide street and house in Ahmedabad. Excitement mounted in Roy's guts. He picked up the phone, and rang the number.

CHAPTER 40

The phone rang with a long, beeping ring tone, clearly connecting to an overseas line. It was a mobile. A female voice answered.

'Hello?'

'Hello. My name is Rohan Roy, Detective Chief Inspector of Yorkshire Police in England.'

He paused to let the words sink in. He heard a couple of voices, speaking in their native tongue. He recognised snippets of Hindi, but couldn't get the meaning. The woman stayed silent, and he suspected she didn't speak any English. Then a man's voice came on the line.

'Hello? Who are you?'

Roy repeated himself, then added, 'This is about Layla Patil. Is this her address?'

'Layla?' The man said, then his tone became agitated.

'Layla? How you know her?' The man spoke in a strong Indian accent, and his English was broken. 'Who you? Where Layla?'

He heard the woman now speaking loudly, saying Layla's name. He knew this was her family, but he had to be sure.

'What's your name, and what relation are you to Layla?'

'Aakash Patil. Her brother.' There was now a babble of voices, and Roy guessed there was a number of people around the phone.

'Layla is in Sheffield, in England. She came to study there, but actually she was trafficked, I am sorry to say. She now works here illegally without a work permit. We have spoken to her, and will see her again. We will arrange for her to be returned home.'

Aakash spoke to the others, raising his voice, and the voices piped down. 'You have Layla? Is she OK? Can she come back?'

'We have seen her, yes. She's...OK. We will get her back to you. Can you please confirm your address? If you have a landline number I want that as well. Also, your local police station details.'

Roy wrote down the details Aakash gave him. He was in a bind now. He wanted to reassure the family, but Layla was last seen with Afzal, a man who could easily be Noor's killer. That didn't bode well for Layla. Roy did the best he could, in the circumstances.

'I will call you again as soon as I have details of her.

She can speak to you as well.'

'When she back? Where is she?'

'I don't know,' Roy confessed. 'But she is here, and I will find her. Then I will get back to you. Perhaps you can come over as well, we can arrange that. I need to speak to the British Consulate and the Home Office. Can I have your email? I can send you some details.'

Roy took down Aakash's email, then promised to be in touch. He heard a voice behind him as he put the phone down.

'You're a keen bean.' He turned to see Natalie. She was dressed for work in her sharp charcoal business suit. She put her portable coffee mug on the table and took a seat.

'I just found where Layla Patil's family is in India. Now we need to find her. Which begs the million dollar question. Where is Afzal Hamid?'

'As long as we're sure Afzal has her. I know she got into his car, but she could be somewhere else now, and not with him.'

Roy shook his head. 'Afzal was one of the enforcers, I think. He was at the restaurant, scaring the waiters into silence, according to Rahul. I don't think Rahul's lying. Hence, I think if Afzal has Layla, we should be worried, and we need to find him asap.'

'What did you tell the family?'

'That we will find Layla and she can be in contact with them as soon as.'

'I can help with that.' Natalie grinned. 'My job really.

Apart from the investigation, I also act as a go-between, linking our government to the country where the person was trafficked from.' Natalie paused, and frowned. 'How did you find her home address? Did we miss something?'

'Yes, there was a discrepancy between the visa application and the college admission letter.'

'I looked at both,' Natalie said, rising from her desk. She looked at the papers on Roy's table.

Roy held up three letters from the Don Valley College. 'This address was only on one of the letters. I'm not sure why. It was the first one sent out to the applicant. The other two letters went to the same address as the visa application. That's why we missed it, I think.'

Natalie shook her head. 'Not good enough. I should've spotted that.'

'Yes, you should've,' Roy pressed his lips together and grimaced. 'I'm disappointed, Natalie.'

For a second, her eyes dimmed and her jaw went slack. Roy smiled.

'Just a little banter. You only got involved in the case yesterday. Don't worry.'

Natalie shook her head slowly. 'I'll get you back for that.'

'I'm sure you will. For now, though, did you find anything more about Ambani and his gang?'

'I don't want to disappoint you, but funnily enough, I did.'

'There you go. You're learning.'

'Quick off the block, me. Sunil Ambani has been on our radar before, as it happens. He formed a company that arranged for students to come over from India for summer internships. That was legal, and the students did enrol in the summer colleges. Like some kids do from USA and Europe. But unlike the American kids, Ambani's cohort stayed back, and vanished. We located some of them when they complained about how they were treated. We found them as far as Dorset, and in Inverness, working for cash in so-called Indian restaurants, fish and chip shops, and in farms.'

'They came forward, which is good. But Ambani wasn't directly implicated, right?'

'He was one of the founders of the company, along with another person called Paresh Mallya. Paresh is a businessman, who on paper imports sand and cement from India to Europe. He owns a house in London. Like Ambani, Mallya wasn't involved in the running of the company. They only donated seeding money, according to their lawyers.'

'Where is this Mallya guy now?'

'Again, I'm sorry to say, I found out.'

Roy grinned. 'That's okay. I won't hold it against you.'

'You better not,' Natalie raised her eyebrows. 'Mallya, as it happens, is in Yorkshire, according to his latest visa stamp. He's an Indian citizen, but travels frequently. His last known address is in Rotherham, where he's renting a house.'

'Does he have permanent residency to live in UK? Otherwise, we cannot subject him to UK laws.'

'Exactly right. He's slippery as an eel. We can't do owt about him, as he's an Indian citizen. We can nab him, and get him a one-way ticket back to India. As you can imagine, his lawyers will kick up a massive fuss. Regardless of nationality, anyone can be arrested of course, but charging them is a different matter.'

Roy rubbed his chin and thought. 'At least we have Ambani, his business partner, in custody. Not that we can charge him with anything, which is frustrating.' He frowned. 'Why would they kill Noor, and make trouble for their business? She must've found something important.'

'Yes. Unless, of course, it's not them. You have Martin Donald as your main suspect, right?'

'And we need to find him today.' Roy glanced at his watch, then looked at Natalie. 'Anything else?'

'That's it for now. Ambani and Mallya have an organisation. I think Mallya handles the immigration, and Ambani is the man on the ground.'

'And the new guy, Afzal, works for Ambani. They will have others. Rahul, the waiter, will have more names.'

''ey yup,' Melanie called out as she walked in quickly. She took off her coat, and blew out her red cheeks. 'Just dropped off the kids to summer camp. We spend more money on their activities in the holidays than when school's open.'

'I know,' Natalie sympathised. 'I don't have children, but my sister and nieces come and stay with me in the summer.'

'Honestly, it's cheaper to go for a holiday. Spend the

same money here. Might as well be in Spain.'

'You went a week ago, didn't you?' Roy asked.

'Yes,' Melanie made a face. 'That's why we can't go again.'

'I take my nieces to taekwondo camp. Maybe your children could go too?'

'You're in good shape. Is that what you do?' Melanie asked, casting her eyes over Natalie's athletic frame.

'Yes. I used to represent my county, in Lancaster.'

Roy noted, not for the first time, Natalie's big hands, and wide shoulders. The martial arts made a lot of sense now. If she got to county level, she must be good, he thought.

'Remind me not to get into a fight with you,' he said.

'I might disappoint you again if I do,' Natalie laughed.

Rizwan and Oliver came in, holding cups of coffee. ''ey yup,' Riz said. 'Did we miss a joke?'

'Yes,' Melanie said. 'The guv took a bet you two can't beat Natalie in an arm wrestle.'

The two DCs looked at each other, confused. 'Well, what do you say?' Melanie teased.

'She's only messing,' Natalie reassured the men. 'I used to do taekwondo. Still do, in fact. We were just chatting about that.'

'And for the record, I never said that,' Roy said to Melanie, who grinned. 'Anyway, busy day, people. We need to find all our missing suspects. Martin Donald being first. Can we please check with uniforms and Traffic for any CCTV evidence?'

As the others got busy, Roy picked up the phone and called Dr Patel. 'If it isn't the man of the moment,' Sheila Patel said.

'Wow, flattery?' Roy was genuinely surprised. 'Doesn't suit you, I must say.'

'Get it while you can, Inspector. I've got news for you.'

'DNA matches, please, if you have them.'

'You have a brain, after all. Yes, it is that.' Her tone became sombre. 'The DNA from the semen sample in the victim shows a match with Martin Donald. Some of the sperm is still alive, which means intercourse was within the last two days.'

Roy noted that down. He twirled the pen in his fingers. 'Anything else?'

'Martin Donald's DNA is present in other parts of her body from where we took skin swabs. She has another DNA sample under her nails for which we don't have any matches from the men you have in custody, or Martin.'

Dr Patel asked, 'Is it safe to assume that Martin is the man who got Noor pregnant?'

'Nothing is safe to assume unless the evidence points to it,' Roy said. 'In my line of work, assumptions ruin investigation. Noor was probably used as a sex worker by the traffickers. There's a chance she was impregnated by someone else.'

'Sex workers use protection, Rohan. Noor was clearly having unprotected sex with Martin, which points to a different kind of relationship.'

'Yes. They were seen together by multiple witnesses inside their estate.' Roy paused. 'Method and time of death is still the same?'

'Yes, no changes. Still waiting for toxicology. Will let you know if anything else pops up.'

Roy went to Oliver's desk and tapped him on the shoulder. 'This man you saw in Noor's estate flat. Can you describe him to me?'

Oliver nodded. 'Short, no more than five seven. Thin but tough-looking, with brown hair and dark eyes. He had a ring on his left hand, third finger, and an earring in his left ear lobe.'

'Did he say anything to you?'

Oliver leant back in his chair and Roy perched his bottom on his desk. 'We talked about Noor obviously. He said that she worked there, and Martin saw her. Hang on.' Oliver frowned. 'When I was leaving he said he'd seen me somewhere before. I denied it and he let me go.'

'Probably saw you on telly. Jimmy Savile,' Rizwan delivered his wisdom from across the table.

'Shut up. Yes, I thought that was a bit mardy. How would he recognise me like?'

'Maybe he saw you around the estate,' Roy said. 'There's one man we still haven't got hold of. Daniel Jones, the landlord of Noor's flat.'

Melanie had overheard the conversation. 'We did a file on him.' She arched an eyebrow at Rizwan. 'Didn't we, lads?'

'Oh yes.' Rizwan fumbled, focusing on his keyboard and tapping quickly. He shot a grateful look at Melanie before he read from the screen.

'Daniel Jones owns two other flats in that estate. Some of the flats were sold to private landlords, despite the estate being owned by the council. There's no record of who he rents them to. He lives in Brinsworth, just to the east of the M1.' The M1 motorway, one of England's longest, formed a loose border to the east of Sheffield.

'And we haven't been able to get hold of him?' Roy asked.

'Nope. We have tried, and left messages on his phone. Nowt as yet.'

Melanie was also staring at her laptop screen. 'He does look like the man Oliver described. Here, look.'

Oliver, Roy, Rizwan and Natalie gathered around Melanie's desk. Oliver exclaimed loudly.

'Chuffin' 'eck. That's the geezer I saw, like. In that flat yesterday.'

'The pimp,' Rizwan said.

'The owner, more like,' Roy said. 'What's the number of the other two flats that Daniel owns?'

Melanie consulted her notes. '627 and 810.'

'I went to 627,' Oliver said. 'Damn, I should've asked his name. But guess what?' He grinned, and everyone waited for the brainwave. Roy didn't have any high hopes, given Oliver's exploits yesterday.

'The radio was on, and his voice was recorded.'

'That's right,' Rizwan said. 'I even heard it, sitting in the car outside.'

'Let's hear it then,' Roy said. Oliver got his radio and found the right channel and recording. They listened attentively. It wasn't a good audio file, police radios were designed for rapid communications, not quality.

'If he was there yesterday, he should be there now,' Roy said. 'Unless your exploits drove him out.' He looked up at the two constables. 'Let's go.'

CHAPTER 41

Roy and Melanie were in the backseat as Rizwan drove at break neck speed, sirens blaring. Ahead of them, a squad car did the same, clearing the road as it streaked through the early morning traffic. A riot van had also been assembled, and was on its way. Three more squad cars were already on scene, patrolling discreetly.

Roy had asked for more support, and he hoped they arrived on time. 'We need the estate on lockdown,' he said on the radio. 'Anyone who matches the suspects' description must be stopped and questioned.'

There was an all-points bulletin or APB out for Daniel Jones and Martin Donald.

'If he knew Martin, then chances are he might know where he is. Martin might trust him more as he hasn't been questioned by us,' Roy had said as they were leaving the nick.

'True,' Riz responded. 'Daniel spoke to Jimmy here, not DC Walmsley.'

'You're just jealous you didn't think of it yourself,' came Oliver's reply.

Now they were both silent as the tension was building. From their hunched shoulders and tense faces, Roy knew both constables were keen on getting the job done. Like them, he hoped and prayed Daniel Jones could be found, but he had an awful feeling the man had escaped. He thought Oliver looked familiar, and that might've spooked him.

Rizwan cut the sirens as they got closer. A knot of riot police had gathered around the main entrance of the estate, obvious in their black padded uniforms, helmets, and long shields. Roy did a quick comms check to make sure they were all on the same radio frequency. Luckily, at this time in the morning, the number of onlookers was few. But Roy noted with unease the men who were speaking on their phones already.

They bunched close together in a team huddle with the sergeant leading the riot team.

'Oliver, you lead as you know where to go. You two come with me, Riz and Oliver.' Roy pointed to two burly uniformed constables, one of whom had the portable battering ram.

'This will be a smash and grab. No warning, no questions. Break down that door and enter. Melanie, you lead the other team in flat 810. Arrest and bring down to the cars.' The cars would enter the compound as soon as they got word from the arresting teams.

'We have company already.' Roy motioned to the few pedestrian on the road behind them. 'Move out.'

No further instructions were needed. One good thing about the riot teams was their high level of training. Many were ex-military, seasoned in conflict zones. Despite their body armour and shields, they ran alongside Roy, Oliver and Rizwan, at full speed.

Within minutes they had arrived on the fourth-floor landing which, mercifully, was empty. The other two exits were covered at the ground level by the uniform teams. They bent low at the waist, and moved in single file. Oliver led them to the door, and the man with the battering room raised the ram high in the air and swung it on the door, as hard as he could. The loud crunch smashed the lock, and a couple of kicks slammed the door inside. They piled in, shouting 'police'. Often, that stopped bullets coming their way, as the criminals didn't fear a rival gang.

Oliver was right behind the uniformed constable who struck down the door, and he put his boot inside a bedroom that was shutting. With his shoulder, he prised it open, pushing back the man behind it. Riz joined him, and the door gave way, and the two men stumbled inside.

Roy caught a flash of a slept-in bed, clothes on the floor, and a table with a laptop on it. The room looked like a storm had swept through it, chucking pizza boxes, chicken bones, beer cans on the floor, mingling with jeans and t-shirts. A pungent waft hit him like a slap on the face, and he crinkled his nose in disgust. The smell was a cloud that seemed to encase the room and coat their faces.

Oliver had grabbed a man around the neck and pushed

251

him against the wall. He was short, but vicious and fought back, kicking Oliver in the legs and snarling. Oliver dragged him to the floor and turned him on his back, but not before enduring an elbow to his ribs, which made him grunt with pain. Rizwan held the man's arms and Oliver put a knee on his back. With Roy helping, they managed to handcuff the man.

'Daniel Jones,' Oliver said, panting, 'You are under arrest.'

'DCI Roy here. And you will be charged with solicitation for sex. We have it on record, and can use it as evidence,' Roy said.

Daniel was face-down, and Roy indicated to Oliver, who raised him to sitting. Thankfully, one of the uniforms had opened a window, and the smell was becoming bearable.

'You own flat 514. One of the girls there, Noor Jehan, died last night.'

Roy saw the fear light up in Daniel's eyes as they widened. 'You knew Noor. Again, we have it on record. We want Martin Donald.' Roy leant closer. He knew if Daniel got a lawyer at the nick, it would be harder to get what he wanted – Martin's location.

'Help yourself, Daniel. I can put in a good word for you. Don't go down for an accessory to murder charge. That's twenty-five years, and you won't get a lighter sentence for good behaviour.' Roy gave him a couple of seconds for the news to sink in. 'Tell us where Martin is.'

Daniel's head sank down on his chest. He didn't reply. 'Right,' Roy said. 'Daniel Jones, I'm arresting you on the charge of accessory to murder. You have the right to remain silent, but anything—'

'Wait,' Daniel said, his voice a cracked whisper. He licked his dry lips. 'I know where Martin is.'

CHAPTER 42

Brinsworth was a sleepy little village outside the formal borders of Sheffield, but sandwiched between the city and Rotherham. Roy instructed on the radio as Rizwan took a turn at high speed.

'Seal off exits to the M1. I don't care about traffic blockage. Set up signs to divert traffic, maybe via the A630 or 631.' Roy looked at the satnav map while Riz drove, and Oliver was helping Riz to navigate.

'Signal all units, if they're not attending a 999 call, to converge on Brinsworth. We can't let him slip through our fingers again.'

It was the three men in the car, Melanie having gone back with Daniel Jones to the station. She would start interrogating him, and there was the small matter of letting Sunil Ambani and Rahul Tripathi free. Roy wasn't happy with that decision, as he knew Ambani was crooked as they come. But Melanie had promised Natalie would interrogate him once before he was released. Roy trusted Natalie, she knew her job well, and her addition to the team was important.

His radio crackled. 'Units two and three in place, behind Whitehill Road. This road is now blocked with car checks on all passengers, save women and children.'

Roy wondered about that. Martin could be in the boot of a car driven by a woman. 'Stop single women without children and check the car. ETA ten minutes.'

Soon their unmarked car was sweeping through the streets of Brinsworth. It was one of those suburbs of Rotherham that seemed to have been built in the Victorian times, when the steel industry was flourishing. After the M1 was built in the 1960s, it was cut off from Sheffield, and was now almost forgotten. Not a soul stirred in the quiet residential streets as the car sped through.

Daniel Jones was a canny property investor. He had a number of flats and houses across Sheffield. All of them were low-priced, but offered good rent. Despite his appearance, and the way he lived, Roy suspected the man was rich. His house in Brinsworth was a nice detached one in a tree-lined avenue, but that's not where Martin was.

Whitehill Avenue was a cramped, narrow residential street. Rows of identical terraced houses were stuck to each other tighter than any fishes in a tin can. It was a ramshackle, poverty-ridden street, graffiti covering its walls, windows boarded up in several houses.

'Junkies' corner,' Oliver muttered. Roy had to agree. Where poverty thrived, so did drugs, heroin in particular.

Sheffield had been ravaged by a heroin epidemic, laying waste to the young population from areas like these.

'On scene,' Roy whispered on the radio. 'Prepare to breach.'

The squad cars had stayed away. Their unmarked car was parked a few houses down from number 84. The upstairs curtains were open, and so was a small window. That was a good sign. Someone was in.

'Units three and four round the corner. Rear of eighty-four is covered.'

'Countdown to five starting now,' Roy said, his hand on the door. In front, he saw Rizwan check his extendable baton. Oliver did the same, and both constables were ready to run out the door.

'Breach units in place,' Inspector Jonty Adams' voice came on the radio. That meant the uniform teams were crouching behind the street corner, ready to rush in.

'Five, four, three, two- shit, Abort! I repeat, Abort!' Roy lowered the radio as he saw a man emerge from the house. The front door opened and the man looked around him furtively, then he shut the door.

'That's him, guv,' Oliver said.

'Grab him, now,' Roy was out of the car as he spoke, and crossing the road. Martin saw him coming, and set off at a run. Roy ran after him, and Martin skidded as he got to the end of the road, and ran full tilt into the waiting phalanx of the uniform team. He screamed and shouted as two burly constables pinned him against the wall.

His eyes filled with hatred as he clocked Roy. 'I'm a

member of a political party. You have no right to do this to me.'

'I don't care,' Roy said plainly, 'If you're the chairman of the Conservative Party. Which, of course, you're not, and never will be.' He stepped closer, bringing his face to within inches of Martin's. 'But Noor Jehan is dead, and you've got a lot to answer for.'

Martin's face mottled even further red, and he spat at Roy, who had expected that move. He sidestepped, and the gob of spit landed on the pavement.

'I want to be arrested by an English officer,' Martin screamed. 'You're not English.'

'I was the last time I checked my bloody passport,' Roy said wryly. 'For better or worse. Anyway, Martin Donald, you're under arrest for the murder of Noor Jehan.'

Martin's face fell, and colour faded from his cheeks. 'You must be joking... I... Never went near her. I've got no idea.'

'Stop lying, it doesn't suit an important politician like yourself.' Roy felt, more than saw, the smiles around him. 'Then again, meeting an honest politician is like seeing the Virgin Mary. Put him in the car.'

The uniforms took Martin away. Roy and the constables got back in their car. Martin had made their job a lot easier by stepping outside. Now they had more time to question him.

'Hate bastards like him,' Oliver muttered as he drove. Rizwan sat next to him and said nothing.

'Let's hope,' Roy said, feeling happy for the first time

the case started, 'That he talks before he gets a lawyer. We have enough against him, but I might be able to trick him into giving more away.'

CHAPTER 43

The station was a hive of activity. Fax machines and printers were humming, constables were busy writing up the endless paperwork that came with arrests, and inspectors were locked in rooms with the CPS (Crown Prosecution Service) legal advisers, to make sure a charge would stick before they went through the whole process of charging someone.

Melanie and Roy were speaking to Jeremy Snape, the paralegal who worked for the CPS. He had listened to the evidence against Martin, and he still had a dubious look on his face. Roy knew that wasn't a bad thing. It was Jeremy's job to examine all the evidence before they rushed into a trial that would cost both manpower and money.

'I know you've got Martin and the victim cavorting around on CCTV. The DNA from the semen sample proves they were together. But it doesn't prove the baby was

Martin's. The DNA makes it more likely the baby was his, but not definite. I don't think there are any medical ways to sample a baby's foetus to check for the father's DNA.'

'Even if there was,' Roy mused, 'it would be too expensive, and the bloody lawyers might kick up a fuss, saying it's not allowed and all that crap.'

'Exactly. It all depends on what the judge sees as feasible. He or she might decide against it, and trying to prove foetal DNA for proof of fatherhood is not going to work.'

Jeremy continued. 'I can see that he had the motive. If she was pregnant, he wouldn't want a child with her, given his political beliefs. He probably had the means, given his criminal record. But the opportunity? Can you prove he was at Thornseat Lodge, between ten and two in the morning, the night of the murder?'

Melanie said, 'His wife says he came home late that night, and she was asleep. Which means we don't know when he came home. She went to bed at half past eleven.'

'Which gives us reasonable doubt, unless he confesses. Yes, that might work, given the weight of the rest of the evidence.' Jeremy nodded sagely. 'I think you've got a decent chance at a trial.'

Roy stood. 'In which case, we better get started. Thanks, Jeremy.' They shook hands, and Melanie said goodbye to Jeremy, who went back to his office in east Sheffield, to the HQ of South Yorkshire Police. As he left, Natalie came into the room.

'I hear you've had a busy morning,' she said. 'You've managed to kill two birds with one stone.'

'Still a way to go. How about Ambani? Did you speak to him?'

'Yes.' The light went out of Natalie's eyes. 'Sorry, he's not giving anything away. He knows we don't have anything against him. The fact that he owns the restaurant and the nail bar where these girls came to work doesn't mean a great deal. The girls, like the waiter Rahul, applied for the position when advertised.'

'Did you speak to him about Paresh Mallya?'

'Yes, and the answer was predictable. He doesn't know anyone of that name.'

Roy stood, and put both hands on his waist. 'You've got a folder on Ambani. He's been on your watch for a while. Did you tell him that? Surely he should be intimidated by that. He might not show it, but men like him don't like it when they find out they're under watch.'

'Oh, he didn't like it one bit. He underestimated me first, but then realised who he was up against.' Natalie smiled, which faded quickly. 'I know what you mean. Wish there was more we could do. But unless you have more evidence against him...' She shrugged.

Roy glanced at Melanie. She shook her head. 'It's what Natalie said, guv. These girls applied for the advertised posts. At least, that's what Ambani will keep saying. Zero hours contract and all that.'

Roy looked at Natalie. He was sure she had tried her best, but, in the end, they didn't have enough to charge him with anything.

Natalie appeared to be in sync with his thoughts. 'You

have to let him go,' she said. 'Far from ideal, but at least he can now be kept under surveillance.'

'Which starts from the second he leaves custody,' Roy said. 'I'll have a word with Nugent.' He made for the door, but turned to face Natalie once. 'Can you please look into Daniel Jones? He had multiple properties across Sheffield, and he was renting them out to people who kept these vulnerable women. He must be known to your crew.'

'That's on my to-do list,' Natalie said.

Melanie also made for the door. 'I'll make sure Martin has a lawyer while you speak to Nugent.'

Roy didn't budge from the door. 'No, leave it. I'll see Martin before he gets a lawyer. Don't tell Nugent anything.'

Melanie frowned. 'That could lead to trouble. Martin can kick up a fuss about police harassment.'

'Exactly.' Roy smiled mysteriously. 'Don't worry, I'm going to keep it perfectly civil. Just keep it to yourself, for now.'

Melanie raised her eyebrows, and there was a worried look in her eyes. Roy took his leave, and waved at the constables who were hard at work. Luckily, Nugent didn't come out of his office to grill him about the morning arrests. Roy ran down the steps to the custody cells. A sergeant called Paul was on duty, and he stood when he saw Roy.

'Which cell is Martin Donald in?'

'Two thirty, guv. I'll take you there.'

'Has the duty solicitor been to see him?'

'Not yet, but I heard he's on his way.'

Even better, Roy thought to himself. He had a plan, and it was falling into place. He felt he could appeal to Martin Donald in a more visceral way, reach into his guts like no law ever could. He signed his name in the book, and Paul led him to the cell.

Martin was lying on the single bed in the spacious cell, and he lifted his head when Roy entered. Then he groaned and his head fell back on the bed.

'I don't want to speak to you. I want an English officer.'

Roy shut the door behind him. He stood by the door, not going in any further. He knew there was a CCTV camera in the wall. Opposite the bed, there was a steel sink recessed into the wall, and an uncovered toilet. The flush button was also recessed into the wall. Instead of a mirror, there was a highly polished steel plate on the wall above the sink.

'That would be me,' Roy said. 'I'm as much British as you are.'

'No you're not,' Martin said, raising himself on one elbow. Then he swung his legs down and sat upright. Excellent, Roy thought happily. Martin was taking the bait.

'You're about as far from being English as I am from whichever godforsaken country you're originally from. Just because you have a posh southern accent, it don't mean owt.'

'You don't like foreigners?' Roy asked innocently. 'Why not?'

'Because you lot are like a swarm, taking our jobs and

money.'

'All of us?'

'Yes,' Martin spat.

'Even Noor?'

Martin looked like he'd been punched in the gut. His eyes flared with a sudden light, then he looked away. 'I don't know what you're talkin' about.'

'Oh, I think you do. The woman you couldn't stay away from. I think you loved her, didn't you, Martin?' Roy tutted slowly. 'What would your friends in the National Front say? Sleeping with a dark-skinned woman.'

Martin clasped and unclasped his hands. He said nothing.

'You didn't just want her for sex. You wanted her as your partner. You wanted to be with her all the time.'

Martin's face morphed into a mask of irritation. 'Shut up, you twat.' He wouldn't look at Roy. And Roy knew Martin was only trying to convince himself, and even at that, he was failing miserably.

Roy sighed, then sat down on his haunches. His tone was relaxed, words slow. 'You know what I think, Martin?'

'I don't give a fuck what you think, like.'

'I don't think you're a racist at all. If you liked Noor that much, you can't be. And I'm willing to bet Noor isn't the first brown-skinned woman that you fancied.'

Martin avoided Roy's eyes.

'I looked at your trial records from the last arrest. The

lawyer who got you off has worked for the National Front for many years. You didn't have money for a good defence lawyer, but they did. Now you owe them, don't you?'

Martin turned his head slowly to glare at Roy. 'Shut your face.'

'Those tattoos on your forearm are new. Your whole ideology is just for show. You just want to please those idiots who saved you from a jail sentence. They want a thug like you, who can fight their cause. How am I doing so far?'

Martin got to his feet. Roy remained on the floor, and merely looked up at Martin.

'Get out of here,' Martin snarled. 'I'm calling the guard now. This is harassment.'

Roy stood slowly. 'Oh, I'm going. I just wanted you to know something before I went.' He paused for a second, to make sure he had Martin's attention.

'Noor was pregnant with your child. She wasn't far gone, about eight weeks.'

Martin's jaws dropped. He seemed to visibly shrink: his head lowered, spine folded, then he descended slowly to the bed. His eyes stared ahead of him, unseeing.

'Didn't know that, did you? Maybe she wanted to tell you, but she never got the chance.'

Martin acted like he didn't hear, and maybe he didn't.

Roy spoke softly. 'She wanted to see you at the Thornseat Lodge. You didn't know what it was about. You had an argument. Maybe she wanted you to leave your wife, and be with her. You ended up stabbing her. I'm guessing you wouldn't have done that if she told you about the baby.'

Very slowly, like an invisible hand was forcing Martin's head, he turned to look at Roy.

'That's why you ran. You heard from us that Noor was dead, and you knew we would come after you.'

'No,' Martin whispered. 'I didn't kill her.'

'Then who did? Why was she there night before last?'

Martin's eyes were as wide as saucers. His head sank down on his chest. 'I-I don't know.'

CHAPTER 44

Martin sat like a statue, staring ahead. He ignored Roy. Then, without a word, he lay down on the bed, and turned to the wall.

'What did Noor tell you that night?' Roy asked, stepping closer to the bed.

'I didn't see her. I didn't know she was there.'

'Where were you?'

Martin was silent for a while. 'At a party meeting.' He meant the National Front, Roy assumed. That could be verified easily. A turmoil was raging in his mind. Martin appeared genuinely griefstruck. He had taken the news of Noor's pregnancy badly. He didn't even try to deny the baby was his.

Roy thought of his next words carefully. As a suspect in custody, Martin had numerous rights. As a previous convict, he would be very much aware of them. It was strange he hadn't asked for a solicitor the moment he saw Roy, or even allowed him into the room. Roy had seen through Martin's shell easily enough, but now he realised Martin was a broken man.

'Why did you run?' Roy asked. Martin didn't move. He rested his head on a folded elbow and faced the wall.

'I knew I might come under suspicion. People had seen us together. I also didn't want the Front lads to know.'

'Can you help us find who did this to Noor?'

Silence again. Martin stirred, turning from the wall and sitting up on the bed. His hands gripped the edges, and his head hung over his chest.

'Aye,' he said hoarsely. 'I'll do what I can, like. But I don't know what happened that night.'

'Did she tell you why she was going there?'

'Nah. She was in some bother, like. Trying to get away from those bastards who got her here. They kept her like a bloody slave. She was workin' for money, that's how I met her.'

'Yes, we heard from Daniel. But you started caring for her, and then it got deeper. Right?'

'Aye. We talked of leavin' this shithole and goin' away, like. I was getting ready to tell Amanda.'

'Did Noor tell you who the men were? You must have seen them around? Or Daniel did?'

'There was a guy called Afzal, who lived with them sometimes. That's the only one I know. There were others, but she was scared of telling me their names. They threatened to kill her family back in India if she did.'

'Who else lived with Noor in that flat?'

'One lass called Layla. She was good mates with her. They were planning to take off, but didn't know how. She wanted my help... I wasn't sure if her mate could come with us. I didn't have any money to give her. I told her to be patient, and she got pissed off with me, like.'

'What plans did Layla and Noor make?'

Martin shrugged. 'Just to leave. But they didn't have anywhere to go. Noor kept sayin' the men would find them. I was also uneasy like, of getting in between them.'

'Who were these men, Martin? You said Afzal, but anyone else?' Martin shook his head, and maintained eye contact with Roy.

'What about a man called Sunil Ambani? Or Paresh Mallya?'

'Don't know those names.'

'Are you sure?'

'Yes.'

Roy bit back the frustration that faced him like a wall. Ambani was in custody right now and he could've charged him with a statement from Martin. At least Martin knew about Afzal.

'There was one thing though.' Martin frowned as if he remembered something. 'Noor said she had seen someone who might be able to help her. That's all she said.'

'She didn't describe this person to you? Who he was, or what he looked like?'

'No.'

Roy thought about that. It was something new, but also very vague. It was possible Noor had met this person at Thornseat Lodge.

'Anything else?'

Martin shook his head slowly, and sadly. 'Wish I could help.'

'Stay here until we find out more. I will need an official statement, and your solicitor will be here soon.'

Martin nodded, and Roy left the room, closing the door behind him. If Martin was the killer, he was pulling an act worthy of an Oscar. He wasn't lying, that much Roy could tell. Roy went upstairs quickly, and found the team in their corner. Melanie looked up at him, her face worried.

'What happened?'

'All okay, don't worry. I don't think Martin did it,' Roy explained quickly. Riz and Oliver were on the phones, but they hung up and listened to him attentively.

'Where's Natalie?' Roy asked.

'She had to go back to her office. Ambani and Tripathi are out. A surveillance team's been sent out to Ambani's home address. We're tapping his phone, but he'll get a burner I think.'

'Yes, but that's expected. The sooner we have eyes on him, the better it is. Did Natalie say anything about Daniel Jones?'

'Nope. He's not been on the Modern Slavery Unit's radar. They have this thing called the National Referral Mechanism, or NRM, where anyone can fill in a form online to complain about how they're being treated. No one's mentioned the name of Daniel Jones.'

'And yet he was renting out flats to known human traffickers. Has anyone interrogated him yet?'

'I was about to do that with one of the lads,' Melanie looked at Rizwan and Oliver.

Roy looked at his watch. 'I've got to drop my daughter at the train station. Then I might swing by Sarah's house to make sure she's okay. Has anyone heard from her?' He meant to call her today but the morning had been eventful to say the least.

A voice from behind answered his question. 'Anyone ask for me?' He saw Melanie's eyes pop open in surprise, looking over his shoulder. He swung around to find Detective Inspector Sarah Botham standing there. She was casually dressed in jeans, a white vest and burgundy jacket. Her blonde hair was tied back in a ponytail, and her sea-green eyes glimmered with the hint of a smile.

'What're you doing here?' Roy asked, pleasantly surprised, but masking it with official indignation. 'You're meant to be on leave.'

'Mum's at home with Matt, and he's alright. I heard that you lot have been busy so thought I'd come to give a hand.'

Rizwan came over and shook Sarah's hand. He said the words Roy longed to utter but couldn't.

'Missed you, guv. Glad you're back.' Sarah gave Riz and Oliver a hug, and looking at their happy beaming faces which bore than a trace of emotion, Roy could see why they were one big family.

Sarah had been with them since their uniform days, and helped them become detectives. He hoped in some small way he was making a contribution to their development into better officers – but frankly they didn't need him. They were a well-knit group before he arrived. He also hoped he fitted in well with them. His old team with Arla Baker was like this – where everyone cared for each other not because they were colleagues, but the challenging experiences they went through together also made them friends.

'Is Matt going to get some counselling?' Melanie asked, when they were seated together. 'Might help him.'

'Yes,' Sarah said, and sighed. Her expression bore the depth of her recent troubles, and the fact that both she and Matt almost lost their lives. 'He's come through alright though, I must say. He's talking about it, and I'm trying my best to support him.'

'Which is why you should be resting at home,' Roy said gently. He knew life wasn't easy for Sarah as a single mother. She took her maternal duties seriously, and she wouldn't be here if Matt wasn't okay. She looked at him, and a silent message passed between them. He didn't know exactly what she wanted to say, but he realised she was at peace, and had come back because she missed them.

'I know what you mean, Rohan. But when you told me about the case, I felt I had to do something.' Roy had spoken

272

to her en route to work, which he was now starting to regret. He had known she would find out eventually, a murder case wasn't exactly easy to conceal from an inspector. He didn't want her to be involved, it just emerged while he was talking.

'We have it under control, actually,' Roy said, a tad firmly, and Sarah glanced at him. 'We do want you back, but you should also take it easy.'

Sarah's eyes flickered over to her desk, where a laptop rested, along with an empty cup of tea.

'Who's using my desk?' Sarah got up to have a look.

'That would be Natalie Scarrow,' Melanie said. 'She's from the Modern Slavery Unit.'

Oliver hastily added, 'There weren't any other desks around.'

Sarah shrugged and went back to her seat next to Roy. She wasn't the type to ever make a fuss, but Roy could see she was a little peeved that her desk was already being used by someone else.

'Natalie's only here for a few days,' Roy said.

'It's good that she's here. You're after a human trafficking gang, and she can help.'

'She already has,' Melanie affirmed. 'Ambani, the man we had to let go this morning, has been on her unit's watch list. Incidentally,' Melanie looked up at everyone else, 'The MSU's folders can be accessed from the PND databases. The lads got there first, didn't you?' The PND or Police National Database in the UK linked all the police forces, National Crime Agency, child protection and sexual offences services together.

Rizwan and Oliver nodded. Rizwan said, 'Actually it was the researchers who came up with it.'

Melanie said, 'Speaking of which, I've uncovered some new facts about Ambani. He owns a couple of other businesses – a fish and chip shop, and also a pizzeria. One of the waitresses there made a complaint about the work conditions, and the sexual harassment. She came from Poland, and was working for next to nothing. What's interesting is that this woman also did hours as a sex worker in one the massage parlours in Attercliffe. Guess who owns the massage parlour?'

Roy frowned. In their last case, they were heavily involved with murders in the city's massage parlours.

'Kevin Rawlinson's gang? The Loxley Boys?'

'The one and same,' Melanie said. All eyes turned to her. In the ensuing silence, Roy knew everyone was thinking about their previous case – the murder of the sex workers in the massage parlours. He recalled the women from Eastern Europe who lived in a house owned by the gang boss, Kevin Rawlinson. He was a despicable character, and had gone free.

Sarah said the words. 'Are you saying there's a link between Ambani and Rawlinson?'

'There could be. Maybe women like Noor were forced to work in the massage parlours as well.'

'In which case,' Sarah said, 'you better track down Rawlinson and ask him. He's going to deny all of it, clearly. But we did suspect he was linked to a trafficking gang,

274

didn't we?'

'Yes,' Roy mused aloud. 'But men like Ambani, and his business partner Paresh, are from India originally, and they seem to source their victims from there. Polish or other Eastern European criminals would be getting this woman Melanie referred to. But both Kevin's gang, and Ambani, could be using them once they arrive here.'

Rizwan said, 'If they are linked up, then our job just got trickier.'

CHAPTER 45

DCI Rohan Roy was in father mode again. He walked down the busy railway platform, talking to Anna over the general hubbub. It was hard to think she'd be gone, he had got used to her being at home with him.

He handed Anna her rucksack, and helped the teenager put it on her back. The usual protests followed.

'I can do it myself, Dad.'

'Just helping, you know.'

Anna wiggled her eyebrows. 'You being helpful? Funny that.' She grinned.

He would miss her like mad. It must've shown on his face, because Anna leant in for a hug. People with luggage bustled past them on the busy platform. They arrived outside Anna's train carriage. It was the direct train to London, and Anna would be there in a couple of hours.

From King's Cross she would take the tube back home to Tooting.

The long blue train's engines hummed, and the platform seemed to buzz along with it. Somewhere, a whistle sounded, and the kinetic energy around them kicked up a notch.

'I better go,' Anna said. Her large, expressive dark eyes were pools of light as they scanned his face. 'Look after yourself, Dad.'

A weight was stuck in his throat, and a pressure built behind his eyes, but he managed an eye roll.

'You're telling me?'

'Yes. Stay off the beer. No more fried chicken or fish and chips.'

'Hey.' He frowned. 'I don't eat that stuff. OK, only when I can't be bothered to cook.'

'See?' Anna got on the train. Another whistle sounded. A man went up behind her, and squeezed past her. Anna stood in the doorway.

'Call me,' Roy said. 'I'm not that far. I need to come down anyway, to get my release papers from the Met. I'll let you know.'

'See you soon. Love you.'

He smiled and waved. 'Love you, darling.'

Anna waved again, then went inside the carriage. He followed her from the platform. The conductor arrived and shut the doors, locking them. Roy watched till Anna got to her seat and sat down. Not because he needed to, but old habits died hard. Besides, saying goodbye to your own child is always a fraught affair. Anna was always in his blood, she thumped in his heart, saw through his eyes. She was growing up into a woman, and had her own life, and while letting go was natural, so was the constant worry about her welfare. Anna caught him standing there, and waved at him. He waved back. The whistle sounded one last time, and, with a lurch, the train moved forward. He caught a last glimpse of Anna, who was busy putting her ear phones in. Roy stood there, watching the line of steel winding its way out into the sunshine. He watched until the rear of the train curved around a little bend, and started to disappear.

He stuffed hands into his pockets, and walked back briskly. He made his mind focus back on the case, and the urgent need to find Jayden. His phone beeped with a message. He took it out, and stopped short. His breath came faster, and he clutched the phone so hard he thought it might snap into two. The text message was from the same unregistered number that had tormented him over the last few weeks.

We have Jayden. Or shall we call him Robin? If you want to see him alive, let Stephen Burns go free.

A roar rumbled in the depths of his chest. He couldn't utter it in this public place, and it became a growl, lashing against his throat.

CHAPTER 46

Layla looked out the window of the farmhouse. The place was almost derelict. It was a small stone cottage with a loft conversion, and she was in the loft. There was a bed and a table, and the windows had thick wooden shutters. She could see the winding black asphalt road that ran like a ribbon through the bracken and heather filled land. The road dipped into a valley and vanished around the bed, hidden by mountains that raised broad shoulders to the horizon. She heard a sound behind and turned to see Afzal stepping in through the door.

'What are we doing here?' she asked, aware she might provoke his wrath, and not get an answer. But a terrible fear was gathering in her guts. Didn't Noor die in an abandoned farm house like this? Her voice wobbled as she spoke. 'I want to go back.'

'Shut up,' Afzal snarled, advancing. She cowered

away, expecting him to hit her. He didn't, but a satisfied, evil smile spread over his face. 'You'll do as I tell you. For now, you stay here. There's food in the kitchen downstairs. Check the fridge. You sleep here. With me.'

Casually, he came forward and squeezed her breasts. It was repulsive and hideous, and she brushed his hands away. He swore at her, and pushed her in the face without hitting her. She stumbled back, the anger and shame sending ripples through her numb body. She didn't look at him, and hoped it didn't go any further. To her great relief, he seemed to have other things on his mind. He looked out the window, and appeared to check around the landscape.

Layla could see the stone cottage occupied a strategic location over a hill, presiding over rolling farmlands that gave way to the wild expanses of the Peak District. Afzal had chosen this place for a reason. He was hiding, along with her. He was also worried, she could tell from the concern in his face.

He was worried about the police asking about Noor. It had to be that. It also meant she had to get back to Sheffield, and get in touch with the police. The threats of these evil men killing her family? *Let them threaten*. It was just another way of them controlling her. Somehow, she had to escape from this place.

Afzal's phone rang, and he moved away from the window. Below, in the courtyard, Layla could see his car. Layla hadn't driven a car before, but she knew the theory. She had to try and see if she could steal the keys from Afzal. He was speaking on the phone in a hushed voice. He went down the stairs, and she let him go down the stairs, then followed him with soft steps. Layla was barefoot, and she didn't make any sound as she got downstairs. There was a large landing, with two doors to her left, and the kitchen and dining area to her right. She went to the kitchen door that was closed. It was open when they had arrived, when Afzal showed her around. He had shut it now, and she could hear his muffled voice as he spoke over the phone. She put her ear to the door.

'Yes…she's here with me, now. The…Akbar doesn't… Really? No escape, no.' The voice got louder as she heard Afzal come for the door. The landing was a long space, and if Azal opened the door, he would see her, and realised she was eavesdropping. Swiftly, Layla ran to the door to one side, and turned the handle. It was locked. She heard the kitchen door behind her opening. In a blind panic, she reached the staircase and ran upstairs. The stairs curved around, and she paused at the bend when she was out of sight. Her heart thumped loudly against her ribs as her breath came in gasps. Afzal went into one of the rooms, still talking on the phone. He returned, shutting a door behind him. She leant out a little, then shrank back as she saw his head downstairs. He was walking back to the kitchen and still speaking on the phone. His voice was lower, like he didn't want anyone to hear.

'Kill her now? Yes, I can get rid of the body as well. Makes sense. She'll only be trouble for us later.' Afzal shut the door, and she couldn't hear him anymore. But she didn't need to. Panic had gripped her entire body, and her spine shook, but she couldn't move. She now knew why Afzal had got her here. To kill her.

She ran to the loft room, and shut the door. She needed to think. This place was now a deathtrap. The longer she stayed here, the worse her chances of staying alive. She sat down on the bed, then got up. She looked down the window. The drop was a sheer one, and there was nothing that she could climb down. She looked at the bed sheets, and wondered if she could tie them together to make a rope like pulley she could climb down. But the sheets were flimsy, and if she tied them to the leg of the rickety table, none of it would take her weight.

She had to think of something else. She looked at the ceiling, but there was no trapdoor for the loft, it had been converted into this room. She made for the door, then heard footsteps heading up. She shrank backward, looking around her fearfully. There was no escape. She was trapped.

CHAPTER 47

The door opened and Afzal stood there. Layla had retreated to the window, and clutched the ledge. She relaxed her grip when she saw him. If he tried to hurt her, she would rather jump to her death. Nightmare visions of being stabbed like Noor came to her mind. It must've been Afzal who killed Noor. Layla cursed herself for getting in the car with Afzal. She should've known when he called to meet her urgently. This had been his plan all along.

Afzal watched her in silence, then stepped inside. His movements were now measured, and there was a quietness about him she found unnerving. He came forward and stood in the middle of the room. He put a hand in his trouser pocket, and she tried not to flinch. Was this it? She'd wait until she saw his weapon, then jump through the window.

Nothing happened. Afzal put both hands in his jeans pocket and simply watched her.

'What're you doing?'

'Nothing,' Layla gulped.

'Come downstairs. You need to make me some food. You need to learn how to use the cooker.'

The kitchen was in the process of being renovated. Wires poked in from the ceiling, but lights were not yet in place. The floor was laid with new tiles. There was a free-standing, cheap-looking cooker which didn't look like it worked. Afzal wanted her to cook her last meal so he could eat before he killed her. The thought made her sick, but it also gave her an idea. Could she poison him?

'Is there anything here to cook?' she asked tentatively.

'Yes. There's meat in the fridge, onions, and spices. Make me a curry. Come on, move.'

Layla's legs were rooted to the spot, and she couldn't move. He wanted her to go downstairs so he didn't have to carry her body. She would cook, then get killed. What could she do? Run out the front door as soon as she got to the landing? How far would she go before Afzal caught up with her? Even if she did manage to get away, she was easily thirty or forty miles away from the nearest village or town. But she could get to the main road and flag down a car. The thought gave her some hope. She willed her feet to move. Head lowered, she moved past him. He followed close behind. She had no hope now of running to the front door. She could try, but he would catch her easily.

She got to the landing, and looked to the end of the long corridor, where the heavy old wooden door looked locked. A bolt was placed across it. She wouldn't be able to lift that and escape in time. Her heart sank, and a cold fear trickled down her spine.

'What're you waiting for?' Afzal gave her a shove from behind. Layla stumbled forward, and made for the kitchen door. The tiles were cold under her feet, and now that she was barefoot, she also felt the wetness. Her eyes went to the sink, and followed the path of the pipes under it. There was a leak, she thought, hence the slick of water on the floor. Afzal walked past her, and opened the fridge door. There was a patio door on her right that led to the garden. This door was also locked, and she couldn't see a key. The window above the sink, and on her right, were also locked. The view outside was stunning, rolling meadows sloping down to a distant green valley. Grey-blue mountains rose in the distance, the afternoon sun shining between them.

The cooker was opposite the fridge. Cabinets hung on the wall on either side of the cooker. She opened them to find the spices and oil. Her eyes fell on the floor, where the electric cooker connected to the wall. The plug was in bad shape, with wires sticking out. One of them was black. Layla didn't know a great deal about electrics. But she knew a black wire was used to earth the electric circuit, and it was a live wire. She suddenly had an idea.

'Come on, hurry up,' Afzal said gruffly. He placed a slab of beef fillet on the kitchen counter next to the cooker. 'Cook it now.'

'Shall I call you when it's done?' Layla asked. Afzal gazed at her for a few seconds. She couldn't hold his stare.

'Okay. Let me show you how to operate the cooker. See that plug below?' Layla certainly had, but she acted like she didn't know.

'Put the plug in that socket and that turns it on. Then use the knobs on the electric cooker. Got it?'

'Yes.'

He went out of the kitchen, and left the door open. She heard him go into the living room, then open and shut doors. It seemed he was making sure they were locked. Layla wasn't going to get another chance to do this. She bent down, and crawled between the cooker and the cabinets to get to the plug. A gentle pull exposed the wires. She pulled harder, then harder still, till, with a snap, the plug came off her in her hand. The wires now dangled free, above the wet floor. She knew what would happen if the live wire touched the water – electrocution, and almost certain death. She put the plug on the floor. She pulled up a chair from the table, and placed it behind her, as if she needed to sit down to chop the onions at the counter.

As she expected, Afzal came back into the kitchen. She ignored him. She had placed the chair so she blocked any view of the plug. Afzal made sure she was cooking, then retreated to the patio door and looked outside. Layla sneaked a look. The wetness on the floor stretched to where Afzal was standing.

She carried on chopping, moving to the meat. She looked behind the cooker. From where she was sitting, she could stretch forward, and plunge the live wire on the wet floor. But would the current travel as far as Afzal?

'I need some help,' she said. 'I can't get the plug in the socket.'

With a curse, Afzal came forward. This was her

chance. Layla remained seated, feet off the floor. She reached out and grabbed the insulated end of the wires. She pulled on them, then stabbed the live end of the black wire on the floor.

A blue and white bolt of electric flared suddenly on the floor, and Layla leaped backwards. The chair rocked, and she realised she was going to lose balance and fall on the floor.

But Afzal was the first to feel four hundred volts of live electric current explode into his feet, and surge through his body. He screamed as his face went rigid, and his hands became claws. His entire body went stiff, and white hot bolts of power shook his body. His screams became hoarse, and he stood there, shaking like a leaf as the current surged through his body, burning it.

Layal felt herself toppling backwards, and she screamed too. But she was able to rectify her balance at the last moment, leaning forward to correct her centre of gravity. She laid hands on the kitchen counter, and leaped up on it.

A horrific sigh greeted her eyes. Afzal's skin was turning black as it burned, and the smell of charred flesh made her gag. His eyes bulged out, and veins stood up in his head till it looked like his skull would explode. He opened his mouth, and took a step towards her. Layla screamed and scurried back along the kitchen counter on all fours. She knew if she fell on the floor she would die.

Afzal took another step, then his knees buckled, and he collapsed on the floor. His body shook and spasmed, then went still. Layla burst into tears. Then she dried her eyes, and scuttled as far back as she could on the kitchen counter. The floor still had the slick of water on it. But there was a small table at the edge of the counter. If she stepped on the table, then she could reach for the door handle. She hoped and prayed the table would take her weight.

She placed her knees on the table and it creaked, but held firm. She leant forward, and was able to grasp the door handle. She heard a sound behind her. It was a grunting sound like an animal makes, and then a shuffle. She turned her head and fear screamed into her heart like a train in a tunnel. Afzal was scorched and burnt, the charred skin on his face peeling off, exposing the flesh and sinews underneath. But he had managed to pull himself to standing.

Like a macabre ghost, Afzal reached out a claw-like hand for her. Layla screamed.

CHAPTER 48

Melanie and Sarah were leaning over Rizwan's desk. Oliver and Rizwan sat next to each other, Ollie pointing at the screen while Riz talked them through it. A black and white CCTV film was playing on the laptop.

Rizwan pointed at a small blue car that had been marked with a red cross over it. 'That's Afzal's car. ANPR picked it up leaving Meersbrook via the A625. We lost it in Netheredge, where Afzal probably knew the CCTV black spots.'

Rizwan also lived in Netheredge, so he knew that part of South Sheffield well. 'The streets where Layla and Akbar lived don't have CCTV,' he said. 'It's possible Afzal headed that way, but eventually he made his way out to the countryside.'

He zoomed in, and although the image quality wasn't great, they could see Afzal sat in the driver's seat with a young woman beside him.

'Layla,' Oliver muttered. Melanie glanced at him. When they met Layla, she had felt Oliver was staring at her a little too keenly. He was professional throughout, of course, but she couldn't help feeling that Oliver was a tad smitten by Layla. She didn't blame him, the girl was beautiful. She didn't need make-up or glam clothes. Melanie felt sorry for Layla, Noor, and vulnerable girls like them who were at the mercy of these evil traffickers. She took out her phone and checked if Natalie had responded to her texts about Daniel Jones. Natalie hadn't replied as yet.

'Matches her description,' Rizwan agreed. The film rolled, following the blue car as it moved down the busy A621, and Riz speeded up the film till the car took an exit on B6054. The CCTV ended abruptly, replaced by a static-filled blank screen.

'Damn,' Riz muttered. 'No cameras on that road.'

Sarah said, 'Pull up a map. I think that road goes past Owler's Bar, towards Nether Padley.'

Rizwan did as Sarah suggested, and the map proved the veracity of her words. 'There's a couple of farmhouses there, down some old roads that aren't used any more. But it's a long road, and it's going to take us a while to search all the off roads.'

'Does the car emerge at the next CCTV spot?'

Rizwan shook his head. 'That would be the A625 junction at Wooden Pole – Traffic have checked already. Nowt over there, and it's not that busy a road, even at the height of summer.'

Melanie looked at Sarah. 'Thanks, guv. That means he's there, in one of those off roads you mentioned. I'll get some patrol cars sent out now.'

Melanie turned to her desk, and spotted a uniform constable hurrying towards her. She was a woman called Emily Hawthorn, and Melanie had spoken to her in the past.

''Ey yup, guv, I got news for you. A lad called Akbar Mahfuz just turned up at the counter. He says he ran away from you guys before. It's to do with the Noor Jehan case?'

'No way.' Melanie could've hugged Emily. 'Is he in Reception?'

The others moved towards her, and Emily was crowded by the four detectives. 'Yes he is. We've put him in a room with a guard. He was flagged as a flight risk, right?'

'He was but not any more, if he presented himself here.'

'He's not in a good state,' Emily said. 'He's been sleeping rough and worried the others might be after him. That's what he said. He wants to talk about Noor and Layla.'

'Excellent. Daniel Jones will have to wait. We'll come over shortly, give Akbar some food and water.' Once Emily left, Melanie glanced at Sarah. She felt a little awkward. Sarah was higher-ranking officer, and if she was here, she should be calling the shots.

'I'm sorry, guv,' Melanie said to Sarah in a low voice. She pulled her to one side, and Sarah looked at her questioningly. 'I'm taking the decisions, is that okay with you? You're on scene, after all.'

Sarah smiled disarmingly and squeezed Melanie's arm. 'Don't be silly. You're in charge. Officially I'm on leave, remember?'

'Thank you,' Melanie said, and meant it. She also felt relieved. She wasn't a person who did office or work politics well. What she liked about the major investigations team was the lack of any politics. The team got on really well, and there seemed to be a close bond between Sarah and the two younger male detective constables. Melanie also suspected there was something between DCI Roy and Sarah. She felt it in the occasional glance and touch exchanged between each other. Melanie wondered if she was mistaken, but she didn't think so. It was palpable, at least to her. Perhaps she could bring it up if they had a night out, which was overdue.

'You get along with whatever you have to do,' Sarah said. 'Don't mind me. I'm going to talk to Nugent, and then be on my way. I might wait for Rohan to come back as well.'

'Okay, guv.' Melanie turned to the constables, who had gone back to their desks. 'Come on, lads. I'll speak to Akbar, while you two chat with Mr Jones, the dodgy landlord.'

Melanie headed out for reception, and Emily directed her to the interview room where Akbar was held.

Akbar looked frightened out of his wits. His shirt was missing three buttons, and had dark stains on it. His jeans looked dirty, as did his shoes. He gaped at Melanie as she came inside, and shut the door. Melanie sat down in a chair on the table, opposite Akbar. His feet tapped on the floor, and his hands moved on his lap. He was on edge, and Melanie felt sorry for him instantly.

'I'm Detective Sergeant Melanie Sparks, I came to see you at your house.'

Akbar nodded in silence. He seemed unsure of what to say. Melanie continued. 'You did the right thing, Akbar. Is it OK if I call you that?'

The young man nodded again. 'Tell me what happened after we came to see you. Why did you run?'

Akbar gulped, the prominent Adam's apple in his scrawny neck bobbing up and down. 'I was told not to speak to any police about Noor or Layla. Or about anyone who...about anyone.'

'Anyone who... Who do you mean?' Melanie seized on the hesitation.

'The others like us, who were brought over from...from our countries.'

'Tell me about them, and you.'

'I came from Faridabad in India, to study at a college here. But there was no college or degree. Instead, I was told to work in a restaurant, and...' He looked down at his hands. Melanie gave him some time, because she could guess what was coming, and she felt terrible for the poor lad.

'I had to sleep with different men. I was taken to houses, or flats, where a man waited, or they came to the house where I lived.'

Akbar remained downcast. Melanie kept her voice gentle. 'Who arranged all of this? The men who brought you here?' Akbar nodded his agreement, but didn't look up.

'Was it Sunil Ambani? Afzal?'

'Yes, it was them. There was another guy called Paresh, who contacted me in India, and came to see my family. He convinced us it was a good deal to come and study here. Ambani, Afzal and a couple of others manage the people over here. There are others who help them.'

'These others, what do they look like?'

'They are English people, from here. They're big, with shaven heads, and they're scary. They used to come to the house.'

That fit the description of the skinheads who belonged to Kevin Rawlinson's gang. 'Did you find out their names?'

Akbar thought for a while. 'I think one was called Charlie. He was around most of the time.'

The name meant nothing to Melanie, but she wrote it down. 'So you ran because you were scared of us, and also worried what Ambani and the others would do to you if you talked to us.' Akbar nodded.

'Then why did you come back?'

Akbar looked up, his eyes sunken deep into his sockets, a despairing look in them. 'Ambani rang me. He said Layla was dead because she'd spoken to the police. She tried to run away, but they got her. He told me the same would happen to me if I didn't come back immediately.'

Akbar licked his dry lips. 'But I didn't want to go back

to them. I think they would've killed me anyway. You see, I started to help them. I was friendly with Noor. Both she and Layla had plans to escape, and live somewhere else, or try to get a passport. But I betrayed Noor. They made me do it. I think it's my fault she's dead.'

He broke down then, covering his head with hands and lowering his head to the table. His shoulders shook as he sobbed. Melanie got up and touched his back.

'You did the right thing, Akbar. I know this wasn't easy for you. Specialist officers will come and speak to you today. One of them is Natalie Scarrow. She works for the Modern Slavery Unit and she will be able to help you, arrange your return to your family.'

Akbar was still in tears. 'I shouldn't have betrayed Noor. She trusted me.'

'What did she tell you?'

'She said she was speaking to someone who could help her escape from Sheffield. She was seeing a man called Martin Donald, and she thought Martin was in love with her. He was going to leave his wife for Noor. But she wouldn't tell me this other person's name. I told Ambani all of this, and then…'

'It's not your fault. You were made to do this.' Melanie frowned as a thought hit her. 'Do you know if Ambani or Afzal have a house in the Peak District. Somewhere down the A625, the long road that goes out from south Sheffield?'

Akbar wiped his eyes on shirt sleeve and looked up at her. 'Yes. I was taken there once, to do some building work. Why do you ask?'

Layla must be there, Melanie thought to herself.

CHAPTER 49

Layla stared at the ghastly, ghoulish figure of Afzal. Smoke rose from his skin, which was charred black in places. Flesh peeled off his face, and his bloodied lips were bent in a snarl. A guttural noise came from his throat as his feet inched forward. On the floor, the live wire still emitted blue-white sparks. Layla knew she couldn't set foot on the floor, and yet Afzal was getting closer. She couldn't let him touch her, in case the electricity conducted itself to her body. She looked around wildly, and her eyes fell on the pan on the cooker. She snatched it up. It was a heavy pan, and she almost dropped it. She held it with both hands. Afzal got closer. She waited, then hurled the pan at Afzal with every last ounce of strength in her body.

The pan hit Afzal in the chest, thrusting him backwards. His lips moved as he tried to shout, but he could only grunt like an animal. He lost his footing, and fell to the floor again. His hands moved like a puppet on a string, a strange, jerking motion. Layla scrambled to the edge of the kitchen counter, and this time, her hand closed over the door handle. She could just about twist it. The door opened. She could see the long hallway from here. The table creaked under her weight, and one side suddenly depressed, like a leg was about to give you.

She screamed in fear. She couldn't hit the floor, she would also be electrocuted. Like a person on a wobbly dinghy sinking at sea, she raised herself on her knees. The table listed further to the floor. Layla hurled herself towards the door. The distance was no more than three to four feet, and she was able to clear it. She landed on a heap on the floor, and banged her head against the staircase. Pain shot across her shoulders and neck, and she cried out. Then she was on her feet, leaping on the stairs to get herself off the floor.

There was no need, the floor was dry. The doorstep of the kitchen prevented any of the moisture from leaking into the hallway. Shakily, she got to her feet, and looked at the kitchen. Afzal lay there, face down, an arm outstretched, the other folded under his torso. He wasn't moving. From outside, Layla heard a sound. It was a car engine. She ran down the corridor, and discovered that she had an ankle sprain. The pain made her pull up, and she looked down to see the left ankle swollen and dark with a bruise. She limped to the window next to the bolted door and looked out. She was worried Ambani had sent reinforcements to check on them. Her fears were confirmed when she saw a black Ford. But a man and woman in suits were in the front seat. Layla frowned as the woman got out of the driving seat, and she suddenly recognised who it was. The female detective who had come to see her at the nail bar. Melania or something her name was. Layla banged on the window, trying to get their attention.

Tears of relief burst in her eyes. She wiped them and hit the window harder, then ran into the living room, which looked over the drive. The bay windows were wider, and she hit them with both her fists, and it was the male detective who noticed first. He came running, his face a mask of concern. The female detective was trying to open the door, and she gave up soon. They indicated to her to wait, and ran around the back. Layla heard a thump on the patio door, and her heart screamed out in panic. She didn't want them to come into the kitchen with the live electricity on the floor.

She ran to the end of the corridor. The kitchen had a rear entrance, and she could lean through, and see the patio door. Without stepping inside, she waved at them. She got their attention, and pointed at the floor. She didn't know if they understood, but they definitely saw Afzal lying on the floor. Layla waved her arm wildly, urging them to try the front windows. The male detective understood first.

Layla heard a crashing sound, which was repeated a few times. She hobbled to the front room to see two bricks on the carpet, and shattered glass on the floor. The windows were locked, and the male detective had to smash the glass a few time before one window pane gave way. He took off his jackets, and wrapped it around his head and face. He climbed on the ledge, then crawled in through the window.

'Are you okay?' he asked, approaching Layla. She felt so weak she had to sit down on the floor. 'I'm Detective Constable Oliver Walmsley,' he said. 'You'll be safe now, don't worry.' She remembered his name. She nodded, so exhausted she couldn't speak.

Oliver took the bolt off the front door, and he had to bend his back to do it. He opened the door, and Melanie stepped inside. She rushed in and knelt in front of Layla.

'What happened?'

Layla went to speak, then her voice got wobbly, and she started to cry. She managed to get some words out finally.

'Afzal was going to kill me. He spoke to someone on the phone, and they talked about hiding my body out here. He told me to cook a dish in the kitchen, and I think after that he was going to drag me out into the garden. There was a live wire in the socket that connected to the cooker—'

Melanie stretched an arm out, stopping Layla from speaking. 'It's okay,' she said. 'I understand. I can see what happened. We will need a full statement from you, but whatever happened was either an accident, or you acted in self-defence. Is that correct?'

Layla nodded in silence. Melanie stared at her as if she was trying to impart a message with her eyes.

'There will be an investigation into this, and what you say will be used in a court of law. It won't go to trial, as Afzal is already dead, and no one will represent him, unless he has family who want a trial. Do you understand? I know this is hard for you right now, but remember what you say is very important.'

Layla understood. Melanie was trying to help her. 'The live wire fell on the wet floor and Afzal was electrocuted. I saw it and managed to save myself by jumping on the kitchen counter.'

'Good.' Melanie smiled and squeezed her arm. 'Akbar Mahfuz has come to the police station. He is now under our protection, and you will see him later today.'

Layla got worried. Afzal had betrayed Noor. Melanie seemed to read the concern on her face.

'What is it?'

'Akbar and Noor...'

'Don't worry. He came clean about what he told Ambani and the others about Noor. He feels terrible about it. He was forced into betraying Noor. I believe him.'

Layla closed her eyes, and her head rested back on the doorframe she was leaning against.

CHAPTER 50

Rohan Roy pressed the digits on his phone, checking the undisclosed number again. He had walked to his car now, and was sitting inside. He banged his fist against his knee and the frustration boiled over. He smacked a fist against the dashboard and kicked the footwell. Then he got out of the car, he had to. He had left the train station, and had parked in an alley close to the city centre. He walked up and down, checking his phone. He was about to ring the traffic department to see if they had any triangulation leads on the phone signal, when there was an incoming call. It was an undisclosed number. He answered immediately.

'DCI Roy.'

There was silence from the other end. 'Answer, damn you,' Roy growled. To his surprise, a female voice spoke.

'How does it feel to find Robin and then lose him?'

'Lydia Moran. Is that you?'

'Oh yes, it is.'

'You have no idea what you're doing. Where are you? Where's Robin?' At the back of Roy's mind, confusion surfaced. Lydia couldn't be working alone, if she was speaking the truth of having Robin. She needed help. Who was it? The same people who helped her to escape?

'So many questions, Rohan, but so few answers.' Lydia tutted. 'Now you know what I feel like.'

'What do you mean?' With his left hand, Roy fished out his personal phone. He thumbed a message to Sergent David Bloomsdale in Traffic, whose number he had saved.

Check the number calling my phone now.

With any luck, Lydia had overplayed her hand. Now the signal could be geo located using triangulation. Roy needed to keep her talking.

Lydia said, 'You put my lover in jail, for life. For a crime he didn't commit. I lost him, just like you lost your brother.'

'You know what Stephen Burns did, Lydia, so don't cover for him. You were his partner, and you aided and abetted him in his disgusting crimes against children. What does that make you? Believe me, you'll be locked up soon, for the rest of your life, just like Burns.'

The laughter on the other end chilled him to the bone. 'Really? Then remember the price you will pay. Your brother's dead body, delivered to your door. And don't forget our network. We have friends all over the country. Your daughter will never be safe.'

'Keep trying, Lydia. Keep looking over your shoulder. You, and your despicable friends will never be safe either.'

'Enough talk!' Lydia yelled suddenly. 'I want you to release Stephen. I will send you details of another person, and you have to admit that they committed the alleged crimes against Robin and the other boys. You made a mistake convicting Stephen.'

'If you're joking, I suggest you try your luck as a comedian. On second thoughts, don't bother. That's the worst joke I've ever heard.'

'I'm laughing at you, Rohan. Do you want to see your brother alive, or not?'

Roy went still for a second. 'What do you mean?'

'Manufacture the evidence against the man whose detail I'll send you now. Stephen will ask for a new trial on the grounds of contradictory evidence. He will secure a release, and you get Robin back.'

'Seriously, Lydia, you need to try better than that.' He gnashed his teeth together. 'This won't end well for you. Where is Robin?'

'Wouldn't you like to know.'

'You're bluffing. So far, you've not sent me any proof.'

Lydia went silent, but he heard sounds on the phone like she was tapping the key pad. A photo came up on his screen, and when he looked at it, he couldn't breathe. It was Jayden, or Robin as he called him now. He was tied up on a chair, head held upright by someone pulling on his hair. There was a gag in his mouth. He had bruises on his cheeks and forehead, someone had roughed him up. Roy breathed fire in his nostrils, and rage ignited in his veins, clouding his eyes.

'Happy now?' Lydia asked sweetly. 'I'll send you the details now. Start the process, or the next photo you get is of Robin's head separated from his body. Then we come after your daughter.'

The phone went dead. Roy stared at it for a few seconds, unable to think. He checked the photo again, zooming in on the face. Then he stuffed the phone in his pocket, and walked up and down the alley. Seeing Robin like that had shocked him, but he needed to get over it.

Where could his brother be? And who had taken him?

He got the phone out again, and leant against the wall. He put a foot against the wall, standing on one leg as he looked at Robin's photo carefully. The background was dark, it was clearly a room, with light coming in from the left, probably the window. Which meant it was taken in daylight. The back wall was dark and bare. So was the floor. The man who held Robin's hair from behind was only visible up to the chest height. Which meant he was a tall man. Roy zoomed in on the photo again. Now, he could see the hand that clutched Robin's hair. On the second finger he saw a ring. A big, round, gold ring with a letter on it that he couldn't read. A distant memory sparked in his mind, then died. He had seen a ring like that on someone.

Who? His mind scurried round like a fox hunting for food. Why was that ring familiar? He could get a closer image if he took it to the cyber lab. Without a doubt, it belonged to the man who had helped Lydia escape, and then capture Robin.

He ran back to the car, and set off for the nick. His phone went off again, and he drove with one hand while he answered. Traffic was thicker in the afternoon, and his old car didn't have a siren. Several times he had to honk and beep, attracting yells from irate motorists.

'DCI Roy.'

Oliver's excited voice came on the line. 'We've got Layla, and also Akbar.'

CHAPTER 51

MIR, or Major Incident Room 1 was full to the brim. Melanie was at the lectern, just in front of the wall projector, the screen showing photos of the farmhouse where Layla was rescued from.

'Layla could easily have been our next victim. She showed real courage in her self-defence. There might be a trial over Afzal's death, but we know the truth of what happened. Afzal's phone is with the cyber lab. The person who called to give the command hid their number. It could well be the same undisclosed number that appears several times on his phone. But there is one number that we recognise already. Sunil Ambani's.'

Melanie went through a few slides, showing Afzal, Ambani, and Paresh Mallya on the screen.

'We now also have the statements of Akbar Mahfuz. It seems Noor was reaching out to someone, and the others discovered that through Akbar. Hence she was killed. Layla confirms that Noor was in touch with someone, but she tragically died before she could share their identity with Layla. In any case, it remains likely that either Afzal or Ambani killed Noor that night. It was witnessed by the teenagers, whom we can call on again for an ID check, once we have Ambani in custody again. They're coming in today to look at Afzal's photos on file.'

Roy was sat in the front row, listening. At the mention of the teenagers, something clicked in his mind. He thought of the statement Marcus had made. He was the first to see the man sitting on Noor's body. Derby and Lucy, the other two, barely saw the man before he went through the window and climbed down the tree.

Short, dark hair. I didn't see his hands.

That's what Marcus said. But was there a chance the man turned around, and saw Marcus as he came up the stairs. A concern unfurled in Roy's mind, and he raised his hand. Melanie stopped speaking and pointed at him. 'Yes, guv.'

'We need to keep the teenagers secure. I want to see Marcus and the others today. When are they arriving?'

'They should be here already.'

'Okay.' Roy stood and walked over to stand next to Melanie. He indicated to Oliver and Riz to open the blinds, then stopped as he remembered how much time they wasted trying to do it. He asked Melanie to switch the lights on instead. The dimness lifted as the spotlights in the ceiling slowly came to life.

'Our job is now clear,' Roy said. In the front row, he

saw Natalie as well, listening to him with close attention. She smiled when their eyes met, and he nodded at her.

'We have enough evidence in the form of statements and phone records, to arrest and charge Sunil Ambani. We know where he is. Apart from the human trafficking crimes, he also had the motive and opportunity to kill Noor. The hunt is on for Paresh Mallya, and we will get him soon. His phone number is on Afzal's, without a doubt. It's just a matter of locating him. Ambani first, then the others.'

He paused for a few seconds. 'I don't want another young life on our hands, so can we please patrol the houses of the three teenagers who found our victim. Marcus especially, as there might be a chance the killer saw him. I'll speak to him myself, and to his parents.'

Roy pointed to Inspector Jonty Adams, who would lead the arrest. 'We need at least three teams for Ambani, one for the back and front of his house, and one to block the main exit road. Does the surveillance report show he's at home right now?'

Adams nodded. 'Yes, just heard from them. He was last seen coming out yesterday evening around ten p.m. He went for a walk, then went back in after half hour. He's not been seen today, so far.'

'Any visitors?'

'Not that the team saw.'

Roy pondered for a while. 'Does his house have a rear exit?'

'Yes, the back garden opens out into an alley that runs across the whole street, and all houses have access to it. The surveillance team patrol the alley once an hour. He's not left through there, guv, I can assure you.'

Roy wasn't so sure, and he was glad they were going to nab Ambani now. 'Let's get moving. Bullet and stab proof vests, everyone. We don't know who's holed up in that house, or what reception we get.'

The meeting broke up, and Roy was the first one out. He had given his phone to Sergeant David Bloomsdale up in Traffic as soon as he arrived, and he was hoping the enlarged photo of Robin would be ready. He called David, but the photos weren't ready.

'A couple of hours they said. Sorry, guv.'

'No worries. Call me as soon as you know.'

'I will.'

Roy hung up. Riz and Oliver were walking past the desk to get kitted up, and he joined them.

'What's happening with Martin Donald?' Riz asked. 'We have to let him go, don't we?'

'That's right. We have nothing against him. Personally, I think he loved Noor. But I still want to check out his alibi. Was he at the pub the night of her murder?'

'Yes. We got CCTV, and I spoke to the pub manager who knows him as a regular.'

'Well then, one of you can do the honours, and sign him out. But make sure he stays in Sheffield in case we need to speak to him again.'

They got to the supplies counter and joined the queue for their gear. With the uniforms, they put on their chest rigs, and checked their extendable steel batons. Roy wondered if they should have an AFO or authorised firearms officer, with them. So far, he hadn't seen any evidence of guns, but one never knew. In the end, he decided against it. He would be the first person in the house, and it would be his chest the bullets would find, not his teams. He could live with that.

Riz drove with Roy in the front, while Melanie and Oliver sat in the back. Natalie remained at the base, and would draw up some paperwork to charge Ambani. Two vans with uniforms went ahead of them, and when they flicked on their sirens and flashing blues, so did Riz. They sliced through the late-afternoon traffic, and arrived at Hillsborough within twenty minutes.

Riz cut the sirens, and they drove quietly to the address. The van had moved to the rear of the property, after dropping a group of uniforms off at the street before. Roy and the others joined. They peeked around the corner house.

'That's the surveillance car,' Melanie whispered, pointing to a white builder's van. It was in need of a paint, and had a couple of dents on the sides. No one could tell there was four tv screens in the back, and a whole portable lab to analyse sights and sounds. Even the most intense scrutiny wouldn't reveal the cameras disguised inside the headlight and wing view mirrors, or in the luggage rail on top of the van.

Only one person was visible in the driver's seat. The van was three doors down from Ambani's house, on the opposite side. The house was at the other end of the street, and they had to walk a fair bit to get there.

'Let's circle around the back,' Roy suggested.

'We already have a unit there. Do you want them to breach?' Melanie asked.

Roy thought, then shook his head. 'No. Let's go ahead. On my count of three.'

He counted, then set off at a brisk jog. As he got to the house, a uniform's car screeched around the corner, and a burly officer jumped out. He had the portable battering ram and Roy stood to one side as the constable smashed the door down with one hefty swing of the ram. He stood to one side and Roy crashed in, shouting 'Police!'. He was in a narrow landing, which was well decorated. The carpets were almost new, and so was the painting. The living room was empty, as was the back room and the kitchen. Roy saw a shattered wine glass on the floor, and some liquid that was almost dry. He had a quick look at the garden. It was about thirty feet, and ivy covered the back fence. Another uniform team was in the path beyond, so he wasn't too worried about Ambani escaping from there.

He swept around to the front, just as Riz and Oliver came in. 'Stay here, let me clear upstairs first,' Roy said. Before he went up the stairs, a mark on the wall caught his eye. A dark stain, almost turning to black. He leant in for a closer look. Blood turned rusty black when exposed, and this was a blood stain. He ran up the stairs, shouting Ambani's name. He found more marks on the wall, as if someone had touched a bloody hand for support as they went upstairs. The bathroom door was open, and a body was slumped on the floor, face down. It was Ambani.

Roy rushed in and, with gloved hands, took the pulse

at the neck. There was none. The skin felt cold, and Ambani wasn't breathing. A blackening pool of blood had spread under his abdomen. His eyes stared at the floor. Ambani was dead.

CHAPTER 52

Roy crouched by the body, having put on shoe covers and a mask on his face. From the skin coldness, and the mottling, he could tell Ambani had been dead for a good few hours. The limbs and chest also felt stiff, which meant rigor mortis was settling into the larger muscles – always a sign that death had occurred more than five to six hours ago. The pooling of blood on the floor meant that he had bled out, and an abdominal wound was more than likely. He didn't want to turn the body over before Dr Patel arrived. The rest of the body had no obvious wounds. The knuckles on the hand had some scrapes on them, which signified a struggle.

He heard the door open downstairs, then footsteps coming up. Dr Patel arrived, prim and proper as ever in her charcoal skirt suit, freshly pressed. She put down her briefcase and snapped gloves on.

'Look on the bright side. It's an older victim. From what I hear, not the greatest of characters either.'

'That he wasn't,' Roy said. 'But my job would be easier if he was alive.'

'That means he was killed to make your life harder. Too much knowledge can be a dangerous thing.' She arched her left eyebrows, then knelt and opened up her briefcase. She removed the rectal thermometer from its casing. Rizwan came up the stairs. He put on a face mask and apron and helped Dr Patel pull the victim's trousers down and take the rectal thermometer reading. Roy took the ear temperature with a digital thermometer.

Dr Patel noted both the readings, which were almost similar. 'Not surprising,' she said. 'We're not in the open, and there's no lake or river nearby. Core temperature is fifteen degrees Celsius, so I'd say time of death was around midnight last night. Did he have any visitors?'

Roy shook his head slowly. He had spoken to the surveillance team already. 'No. Their microphones picked up voices inside the house however. Ambani was living here on his own, so someone was here last night. The only way they could've entered is the rear. I think he opened the kitchen back door to let this person in – there's no sign of breaking and entering. There was a fight in the kitchen, hence the smashed glass and liquid. On the carpet in the landing, there's drops of blood. The carpet's dark, so I didn't see it at first. Riz pointed them out.'

'That's right,' Riz said. 'Ollie and I saw it, and also blood stains on the landing wall. He was probably pressing his abdominal wound to stem the bleeding as he went up the stairs. But why didn't he go out the front door?'

Dr Patel said, 'Maybe his attacker stopped him, and it was locked.'

'Anyway,' Roy said, 'He staggered up here, then collapsed. MO is the same as Noor's, so I think it was the same person. He also had to be physically fit to climb the back fence, and overpower Ambani. Fits the profile of Noor's killer.'

Roy stood. He heard Justin Dobson's voice, the head of Scene of Crime. He went up to the landing to see Justin clambering up the stairs, fully clad in his sterile blue Tyvek coating. He stopped when he saw Roy.

'We've got to stop meeting like this,' Justin said.

'You owe me a detailed report on the first victim. There must be more from the rest of the site.'

'There is, but you don't have any patience. I have to help out Derbyshire Constabulary as well, don't forget.' Justin came up the stairs, and Roy moved out of the way.

'I haven't forgotten, but we've now got two dead bodies, not one. Double trouble, and this one was unexpected. So stop making excuses.'

Justin appeared to take that on the chin. He frowned. 'Hang on, there was something. Oh yes. Multiple hair strands which don't belong to the victim. Must be the killer's. So we do have some DNA samples from the hair follicles. However, no match on the database. Sorry,' Justin shrugged.

Roy nodded his appreciation. 'At least we have some DNA, that's good. Unfortunately, our main suspects are both dead.'

Justin frowned and looked at Ambani's prone figure. 'Double vision? You really need to stop the LSD.'

'He's not here, Einstein. Have you been to the farmhouse to see the electrified stiff? He was our other suspect.'

'Ah yes. Mr Toastie, I called him. He's on the slab now. Gosh, you're racking them up, Rohan. Who's next?'

'Might be you if you don't hurry up,' Roy muttered as he went down the stairs. He was gutted, in fact. A confession from Ambani would've meant the end of this case. Layla's family was aware of her now, and she would be flying home soon. So would Akbar. Natalie would sort out all of that. His phone rang and he answered.

'Speak of the Devil. I was just thinking of you.'

Natalie sounded surprised. 'Really? Maybe you need my help after all.'

'Ambani's dead. Now we have to find the real killer, who probably killed Ambani to hide his own identity.' As he said the words, an uneasy sensation flared at the back of his mind. The hair stood up on the back of his neck, and he looked around. He was out on the road, surrounded by police cars, and blue lights. And yet, he felt like someone was watching him. A couple of onlookers had arrived, but the uniforms were moving them along. No, he felt something else. He glanced at the houses opposite, where he could see shapes behind the net curtains. Roy didn't like the weirdness of it. He shook his head, got back to Natalie.

'The search for Paresh Mallya heats up now. Did you

get any leads from Daniel Jones?'

'None, sorry. But we'll find Paresh, don't worry. He can't be far. I looked in the Home Office records, and he hasn't left the country yet.' There was a quiet confidence in Natalie's voice that Roy liked.

'Thanks,' he said. 'Are you sticking around? If not, I'll see you tomorrow.'

'I might be here, depending if you're back by six. If not, hasta manana.'

Roy's Spanish was practically non-existent, but even he knew what that meant. 'Till tomorrow,' he said, and hung up.

He did a 360, taking in the scene around him. That odd feeling was still there, like he was missing something right in front of him. Or someone. And that person was here, watching him. He got this feeling late in an investigation. He couldn't explain it, but his senses were tingling, and there was something here, just out of reach.

What was he missing?

CHAPTER 53

Ambani's body was getting loaded onto the ambulance. Roy's phone rang again, and it was Sarah. He answered swiftly

'You okay?' He was on edge, the portent of something evil just around the corner sticking to his skin like a burn.

'Yes, are you? I heard from Mel you guys were out to arrest Ambani.'

'He's dead,' Roy sighed. 'Been that way since last night. The surveillance didn't stop it. No one saw the killer, and it looks like it's the same guy.' Roy described the crime scene to Sarah.

'To get in, and get out, he had to leave the same way. Nothing in the back garden? Or the fence? One of the neighbours might've seen something.'

'Nothing in the garden. Maybe tomorrow with fresh

eyes Justin and his boys might pick something up. Door to door has started, no sighting as yet.' Roy stifled a yawn. He realised he was starving, and knackered.

'Sounds like you need to go home.'

'No way. Both the suspects are dead.'

'Yes, Mel told me about Afzal.' She paused. 'Any news of your brother? Or Lydia?'

Roy walked to one side, and lowered his voice. 'Yes.' He told her about the recent call from Lydia.

'Bloody cheek,' Sarah hissed. 'That bitch needs to get locked up for life. Are you sure she sent you Robin's photos?'

'Yes, definitely. I'm waiting to hear from cyber-crime.'

'Do you want me to come over? Two heads are better than one.'

Suddenly, Roy really wanted Sarah to be there. She was his island of calm in a storm. He didn't want to admit it, but he missed her terribly.

'No, it's fine,' he lied. 'You've got to be there for Matt, and you need a rest yourself. Don't worry, all under control here.'

'Rohan,' Sarah said quietly. 'Don't do anything rash, OK?'

'Not had a rash in ages. All good.'

'Shut up, will yer? Did you hear owt of what I said?' Sarah's native Yorkshire accent became stronger when she was annoyed.

'Yes, I did. I'll call you, don't worry.'

He hung up, and saw Dr Patel coming out of the house with Melanie and Rizwan. Oliver had already left to start the paperwork. Inspector Adams walked up to him.

''Ey yup. Got a report back from the door to door. Early days yet, but so far, no one's seen owt.'

'Great.' Roy shook his head. 'So someone just pops in, kills a man under surveillance, and no one's see him. Must be a ghost.'

He turned to Mel and Riz. 'Let's check out the rear.' He bid Dr Patel goodbye, and she promised to work on the body first thing in the morning.

'But I think we know already that the MO is exactly the same. A deep stabbing wound in the abdomen. The killer left no fingerprints. Chances are it's the same person. By the way, Justin has found hair samples that might belong to the killer, and I have some skin scrapes from under the nails. I will see if there's a match with the skin samples I got from Noor.'

'Thanks, doc. See you tomorrow.'

Roy and the others walked to the alley at the rear of the street. He saw the park behind immediately, with the waist-high fence. It was getting dark now, and at night, anyone wearing black clothes would be virtually invisible. Now he knew how the killer had escaped.

He went to the house fence and examined it. He could see some boot marks on it, but they needed closer inspection in the morning. All the houses had similar fencing, some with trellis and ivy on top. Ambani's house had a simple fence, without any spikes or trellis. Under cover of dark, he imagined a strong man could easily climb this fence quickly.

'Ask uniform to do a search here,' he said. 'I doubt they'll find anything and the park's too dark now anyway. But I want this place turned inside out tomorrow.'

'I'll tell Justin,' Rizwan said, and left. Roy stifled a yawn and put both hands on his waist. He rubbed his forehead.

'I guess the teenagers have been and gone?'

Melanie shook her head. 'They've just turned up now. Do you still want to speak to them?'

'Yes, and also to Daniel Jones. He must know more than he's letting on. I mean, he took cash payments for the rent, and didn't tell the council who his tenants were. That's dodgy enough. Given how much he knew about Martin and Noor, I suspect he was deeper in with Ambani and the others.'

'How about Martin, in that case?' Melanie asked. 'Surely he knew more about what Noor was up to?'

'Martin's all bark and no bite, to be honest. I think he was genuinely in love with Noor, but she didn't trust him totally. She was up to something, and didn't tell Martin, or Layla anything.'

'She found out something she had to be killed for, you think?'

'Yes, just like Ambani was. I think Noor found out who the real leader of the human trafficking gang is.

Ambani obviously knew who he was. He could be Paresh Mallya, Ambani's business partner. It's time we dug more into him.'

Roy set off with long steps, then turned around to face the others as a disturbing thought struck him again.

'Before he gets any of the teenagers, especially Marcus.'

CHAPTER 54

Natalie placed a tray of four steaming hot mugs and an assortment of biscuits on the table. Her action was met with murmurs of approval from Roy, Melanie, Riz and Ollie. The tea was malty and strong, just what Roy needed.

'You get brownie points for that,' he said, picking up a chunky biscuit and dunking it, then taking a bite. 'No pun intended.'

'Thought I'd make myself useful. I've spoken to the Home Office, and got visas arranged for Layla and Akbar to go home to their families. They will be escorted back, and handed over to my Indian counterpart there. It's late now, but I'll speak to the guy in India tomorrow.'

'You've been busy.' Melanie smiled. 'No wonder you stayed back.'

'And we'll find Paresh Mallya as well,' Natalie said,

her face getting serious. 'He's the only missing cog in the wheel now. And probably the most important one.'

The others nodded. Natalie was standing, a formidable expression on her face. 'I made some enquiries with my Indian counterpart. He's called Inspector Kohli. He said Mr Mallya is well known in the state of Gujrat. He's close to the chief minister's son apparently. It's one of the reasons why he's managed to escape the law so far. The IPS, or Indian Police Service is interested in him, as one woman implicated him in trafficking her to Bangladesh. She managed to escape back to India, which is easier from Bangladesh. The police interrogated Mr Mallya, but nothing happened after that.'

Roy sat back and folded arms across his chest. 'That's very interesting. And now Mallya is hiding here, and could well be the man we want. Well done, Natalie.' He looked at his watch, then at the others. 'Where's Marcus?'

'In the family room in reception, with his parents,' Rizwan replied. 'Shall I tell them you're on your way.'

Roy drained his cup, and stood. 'Yes please.' He was about to leave when Natalie called him back.

'I've got some photos of Mallya which you might want to keep, and distribute.' She handed all of them passport photos of the man that they could store in their pockets.

As Roy walked towards the reception, he checked his phone. Sergeant Bloomsdale had left a message, and so had Lydia Moran. He checked Bloomsdale's text first. He had found data on the photos sent by Lydia, and he had left an envelope for Roy on his desk. Roy's heart rate kicked up a notch. He thought of going up to Traffic, but he needed to speak to Marcus's parents first.

Lydia's text was more cryptic. *How long do you want to wait for before you lose your brother for good?*

Roy ground his teeth together, and hurried over to the family room. A middle-aged couple looked up as he entered, with Marcus sat between them. Emily, the FLO or family liaison officer nodded at Roy and left. He sat down and clasped his hands.

'Thank you for coming in. We think the man who killed the young woman is still on the loose. I don't want to alarm you, but I do want you to be careful where you go, and who you see. Get home early in the evening,' Roy looked at Marcus, who seemed worried. 'And always tell your parents where you are. Don't meet strangers. The man we suspect now is called Paresh Mallya. I have a photo of him.' Roy showed the passport photo Natalie had given him.

'Keep a copy for yourself,' Roy handed over three photos. 'If you ever see this man, or anyone similar to him, report him to us immediately.' Roy gave Marcus and his parents his number. Then he fixed upon Marcus.

'I'd like you to think back to that night. When you saw the man sitting on top of the woman, did he turn to look at you?'

Marcus stared back at Roy, then his eyes flickered down. He blinked a couple of times.

'Yes. Yes, I think so. He was half turned when I shone the torchlight on him. I shouted, and that's when we he got up and ran.'

'So it's possible he saw you. Now think about that moment carefully, Marcus. You said he wore a black jacket, he had short black hair, and you didn't see his hands, or any bare skin. Is that correct?'

'Yes.'

'What skin colour do you think he was?'

'White,' Marcus said without hesitation.

'How can you be so confident when you didn't see any bare skin?'

Marcus gaped at Roy again, then realisation dawned on his face. 'No, I see what you mean. He had short hair, which tapered down to the back of his neck. His neck was white.'

Roy frowned. Paresh Mallya was a reasonably fair-skinned North Indian, would he really pass off as white? Maybe.

'Thank you. Did you see any other part of his body?'

'No, sorry. Now that I think back, maybe he wore dark gloves hence I didn't see his hands.'

Roy was thoughtful. 'How big was he? Really huge, like a rugby lad?'

Marcus shook his head. 'No, not like that. He was slim, but wide-shouldered. He was quick on his feet.'

'Hmm. Anything else?'

'Not that I can think of.'

'OK. Please be careful as we discussed.'

Roy left, and hurried up to Traffic. His mind was

churning again. Did Paresh Mallya have a partner they didn't know about? It would make sense as Mallya was an Indian national, after all.

Roy strode into the Traffic main floor, where the desks were all empty. In one corner, the duty team were sat around chatting and looking bored. Roy waved at them, and they waved back. He went to Bloomsdale's desk, and saw an envelope with his name on it. He snatched it up and tore into it eagerly.

Inside, the photo Lydia had sent of Robin was printed out and enlarged.

Roy looked carefully at the close-up of the hand that gripped Robin's hair. The ring now stood up in sharp relief. The gold ornament had a circle on it, with the initial LB on it.

Roy stared intently at the ring and scoured the depths of his memory; all the nooks and crannies. He had seen that ring. Where? And then, suddenly, in a brilliant flash of light, he knew.

A few weeks ago, when he had interrogated the vile Kevin Rawlinson, the man had made a meaty fist several times, placing his hand on the desk. Light had glinted off the ring, drawing Roy's eyes to it.

LB. Loxley Boys. The gang that Kevin and his dad ran.

The jigsaw pieces were now falling into place and a truly horrific picture was emerging. His breathing was harsh and fast as his heart boomed against his ribs.

Kevin had helped Lydia escape. He had provided the muscle to kidnap Robin. Which meant….

Feverishly, Roy looked at the rest of the documents in the envelope. On an A4 piece of paper he found a map of Sheffield, with an area marked in red. On the side, David had scribbled a message.

When the photo was taken, location services was turned on. It was in Hillsborough. I put the coordinates on the map, marked in red. Hope this helps. Cheers, David.

Roy put the papers in his pocket, then ran out of the office. He took three stairs at a time, deciding not to wait for the lifts. After four floors, he jumped on the last landing, and ran out of the rear doors into the car park. It was dark, and the headlights of a car blinded him as it came into the car park. He was exhausted, but the adrenaline now bubbling in his veins powered him on.

He got into his car and zoomed out of the car park, heading for the location in the map.

CHAPTER 55

Roy drove fast, jumping traffic lights and getting flashed by the cameras. He didn't care. He also knew he couldn't generate a welcoming committee courtesy of sirens and blue lights. He needed a realistic chance of getting Jayden, or Robin, back and stealth was vital. He expected Jayden to be guarded. He had to overpower whoever was there, and for that he needed the element of surprise. Kevin and his men weren't expecting him. That was his main weapon.

He thought of who he could call for help. Riz and Oliver would be going home soon, and he didn't want to disturb anyone else. In the end, he decided to call Sarah. He told her what was happening.

'You can't go there alone,' she said immediately. 'Let me come with you.'

'Don't be daft. It's going to be tricky. I'm going to call

for help if I get into trouble. What I don't want to do is alarm them, and they move Robin someplace else.'

Sarah was silent for a while. Wind whistled in through the window as the car sped down the quiet streets. Drops of rain landed on the windscreen.

'I've got a bad feeling about this,' she whispered.

'Let me check the place out first. I might be able to get him out. I'm almost there.' He checked the satnav, he was about five minutes away.

'Give it an hour. If you don't hear from me, then send an alert to the duty traffic team. I'll send you the coordinates when I arrive.'

'Be careful, Rohan.'

He hung up, and slowed down as he approached the address. The residential streets had flown past, and he was now in the outskirts of Hillsborough, in an industrial estate. He killed the headlights, and drove past it slowly. The hulking, menacing shadows of a large warehouse stood in the dark. Roy parked the car and got out. He put his radio on silent. The extendable baton was on his waist, and that had always been good enough for cracking skulls and breaking windows.

He went to the steel fence and peered inside. Grass and shrubs grew wild, but the paths were clear. A couple of vans and fork lift trucks were parked outside. This warehouse was in operation. No lights were visible, and the place looked deserted. Clouds had blanked out what little starlight remained, and Roy could feel drops of rain on his face. He ran along the fence, which was too tall for him to climb, till he found a gate. It was padlocked. He ran further till he found a thick oak tree that grew over the fence. He climbed the tree, and edged along a thick branch that reached out over the other side.

The branch creaked and bent under his weight, the further he went along. He didn't want it to break. The ground was almost ten feet below him. A fall would land him in the tall grass, that should provide some meagre support. The branch made a cracking sound and dipped again. Roy grit his teeth, and jumped.

He landed on the balls of his feet, and rolled over quickly. He hit the vegetation, and leaves and tall grass slapped him in the face. Pain flared in his ankles, but he was up on his feet swiftly, ignoring the pain. He could weight bear, and the pain was bearable.

He half ran, half limped to the rear of the warehouse. There was a door at the back, which was locked. He leant on it, but it was solid cast iron, and wouldn't budge. He looked up, and saw a steel walkway that went around the warehouse. There had to be a staircase leading up to that. He moved as fast as he could, but couldn't find it. He was starting to lose hope, and patience. His only path seemed the front door, which he knew would be locked.

Then he found something hiding beneath thick ivy on a rusty part of the wall. It was a latch key, and when he released it, a fire escape ladder slithered down in parts, like a loft ladder. He lowered it all the way to the ground, then climbed it slowly. He reached the walkway, and peered in through a crack in the steel wall. Rain dribbled down, obscuring his vision. But he could now make out the glow of lights inside. The cracks weren't wide enough for him to see much else.

Taking care of how much sound his heavy boots made on the walkway, he circled around. The warehouse was big, and it took him a while to go around the first bend. Several trees leant in across the fence, and the leaves brushed his face as he ran on.

He came across a door. There was a latch on it, but he unlocked it easily enough. He opened the door a crack, and waited. His eyes were now used to the dark, and he could see another walkway that circumnavigated the upper floor of the warehouse. There was an office a couple of hundred yards away, but it was empty. On the ground floor, he could see stacked pallets with wrapped boxes of various sizes. Lights were on in the middle, and he saw a man walk across the floor, and disappear behind some pallets. He could hear voices. Suddenly, a sharp cry came from where the man had gone to.

Roy opened the door wider, and stepped into the walkway.

CHAPTER 56

R oy bent low at the waist and ran silently along the
walkway. The steel structure was hard enough to take
the weight of several men at the same time, but he didn't
want it to creak. He considered taking off his shoes, but
discarded the idea. He would only have to put them on
when he reached the floor, and that might be too late.

He saw another man crossing the floor, and headed to
the same spot the earlier man had gone to. Another
skinhead, burly and barrel-chested. Roy waited till the man
had gone past, then went down the staircase. The stairs were
long, and he moved as fast as he could. He was in the light
now, and could be spotted easily. A bloodcurdling scream
stopped him in his tracks. Then he heard a high-pitched cry
like before, followed by someone pleading. 'No, no. Please,
no.'

The scream came again. Roy ran down the last steps,

throwing caution to the wind. He could hear the man being tortured now. He knew that voice, it was Robin. He ran forward to a stack of pallets, flattening himself against it. He recognised another voice. A female one. Lydia Moran.

'Talk to him. Just do it, if you want to live!' Lydia hissed loudly, then Roy heard the sound of flesh hitting flesh, followed by a wail of pain. Rage spiked in his blood, and he gnashed his teeth together. He crept out of the stack and peered out. The crates of pallets were placed at regular intervals, and through them he caught movement. A thick-set, tall man stood with hands on his hips. It was Kevin Rawlinson.

'He won't talk. I'm not sure if this is worth it,' Kevin said to someone Roy couldn't see. Then Kevin moved, and his heart lurched against his ribs. Jayden was tied to a chair, and his face was masked with blood. His eyes were black shadows, and they were swollen. Blood had soaked his shirt, caked his chest with darkening crimson shades. He was still breathing, but he was in terrible shape. His head rolled forward.

Roy retreated and leant back against the pallet. He looked around him wildly. How many men were here? Two that he had seen, and Kevin. Three at least, four including Lydia. But there might be more. He caught a smell in the enclosed air of the warehouse. A deep, distinctive odour. He inhaled deeply, and recognised it. Gasoline. Somewhere in the warehouse there was a store of gasoline.

He went to the other side of the pallet he was hiding behind, and looked. He could now see he main entrance. There was open space between where the line of pallets ended, and the door. He couldn't rush out there. But he saw a jacket hanging on the last pallet, next to a forklift truck. Roy stole up to it, bent low at the waist. He heard steps, then saw a man coming up to the forklift truck. Roy dived in between two pallets, on the brink of being seen. He went still, his heart banging frantically. He breathed through an open mouth. Had he been spotted? He heard footsteps, then they got closer. He moved further back. His back slithered against some plastic, and he stopped.

He was now going back the way he had come, closer to where Robin was being held. He hoped and prayed the man didn't hear him. He hid behind another pallet, and listened. He heard the steps fading, then another scream split the air.

Roy went out to the forklift truck, stopping behind a pallet and looking around first. Behind the truck, he could see the ring of three men, and a slighter shape that was Lydia. One man was holding Robin's head up, while the others watched.

Roy looked inside the jacket that hung next to the truck. He found a packet of cigarettes and a lighter. He had a penknife in his pocket. He ran back to his original position. To his left, behind the shadow of the steel walkway, he saw the plastic flaps of a partition. He darted towards it. The smell of gasoline was now stronger. He went inside, it was pitch black. Cupping the torchlight, he moved the beam around. Two floor-to-ceiling plastic tanks stood in a row. They stored the petroleum needed to run the factory.

He went to the nearest, and felt it with his hands. It was tough, but it also moved. He took out the pocket knife and selected the tallest blade. He plunged it into the plastic. He had to do it three times before he felt the plastic give way, and the knife go through. Then a trickle of dark liquid appeared. The smell of petrol filled the air.

'Bingo,' Roy whispered.

He went into a stabbing frenzy, smashing the knife to the hilt into the plastic. Sweat drenched his head, and his shirt stuck to his back. He kept going till his arms were like lead, and his breath came in gasps.

Now there was a pool of gasoline on the floor, a black river flowing into the warehouse outside. Roy went back outside. He fished out the lighter, and held it in his palms. Then he went to the pallet nearest to Robin. He heard Kevin's voice.

'If he's not going to talk to his brother, then no point in waiting. Get rid of him.'

Roy lit the lighter flame, then hurled it towards the slick of gasoline. At the same time he broke into a run, heading for Robin. Kevin was the first person who heard him coming. He turned around and his mouth opened in surprise as Roy launched himself at him in a rugby tackle.

As he slammed into Kevin, propelling him backwards, an explosion ripped through the warehouse, knocking everyone off their feet.

CHAPTER 57

A red-yellow fireball of heat exploded behind Roy, singeing his back. He had knocked Kevin to the floor, but was dazed himself. The lights had disappeared, and the entire place was smoky and hot like an active volcano crater. Kevin lay still on the floor, and Roy scrambled off him, coughing and spluttering, his eyes burning. He fell to his knees, fumes choking his breath.

'Robin!' he cried out, then realised his folly. 'Jayden!' He got to his feet, swaying with his hands out for balance. He heard the furious crackle behind him, and the heat of the approaching fire. It was a terrifying sight when he glanced up; the pallets had caught fire and huge yellow plumes licked all the way up to the ceiling. He had no time to waste. He remembered the most important thing from his fire-management training – fire sucked out the oxygen, making it impossible to breathe.

He tore off his shirt, and tied it around his nose and mouth. He stepped forward, where the chair had been, groping in the darkness like a bland man. Debris filled the air, and the stench of gas was like a tidal wave, submerging his senses. He stumbled across a body. It was lying still. He felt for the face, and, in the light, he saw an inert skinhead. One of Kevin's goons. He got up and stumbled ahead. Behind him, he heard a cough. He saw the outline of the chair, and rushed towards it. It was on the floor, and Robin was still tied to it.

He sank to his knees and felt Robin's carotid pulse at the neck. It was present. Feverishly, he tore at the ropes. The chair legs had broken, and he snapped them off like twigs. The knots around Robin's hands and ankles were tight, and he had to dig in with his fingers. Sweat blinded his eyes with salt, and he wiped them, coughing into his makeshift mask. The lack of oxygen was starting to make him dizzy. The heat was now like the mouth of a furnace, burning his face.

His fingers got fatigued, and he had to take a break. He patted Robin's face, but he didn't stir. He was still breathing, he could tell by the chest movements. His brother was unconscious, and he wasn't a light man. Somehow, Roy needed the strength to carry him out the front door. If they didn't get burnt alive before that.

He managed to get the knots off, and the hands and ankles free. The process had exhausted him, but he had no time to rest. He pulled Robin towards him, and stood up, yanking his brother into a sitting position. He felt more than heard the sound above him. The burning pallets crackled loudly, had disguised sound. He whirled around as a meaty fist swung at him, and he ducked at the last minute, the fist catching his shoulder. Then a burly shape barrelled into him, and breath burst from his chest as he was flung backwards.

He crashed on the floor, the man trying to get astride his chest. Roy skidded on his back, and his head bumped into the soft form of a prone human being. He rotated his waist, and managed to dislodge the man above. A fist crashed into his skull, sending rocket waves of pain cascading down his spine. His eyes went dim, the dark, burning air shimmered and blackened. Another blow to the side of his face made his body go numb.

'You fecking bastard,' he heard Kevin's raspy voice. 'This is the last time you mess with me.'

Roy could feel the blow coming, a whishing in the air. His survival instincts surged, like a drowning man thrusting above water. His hands groped around, and closed in over a loose chair leg. He raised it like a club, and smashed it over Kevin's head. The blow dislodged Kevin and Roy rolled around, getting to his knees. He could see Kevin's shape, and he hit him again, aiming for the head. The chair leg jarred in his hand as the blow cracked on Kevin's skull. Roy roared with rage, and hit Kevin again, till the body went limp.

He almost collapsed with exhaustion himself. He stood, swaying. He stumbled over Kevin, and got to Robin. Grunting with the effort, he managed to lift Robin on his back and went forward, one hand outstretched as he groped his way through the darkness, debris swirling around him. An explosion drove him to his knees, another red-yellow fireball that detonated across the warehouse space like an incendiary weapon. His arms went limp, and Robin fell to the floor. Roy couldn't breathe, nor could he see. Wave upon wave of exhaustion washed over him, and his body refused to obey his commands.

He groped on the floor, and found his brother. In the blazing yellow glow, he could see Robin's face. His nostrils flared as he breathed. It had taken Roy almost thirty years to find him. Was he about to lose him again? If he did, he would go with Robin. He couldn't bear the pain any more, he would rather die himself.

A voice spoke to him from the hidden recesses of his soul. It was his mother, gently admonishing him.

Bring my son back. I want to see him before I die. Bring him back, Rohan.

Emotion clogged his throat, and he felt moisture creep in his eyes. He had to move. From somewhere, he gathered the strength. He couldn't lift Robin any more, but he could pull him. He stood, and grabbed his brother's feet at his waist, and pulled him like a wheelbarrow. The smoke washed over his eyes, blinding him. The shirt had long fallen from his face, and he was now breathing in all the fumes that made him cough and retch, watering his eyes.

He dodged the burning pallets and, finally, the space opened up. He couldn't see anything yet, apart from the bits and pieces of flying rubbish, but he could feel the space. He picked up his pace with renewed vigour. He managed to get to the front door, and sagged against it. He beat it with his fist, but his strength was ebbing. He wiped his burning eyes and tried to find the best way to open the door. He pushed at the lever on the door, which was a single steel beam across it. The beam wouldn't budge, and the door remained locked. Roy kicked at it, but his legs were like lead. There was another explosion behind him, and another fireball tore and ripped at his back, flinging him against the door. He fell next to Robin, and gathered his brother to his chest. The light was fading in his eyes. The murky-yellow air darkened, and his eyes flickered.

'I'm sorry,' he whispered to his brother. 'I'm sorry.'

Then his eyes closed, and darkness encapsulated him.

CHAPTER 58

He heard a buzzing sound, like a swarm of bees attacking him. The sound grew louder, banging against the doors of his consciousness. He frowned, and tried to open his heavy eyelids. There was a dull glow somewhere, and the buzzing sound was more insistent. He forced an eye open, and all he could see was the yellow dimness. He was next to the door, and Robin lay next to him. The buzzing sound came again, and it was from the door. He craned his neck with difficulty. A red line was spreading across the top of the door frame, and it spread down in a straight line, making a square shape.

Fatigue made his eyes close again. The buzzing stopped and all of a sudden he felt a trickle of fresh air on his face. He gasped, and sucked in the air greedily, but he only convulsed into a fit of coughing. He heard another cough, it was Robin. He stirred, trying to pull Robin towards the source of the air.

A yawning, crashing sound filled the air. Something fell to the ground, shaking the earth. The fresh air was now an icy blast, cooling his fevered nerves. He moved more, still on the floor, pulling Robin with him, inching towards the open air. He heard voices, shouting, chattering, and distant sirens, their twisting whines getting louder.

Strong arms pulled him to safety, but he fought them as they tried to separate Robin. A shape dropped in front of him, and he heard a familiar voice.

'It's okay, Rohan, let go.' It was Sarah. 'They'll look after him.'

'Sarah, I…' he gasped, trying to reach for her. She took his hands and pressed them to her chest. He tried to stand, and she stopped him.

'Just rest.'

'No.' He coughed and turned around, retched. He went into a coughing frenzy, trailing mucus from his mouth in the grass. He looked up to see Robin being helped into a stretcher, and lifted into an ambulance.

'He's OK,' Sarah said. 'You need to go to hospital as well.'

He reached for her again, and managed to stand on his wobbly legs, almost leaning against her. She wiped the soot and muck from his face with a tissue. It was so good to see her. He looked at the burning warehouse. With a crash, a section of the ceiling collapsed. He was lucky to get out of there alive. The ambulance took off with sirens blazing.

'I need to go…go hospital,' he spluttered and coughed again.

'He's going to be fine,' Sarah said in a firm, calm voice. 'You also need to go there. Come on.'

Even in this weakened state, he could tell she knew he wouldn't get into an ambulance. She would drive him to the hospital. Then he thought of what just happened, and the immensity of that realisation landed on him like the Atlas mountains, crushing his senses.

All these years, he had waited for his brother. Never given up hope. Never believed he was dead. Never stopped searching. Now he had found Robin. After all these years.

The pain sharpened to a sword's tip, and drove into his heart. It spilled out all the hurt and suffering, and it burst out of his eyes in hot, saline waves.

'I found him,' he said, and to his own ears, his voice sounded strangely like a wail. But he didn't care. Tonight, he didn't care about anything. 'I found him,' he repeated, and fell into Sarah's arms.

Petite woman she was, half his size, she held him up with arms of steel, bore his weight without taking a step back, without flinching.

'It's OK,' she said in his ears. 'It's alright.'

He fell to his knees, and his arms encircled her waist. He gripped her hard, like she was the rock in the middle of a stormy sea, and his only lifeline.

CHAPTER 59

Roy closed his eyes and breathed gently. Sarah had stayed after the others had left, but now she too had gone. The nurse wanted him to rest.

He should be feeling bruised and battered and, physically, he was, but mentally he felt different. There was an open space in his heart now, a window through which light and sunshine poured in. He felt like he was looking at the hills of the Peak District, standing in his garden at Dore. That vast, wide view where the green, brown and distant blue hills claimed the horizon, spoke to the clouds. That deep, earthy smell of bracken and heather, borne in the wind, invigorating his lungs. Yes, he had looked upon the magnificent scenery, but he had not felt this calmness before. He didn't know it existed, to be honest.

All his life he had felt the absence of Robin like a knife in his guts. It felt strange not to feel that knife anymore. It sounded weird, and it was – but he had grown used to the hurt and pain. Over time, he had learnt to look upon his life in parallel – one without his brother, his real life. Sometimes, through a mist of pain, he would think of another life where Robin was alive, saw his parents, and they had a normal life.

Now that Robin was back, he didn't know where to start. What to say. How to explore the decades they had missed, and would never get back. But at least they could now do that. Now he could tell his parents, and he had to do that without delay. He would never forgive himself if either of them died without knowing Robin was alive.

He took the mask off his face. Then he screwed his eyes shut, and grimaced at the headache that lanced across his neck and back. But he forced himself to sit up in the bed. His feet searched for the slippers, then he stood. The door opened, and the nurse came in.

'You should be in bed.'

'I need the loo.' He turned to face her. She walked past him and tapped on the screen above the bed, silencing a bell-shaped red button that had clearly rung on her desk.

'Will you be able to get there?' The nurse faced him. He towered above her, and in the half light of the room, tried his best to look normal. As normal as possible in a lime-green NHS hospital gown, a bandage on his head, and slippers.

'I've been there before, so yes.'

Her eyes searched his face. 'You had quite the concussion. Not feeling dizzy, are you?'

Roy held up two fingers, then three, and counted them. The nurse shook her head. 'Not funny, DCI Roy.'

He shuffled towards the door, and the nurse followed him. He turned left on the corridor, and she went right. From the corner of his eyes, he made sure she was heading back to the desk at the other end of the corridor.

He had been to the Royal Hallamshire Hospital before, and knew the layout of the wards. There was a door before the bathroom that led to the staircase, which the doctors often used. He slipped through it, and emerged on the landing. So far, the nurse hadn't noticed. He climbed up a floor, and came out on the wider space of the fifth floor, with the triple lifts in front of him. He walked across to the right, to Duke Elder Ward, where Robin was staying. It was almost the end of visiting hours. A few people came out of the ward, relatives heading back home. No one questioned Roy as he walked in slowly, and headed for Robin's room.

He looked in through the glass panel, lowering the blinds. Robin was in his bed, and he looked asleep. Roy pushed the handle, and went in. He shut the door with a soft click. He watched Robin for a while. He had stitches on the right of his scalp, which was bandaged. The left side of his face, with the eye, was swollen in an ugly black bruise. But the right eye flickered open. It widened when Robin saw him standing there.

Roy dragged a chair and sat down next to the bed. A tube ran from Robin's right hand to a small bag on a stand. The bag was empty. He cleared his throat.

'How are you feeling?' Roy asked.

Robin was staring at him, the left eye barely open, but

Roy could tell both eyes were working. Robin licked his dry lower lip.

'Better,' he whispered. 'You're DCI Rohan Roy, is that right?'

'Yes.' Roy thought about his next sentence, then decided just to get on with it. 'I'm your brother. Your real name is not Jayden, it's Robin. Robin Roy. You were abducted when you were seven years old. A man called Stephen Burns took you, but he told you his name was Jerry Budden.'

Roy stopped. Robin's eyes glinted, and his nostrils flared. His jaws were clamped tight together, and his hand now clenched the bedsheet.

'Take it easy,' Roy said. 'It's alright. You're safe here. No one's going to hurt you.'

Tentatively, he reached out and touched Robin's forearm. It was stiff, and it didn't relax under his touch. Slowly, Roy withdrew his arm. As he did so, he noticed a change in Robin. He was tense, but in a different way. More curious than afraid.

Roy knew it was going to get harder to talk, and he wanted to get it over and done with.

'You were taken from me while we were playing in the woods. Our parents and the police searched, but you disappeared. The police found the bodies of the two missing boys that Burns had taken. But you were never found.'

He stopped. Robin was trying to sit up. Roy reached forward. 'I wouldn't do that if I were you. Do you want something?'

Robin glanced at the glass of water on the table next to him. Roy helped him drink, then put the glass back.

'Now we know that Burns took on a fake name, Jerry Budden, and he moved up here. He had a friend called Keith Burgess who helped him. We looked for you everywhere. I joined the Met and never gave up searching for you. When I heard that another child was abducted in Sheffield in the same way that you were, I decided to come up here. I managed to capture Burns, and Burgess. Burns wouldn't confess about you, and we still didn't know where you were. But I believed you were still alive.'

Roy lapsed into silence. He was getting tired again, and his headache was pounding harder. Robin had closed his eyes, but then he looked at Roy.

'I met you by coincidence. I saw you where that woman was murdered, and we spoke. Did you know then?'

Roy shook his head. Robin said, 'I kind of felt I had seen you somewhere before. But when I met your daughter, Anna, I felt a connection. Like I'd known her before.'

'She's your niece,' Roy said, his voice hoarse.

Robin nodded. Then his forehead creased like a thought had occurred to him. 'Do you have any proof of this? I mean—'

'There's DNA evidence,' Roy cut in, 'that's conclusive. You and I are definitely first blood relative, and we share the mitochondrial DNA that comes from our mother. These might be big words for you right now, but when you look at the evidence, you'll see.'

Robin stared at him for a while, then his eyes shut

briefly. He said something inaudible. Roy could imagine the storm churning in his mind, reflecting his own. Robin had a million questions, and he wanted to sit down with him, and answer all of them. He had waited all his life to do that. He could wait a few more days.

There was a knock, then a nurse bustled in. She gaped at Roy. 'Who are you? What are you doing here?'

Roy stood, his back and legs stiff. 'I came to see my brother. I'm admitted in the ward downstairs.'

The nurse came forward, and squinted at Roy. 'Are you the police officer who's gone missing from his ward?'

'Might be. Is there another one?'

The nurse looked like she had swallowed a goldfish. 'Do you know the amount of trouble you've caused us? Security are searching all over for you.'

'And here I am. Thank you for your concern. I'll go back to my bed now.'

The nurser folded her arms across her chest. 'You better.'

Roy edged closer to the bed, and looked down at Robin. 'I never gave up on you. I just wanted you to know that.'

Then his throat closed up, and he couldn't talk. Robin seemed to sense it. He raised his hand, and Roy grasped it. It was a strong, warm hand, and Roy cherished the touch.

'Thank you,' Robin said.

CHAPTER 60

The Next Morning

Some storms never abate. They only die down, stirring the reeds, ruffling the waves. But they never disappear. The calm that follows them is tense, uneasy. The skies breathe, but slowly, like they expect nature's rhythm to be disrupted again.

Roy felt like that now as he lay on the hospital bed. He pulled off the oxygen mask gently. So many questions remained to be answered. He could only imagine the horrors Robin had to endure during his childhood. He had tell his parents that he found him. Then the process of integrating Robin back into his life, and with his parents. He had to take Robin down to the nursing home where his parents lived, and introduce him.

He was looking forward to that, but it would also be difficult. Robin was now Jayden, a man, not the child his parents had lost. Would they recognise him? Something told his parents would, especially Maya, his mother. A mother never forgets her child.

The pain lanced against his ribs again, shredding his heart. A shadow detached itself from the corner of the room, and he jerked his head, suddenly awake.

'Sorry,' Sarah said, coming forward. Her cheeks were pale and drawn, eyes deeper into their sockets. She had no make-up on, and she had never looked prettier. She leant over him, and her concerned eyes scanned his face.

'I didn't mean to scare you.'

'You are very scary.' He smiled, and his lips hurt as they stretched.

Sarah's grin was tired, but genuine, like the relief on her face. 'Robin's alright,' she said. She had informed him already, this was an update. 'His brain scan was normal. Chest X-rays show some lung damage, and so does yours.'

'Inhalational lung injury,' he said.

'Yes, Dr Roy. Now stop talking and relax, will yer?'

'I'm always relaxed. Can't you tell?' He coughed and she put a hand on his chest. Her touch, through the bed cover, felt nice and warm.

'See?' She put a finger on her lips. 'Shh.'

There was a knock on the door, and a nurse poked her head. 'Someone to see DCI Roy. A Sergeant Melanie Sparkes, and Detective Constables Rizwan and Oliver.'

Roy finished coughing, and waved them in. Sarah protested, but he didn't listen. 'Help me sit up,' he croaked.

She wasn't happy, but helped him, along with the nurse. The nurse gave him some water, which he sipped.

The team stood in front of him, everyone a little shocked.

'Bloody hell,' Roy rasped. 'No one's died, have they? What's with all the long faces? Looks like you lot have just been to a wake.'

'Glad to see you're alright, guv,' Melanie said quietly.

Rizwan said, 'And you found your bro. Nice one.'

Roy nodded. 'Thank you. Now what do you want?' He grinned and then coughed again.

'Layla and Akbar are returning to India tomorrow. Visas sorted by Natalie, and tickets booked for flights tomorrow.'

'What's happening with Ambani's case?'

'Door to door hasn't revealed anything. Uniforms and SOC still looking in the park beyond the house. But the skin and hair fragments from both crime scenes show a DNA match. Which means the killer was the same person, more than likely.'

'Any report from Justin?'

'No. Dr Patel says cause of death was blood loss. Same as Noor.'

'So we're none the wiser. Any sign of Paresh Mallya?' Even as Roy said the words, what Marcus had said flashed across his mind. Noor's killer was white. How could it be Ambani, Afzal, or Paresh?

'Natalie and I are going to a couple of addresses in Sheffield today, where Mallya had lived in the past. See if we can get something from the neighbours.'

'They have another member of the team. That person is the killer.' Roy sagged against his pillows.'

Oliver said, 'You mean it's not Mallya? Someone else?'

'Marcus said he saw a white man on top of Noor. The neck skin was exposed and I think he saw part of the face as well.'

Melanie, Riz and Ollie looked at each other. Sarah said, 'We need to find the killer. But at least Layla and Akbar are returning to their families. Imagine how they must be feeling. You lot did well here.'

'But we haven't solved the case,' Roy grumbled. He frowned, as that odd feeling surfaced again, a sensation he was being watched. He looked around the room, then dug his hands on the bed and sat up straighter.

'What's the matter?' Sarah asked, turning to him. She had her hand on the bed. He looked at her, and they held each other's eyes.

'I don't know,' Roy grimaced. 'I just don't know. Feels like I'm missing something about this case.'

Melanie said, 'Natalie thinks we'll get some leads on Mallya's whereabouts today. That's going to help.'

'Natalie's been a great help. Yes, make sure you get hold of Mallya. Report back to me today, please.'

CHAPTER 61

Melanie was sat next to Natalie as she drove her black Ford Focus. It was a company car, and brand new, kitted out with all the mod cons. Melanie couldn't help feeling envious at the lovely new speakers, and the dashboard linked to Natalie's phone.

'Nice bit of kit,' Melanie said.

'Oh thank you. Nice to drive too. Why don't you get one? Not expensive on finance. I get it with work obviously. But you can get it for £200 per month, I think.'

'Nice. Might try, but I need a bigger car with the girls and the dog. I've got a Nissan six-seater.'

'Yes, that makes sense. I'd need a bigger car if I had a family.' She smiled at Melanie.

'We will get Mallya today,' Natalie said, becoming serious. 'I can feel it.'

'Yeah?'

'Yes. He's not left the country, unless he has another identity, which we know he doesn't. He's living on cash, but he's bound to run out soon, and use his cards. Then we'll nab him. But he's sticking close by, watching how far the investigation goes. He had to get rid of Ambani, or Ambani would've exposed him.'

'That's why he killed Noor as well. But you know what? The boss thinks it was a white guy. That's what Marcus said. And it can't be Mallya.'

Natalie's big hands gripped the steering wheel tighter. Melanie couldn't help but notice how strong her hands looked.

A phone rang, and the call was automatically transferred to the dashboard. A person called PM was calling. As soon as the call appeared, Natalie cut it. The call came again, and she did the same thing. Then she took out her phone, and powered it down.

Melanie wondered who that was, but didn't say anything. She felt uneasy about the initials however. PM... Paresh Mallya. No, that was silly and she was jumping to wild conclusions.

'Who was that?' she asked.

'Oh, just a friend of mine. I'll chat to her later.' Natalie took a bend on the road, then the car straightened. Her knuckles were white on the steering wheel, her wide shoulders hunched forward.

'Marcus is that tall teenager with long hair, correct?' Natalie asked.

Melanie frowned. 'Yes. How did you know? You haven't seen him.'

Natalie was silent again. When Melanie looked at her, she was staring forward, her jaws set in a hard line.

'The teenagers arrived at the station after you left,' Melanie said. Suddenly, she was feeling sick to the pit of her stomach. A cold, icy fear was spreading across her body, numbing her hands and toes.

The killer was wide-shouldered, physically agile...but was it a man, or a woman?

Natalie was a taekwondo martial arts expert – did Marcus see Natalie killing Noor?

Melanie thought how the killer had always evaded their grasp, and stayed one step ahead. Natalie knew when and where Ambani would be after he was released. She also knew where the surveillance team were, and how to avoid them.

She stared at Natalie, who casually took out another phone, and called a number. She spoke in a foreign tongue with an accent. Melanie didn't understand what she said, but the words struck her as being of an Eastern language, and not Chinese. Urdu? Hindi?

Natalie hung up. Melanie gasped. 'Natalie? Was it you? All along...you did this?'

She got no response. Natalie turned the wheel savagely and sped down a road that connected to a country lane. She pulled into the back of a large, derelict building. A van was waiting, and two men stood outside. Natalie pulled in alongside them, and lowered the window.

Her steely eyes didn't blink, and her face was hard and cold. 'Give me your phone.'

'Natalie, I—'

'I said give me your damn phone!' Natalie shouted, making Melanie jump. She looked at the two men, who were now standing right outside her window. She had no choice but to obey. She gave Natalie her phone, hands shaking.

'Now get out, and get in the van,' Natalie said. Melanie didn't have her radio on her, it was with Natalie. She felt completely helpless.

Natalie got out of the car, and one of the men opened Melanie's door. He grabbed her by the collar and pulled her out roughly. She looked at Natalie in shock as she was bundled into the van, and the door slammed shut.

CHAPTER 62

Detective Chief Inspector Rohan Roy furrowed his brows, wondering if he was hearing correctly. It was the morning after his hospital admission, and he had a coffee and an NHS breakfast, which was barely edible. Still, his headache was receding and he felt better after a good night's rest. The news that Sarah had just given him however, threatened a new migraine.

"What? What do you mean abducted? She's a police officer on duty, for crying out loud." He was referring to Detective Sergeant Melanie Sparks, a member of their Major Investigations Team.

"Melanie's been missing since yesterday, with Natalie Scarrow from the Modern Slavery Unit," Sarah said. Sarah was now back at work, which was great news.

"Neither of them is answering phones. Traffic located Natalie's last call to a warehouse outside Dore, on the way out to the Peak District. The warehouse had security cameras." Sarah stopped, and Roy could hear the concern in her voice. That worried him.

"Natalie and two men put Melanie inside a van, guv. One of the men match the description of Paresh Mallya, the human trafficker we're trying to get hold of."

Roy's mouth opened in shock. He couldn't speak as his mind ran loops, trying to see all the different angles. "What're you trying to say?"

Sarah's voice had an edge of steel. "I mean Natalie was behind all of this. She's the one we've been trying to get our hands on. She killed Noor Jehan. Think about it. Natalie used to be a national Tae Kwon Do champion. She's tall. She's got the physique of the killer who climbed down the tree that night."

Roy was lost in his thoughts, which he uttered out loud. "And she pointed us in the direction of Sunil Ambani, the restaurant owner where Noor and the others worked, then killed him too. She knew when Ambani was getting out of custody, and exactly where he'd be."

"She even saw Ambani while he was in custody, Rohan. No wonder Ambani never cracked. He knew all along Natalie would keep him safe, till she killed him. That's why there's no sign of breaking and entering at Ambani's house. Natalie climbed over the fence. Remember the boot prints we saw on the fence? Well, they match with the prints where Noor died. And guess what we found when we raided Natalie's flat this morning?"

"Boots matching with prints obtained from both crime scenes?"

"Bingo. And the DNA from the skin samples under both victim's fingernails?"

"It shows a match with DNA from Natalie's clothes? Her underwear, maybe?"

"Exactly. When I looked at the results on my screen, I couldn't believe it."

"Oh god." Roy cradled his head in his hand. "How could I have missed this?"

"You had a lot on your plate, Rohan," Sarah's words were soft. "You and Robin almost died getting out of that warehouse."

"But still," Roy shook his head. "I should've thought about it more. I kept getting the feeling something was wrong. That someone was watching me. Odd I know, and I couldn't explain it myself. My gut was telling me…" he lost his words. Then he cursed himself in silence. He had a habit of being hard on himself, and this time, he felt it was justified. Melanie was missing because of his mistake. He had to get her back.

"And your gut is rather big, so good job you listened to it," Sarah said.

"I'm coming back to the nick. See you soon."

She raised her voice immediately. "Whoa, whoa, take it easy. You're meant to be in hospital for another day."

"Like hell I am," Roy growled. He stood, and tugged at the neck of his gown. He needed to get out of this and into his clothes. He had checked on Robin already this morning. He was well, and would remain admitted until tomorrow at least. Roy sighed. At least he had his brother

362

back. He had waited all his life for that to happen. He was never letting go of Robin again. But first things first.

Sarah said, "Rohan, just listen, will yer?"

He had already taken the gown off, and was reaching for his trousers. The machine on the wall had started flashing silently, as the soft alarm went off in the nurse's desk.

"I'm on my way." He hung up. He put his shirt on slowly, grimacing in pain as he raised his shoulders. The door behind him opened and the nurse stepped in. She bustled up to him.

"Where are you going now? Honestly, Inspector, you have to stop running around. You're meant to be resting."

Rohan sat down on the chair, and clamped down on his teeth as he put his shoes on. His limbs and spine screamed in pain. Somehow, he managed to get dressed, and stood, stiff and bent forward slightly. He felt tired and awkward.

"You need to rest," the nurse repeated, glaring at him.

"No rest for the wicked," Rohan said darkly, then shuffled past the nurse, towards the open door.

To be continued in Book 5, HOLD YOUR BREATH.

Made in the USA
Middletown, DE
14 October 2023

40781274R00217